Born in Paris in 1969, Sophia Creswell attended Durham University and graduated in 1991. Subsequently, she lived in St Petersburg, working as an English language teacher and an art publisher. She has travelled extensively in the Far East and Africa, where she worked for the Namibian Broadcasting Corporation. This is her first novel.

∫

SCEPTRE

Sam Golod

SOPHIA CRESWELL

SCEPTRE

First published in 1996 by Hodder and Stoughton
A division of Hodder Headline PLC
A Sceptre Paperback

British Library Cataloguing in Publication Data

Creswell, Sophia
    Sam Golod
    1. English fiction – 20th century
    I. Title
    823.9'14 [F]

    ISBN 0 340 66640 4

Typeset by Palimpsest Book Production Limited,
Polmont, Stirlingshire
Printed and bound in Great Britain by
Cox & Wyman Ltd, Reading, Berkshire

Hodder and Stoughton
A division of Hodder Headline PLC
338 Euston Road
London NW1 3BH

For Pilot

Acknowledgments

Many thanks to my family, Clare Allan, Katie Higgingbottom, Nicki Symington and Dug Falby, Kate Symington and John Whiston, Gavin, James and Corinna Hamilton, Nicholas Miles, Chris Wood, Nick and Felicity Barren, Anna Powell and Judith Wood for all their kind support.

ſ

I am sitting at the table by my window trying to write a letter to my parents. I've been holding my pen too tightly and it has worn a groove in the top joint of my second finger. When I first arrived here I described everything in my letters home to my parents and then slowly, as I became more involved with the artists, I began to leave things out. I didn't tell them about Tornikov, then I didn't tell them about Oleg and his black market nickel. The omissions became bigger. I didn't tell them about Pyotr because it was too personal and I don't tell my mother about that kind of thing. Now I want to confide in them but I can't, there is too much to explain. It seems an impossible task to tell them everything that has happened, and I don't think that I've got the strength to begin.

Instead I've told them about my holiday in Berlin and how spring broke in St Petersburg while I was away, and I've made a joke about the mosquitoes developing a taste for English blood.

My father is an accountant, he pushes himself into a crowded tube at quarter past eight every morning at Clapham North station and takes the Northern Line into the City. He reads the sports pages of the *Daily Telegraph* on his way to work and has a go at the crossword at lunchtime while he's eating a sandwich at his desk. Maybe

I'm underestimating him, but I don't think he'd understand what's been happening here.

I used to sit like this by the window and listen to the evening sounds when I first arrived. It was late autumn then, and the city was wet and sodden and waiting for snow.

To begin with I didn't know anyone in St Petersburg. Each night after my last lesson I cooked myself cabbage and potatoes and sat staring out into the courtyard. I listened to the televisions and the family arguments. The windows on the corner of the third floor opposite belong to a communal kitchen, and I filled the hours during those long black nights watching women in housecoats gossiping and preparing meals. As we moved further into winter the snow brightened the courtyard and the echoes grew stronger with the cold.

I got to know the courtyard but the city outside remained a stranger for much longer. St Petersburg. Three million or more people living behind windows whose squares of light floated in the dark night. Some nights I would let my mind wander out beyond the suburbs and into the forests, and I would think of the hundreds and hundreds of miles of trees that were out there, standing patiently waiting for the spring.

I am feeling some of that sense of isolation again now. This letter will travel across a whole continent from this narrow room and its tall, blank window before it reaches my parents in South London. There is a world of windows between us, of people that neither my parents nor I know exist. In the autumn I used to think of those unknown people and unknown lives as a force, an anonymous pressure like water or air. I looked out into this strange city and imagined all its inhabitants as an enormous weight, reducing me to a tight, hard, lonely atom.

Babba Lenna, who lives next door, was always company,

shuffling up and down the corridor in slippers that are too big for her. I'm very fond of Babba Lenna, she's a constant, she's been here through everything and she's endured more than I can even think about. She calls me *dotchinka*, little daughter. I really like that, it makes me feel that I have some sort of base here, however tenuous it might be. At the moment Babba Lenna has a friend around from one of the other staircases and they are watching television together. They have turned it up loud because they are both a bit deaf and I can hear it through the walls; it's one of those melodramatic black and white films in which men go to war and women sob.

Babba Lenna is a *blokadnik* – which means she survived the seige of Leningrad during World War II. She's very proud of her status as a *blokadnik*. She told me once what happened: the Germans surrounded them for over three years. She says millions of them died from shelling, disease and starvation. By the end of it not much of the city was left. She doesn't approve of the city calling itself St Petersburg. For her, Leningrad is the hero city, the city that survived the starvation and the artillery. In our kitchen nine great sacks of baked crusts sit on the top shelf waiting for another famine. 'Hunger is the worst way to die,' she told me once.

I've never been hungry here, but food was short during the winter. Most of the shops were empty and I spent all my spare time queuing or searching for food.

They liberalised the prices at New Year but supplies didn't reach the shops for a long time after that. Annya, the other English woman at the school where I teach, blamed it on the communists still in control in the countryside. She said that they were trying to provoke food riots by preventing supplies reaching the cities.

There was never anything as dramatic as a food riot, but all through January there were little spasms of trouble in shops across the city. I witnessed one in a *gastronomia* on Nevsky Prospect. A rumour ran down the queue that they were selling *kalbasa* – sausage. A few moments later I heard shouting coming from the counter. A solid woman in a venerable blue coat with a fur collar was accusing the sales assistant of profiteering and black market dealing in food. The assistant responded by hustling us all out onto the ice-packed pavement and shutting the shop. We stood in the street grumbling at each other, disgruntled and cheated of our sausage.

I pulled my arms through my rucksack and began to make my way home. When I turned the corner by the Metro the woman in the blue coat and a dozen other people from the queue were standing in the middle of the road, shaking their fists at the passing motorists.

Later that week, Annya came to see me. I was in my room preparing a lesson. She had a hangover, it was one o'clock and she had just surfaced, rumpled and bleary with bloodshot eyes.

'I feel like shit,' she informed me, hunched over a glass of tea at my table. 'They say they put tranquillisers in the vodka to keep us all quiet. Fuck, I can believe it. Even my fucking bones ache today.'

Outside, Babba Lenna was making her way across the courtyard carrying a tin pail of potato peelings to empty into the main bins. She'd sat in the kitchen that morning peeling them, the pail on the ground between her big arthritic knees. 'Before,' she said, 'potatoes were as big as a fist, with clean flesh. How do they expect us to eat these?' She waved a black, shrivelled ball at me in disgust.

'Where were you drinking?' I asked Annya.

'In a studio in the squats on Ulitsa Pushkinskaya. I bumped into Nikita and Pyotr, a couple of artists, and we scored some vodka. Jesus Christ they were being funny, you should have been there. I was in fucking hysterics.

I've decided I'm going to persuade Pyotr to take part in my exhibition, his work is fucking excellent.' Annya was trying to organise a joint London/St Petersburg art show.

'And another thing, there is this exhibition coming up next week that's been set up by their agent. Do you want to come along with me? The artist is a guy called Tornikov. I've met him; he used to be the wild man of Petersburg. He's only just got back from the West, and apparently they fucking worshipped him there. He was like this way-out Russian and they thought he was just brilliant.'

Babba Lenna was now slowly retracing her steps. Halfway across the courtyard she rested, planting her legs curiously far apart under her stiff hips. Another old woman with a string perhaps-bag full of bread stopped to talk to her. The two brown-wrapped heads nodded together.

Annya was still telling me about Tornikov. 'This is like his triumphal return. The artists at Pushkinskaya said he would never come back. Once he'd gone West that would be it. But he's returned and proved them all wrong and now he's having an exhibition at the Ethnographic Museum. That's as high as you can go. I mean it's so fucking respectable you can't touch it. And Tornikov, the original king of the underground, is doing a show there. I'm not at all sure about it, I mean I reckon he's selling out, but I want to see it all the same, it'll definitely be interesting.'

We went out to a *molochnik* on Maly Prospect to get some lunch. *Molochniks*, according to Annya, were first started by grand ladies after the 1905 revolution, to provide milk products for people too poor to afford meat. Now they were the only places you could find any kind of milk products at all.

It was a cold day and the air coming off the Baltic was heavy with snow, thick and damp to walk through, like a towel that's been left in an unheated bathroom. We reached the *molochnik* through an unmarked corrugated iron door.

The dining hall was a long room, painted a sanatorium blue and set below the level of the street so that the windows, displaying the feet of the passing pedestrians, were pushed up against the ceiling.

Annya negotiated her way between the iron chairs towards two young men sitting in their overcoats at a table in the corner and I trailed behind her. It was past lunch hour and there weren't many other people in the room. A group of factory women sat in one corner, with big felt boots and white elasticated mob caps covering their hair. Two old men sat at separate tables.

'Look who's here,' Annya bellowed. 'Nikita, you devil, I hope you feel like rat shit, you don't deserve to be alive after what you put me through last night, and you neither, Pyotr.'

Pyotr gave a one-breath laugh. He had his back to me, and was wearing a long brown leather coat, a green beret and a gaudy red and yellow scarf. He turned his head slightly. Although the laugh was over he was still smiling and a gold tooth flashed from underneath the top corner of his upper lip.

'Annya, I feel better for seeing you, and who is the other angel?' he asked. Annya introduced me and we pulled up some chairs and joined them.

Nikita was smaller, with a drooping red nose. 'Nice to meet you Natalie,' he said. 'Tell me, are all English girls as good at taking their vodka as Annya?'

I smiled and sipped my ersatz coffee. The three of them bantered together and then Annya began talking about Pyotr's painting. 'You see,' she explained for my benefit, 'he's invented this new mythology and a new god called Sam Golod. It means hunger, self-causing, self-fulfilling hunger. Pyotr says that this is the new religion now that communism is dead. He's fucking right you know, this country's always had some kind of big idea to look up to and what's happening now is just as fucking mental as what's gone on before.'

'Don't listen to her Natalie,' interrupted Pyotr. He swivelled his body to face me, the grey light from the street flowed in over his head and a smile breathed onto his face.

'Annya is obsessed. All of this is a joke, you understand. In the United States they worship Greed, in Russia we are a bit contrary and so we worship Hunger.' He leant across the table and helped himself to a pancake from my plate.

'Now you are coming with us, aren't you?' he continued once he had finished his mouthful. 'We have to help our friend Alexey hang the paintings for Tornikov's exhibition. We need your help. I insist. Annya, you've got to make your friend come with us.'

'Why not, Natalie?' added Annya and they all looked at me expectantly, assuming that of course I would. But I couldn't go with them. I had lessons to teach that afternoon, so an hour and a half later I reluctantly left.

2

I first met Yelena and Arkady in Pushkinskaya on the night of Tornikov's exhibition. And if what Arkady has told me is right, then that night was the beginning of everything. I didn't go out very often in those days and I remember being very excited.

I had a headache when I left here; I always used to get them before it snowed. My hat felt tight across my temples, there was a heaviness in the atmosphere and the sky was sagging low between the lines of Sredny Prospect. It was four o'clock and the sun had already sunk back into the Gulf of Finland. The lightless air that it left behind flickered in front of my eyes.

There were people waiting outside the bread shop and more at the stall on the corner that was selling cabbages and jars of tomato sauce. Normally I would have joined them, but I was already late for my meeting with Annya.

By the Metro there were flower sellers' stalls offering glass boxes of red carnations and roses. Each box was lit up like an icon against the dusk and the dirty snow, by a candle burnt to protect the flowers against fifteen degrees of frost. I pushed through the glass doors into the station. Inside, the hot, sour atmosphere was ringing with the fractured tones of boots on wet stone, fifteen kopeck pieces in the ticket machine and rattling escalators. I got out at Gostinny Dvor, jostled through the thick-packed bodies in the corridors and emerged into the air at the Canal Griboyedova exit. Nevsky Prospect was empty. It was dark and the bellies of the snow clouds glowed yellow in the city lights.

Annya was waiting for me on the bridge. She's short, even shorter than I am. She was rolled up in an overcoat with a black and red Eastern skullcap jammed onto the top of her large head. She was facing me, her back to the wind that was searing down Nevsky off the river, her hands cupped around a Belamor cigarette that she was trying to relight. Her veined cheeks had turned purple in the cold.

Belamor are the local brand of Russian *paperossi*. They are the cheapest cigarettes that you can buy, workers' cigarettes, and they consist of a plug of tobacco and a cardboard tube. Annya says they are A-grade pure and better for you than anything else. Annya, who has lived here on and off for two years, likes to proclaim the wonders of Russian manufacturing, even of the shoddiest things like cigarettes and ersatz coffee, and then she implies that I'm too narrow-minded to appreciate their true quality. Belamor taste like you are inhaling a cigar, the tobacco might well be pure but it's so strong that my poor lungs can't take them.

Annya suffers from a severe squint and right then half of it was directed at the best London loafers which I had worn especially for going out. 'Call those shoes?' she sniffed as she tapped the little army boots that she always wore against the wrought-ironwork of the bridge, in order to dislodge the snow clogged under her heels.

I examined my feet. The snow had begun to seep through the thin leather. I was annoyed with her for being right.

'Never mind,' she said, tugging abruptly at my arm and hustling me down the pavement. 'Let's get going. This will be great. Things always happen at Tornikov's openings.'

We entered the Ethnographic Museum via a dark marble

foyer. The noise of the guests in the main hall rattled down the steps to greet us. We handed over our coats and joined them in an immense room crowded with cocktail party clusters. Near the head of the stairs there was a thickening around a table bearing bottles of sweet Soviet Champagne.

I hung awkwardly at Annya's shoulder for a few conversations until Nikita arrived to relieve me. He grinned and cocked his head as he said hello. His brown eyes had a sheen on them like the yeast on grapes. 'Ah,' he exclaimed with satisfaction, 'this is very good, now we have two English girls.' I smiled in return and looked at the floor. On his feet he had a pair of worn old Chelsea boots, thinner and even less practical than my footwear. He handed me a glass of champagne and, leading me through the chatting groups, took me on a tour of the room.

All the work was recent; the oldest painting there was dated September 1991, which made it just over three months old. In those days I hadn't seen many contemporary paintings and knew very little about art. I didn't like Tornikov's work, which consisted of semi-abstract faces in thick brown and yellow oils. I found them depressing and ugly. Nikita didn't bother to look at the paintings. Instead he gave me a run down on all the people we passed.

When we drew to a halt he asked me why I had come to St Petersburg. My students were always asking me the same question and I gave him the answer that I gave them: that I'd seen an ad for the job in a newspaper, and it had seemed like a good idea at the time. It was a simplistic answer but, just then I didn't feel like going into graduate unemployment or the boredom of London with no cash. 'Where did you learn your English?' I asked.

'From an American woman I knew.' Again he smiled and tipped his head sideways. 'And now all my friends want to learn English.'

The sound of shouting interrupted us. I pivoted. In the middle of the room a man was roaring at a character who looked like the ringmaster at a circus, small and neat with a goatee beard, an elegant shine on his balding head and a flat smile. His attacker's face was a furious red, the ridges in his neck standing out hard, like tree roots, his eyes starting from his skull in rage. My Russian wasn't good enough to understand everything he was saying, but from what I could catch it was rough and abusive. The man with the goatee beard was being remarkably cool. He hardly responded, he just stood there and smirked. The entire hall had stopped talking, everyone was watching them and nodding knowingly. The scene was very public but the large man was so incoherent that I don't think he was aware of us all watching him.

'That's Tornikov, the artist,' whispered Nikita, pointing to the florid big man. 'And the other one is Alexey Andreev, our patron. He's the man who organises these exhibitions.'

'Looks as if Tornikov's had too much to drink,' I commented. 'I suppose with the first night of his exhibition and everything he must be under a lot of pressure.'

'Maybe, but Tornikov's got a vicious temper anyhow. He's well known for it. He's fought with practically every critic in St Petersburg. He's got some extremely influential enemies but he is making a big mistake quarrelling with Alexey. Seriously, I mean Alexey's helped Tornikov a lot and he's the one enemy Tornikov really doesn't need.'

Alexey left the hall. It took a moment for Tornikov to realise that his opponent had disappeared and then he, too, stamped out. The guests turned back to their conversations and the noise swelled again. Annya came up to us. Behind her, and towering way above her, strolled Pyotr. 'Boring, boring, boring as fuck,' fumed Annya. 'I'm sorry Natalie, I shouldn't have dragged you along. You might as well be in a Piccadilly gallery, turgid fucking paintings. I tell you, the floor show is all the excitement we're going to have here tonight.'

I hadn't registered how tall Pyotr was when I had met him before. 'Hello,' he said, smiling slowly down at me, his gold tooth flashing. 'Nobody told me that you were going to be here.'

'I dragged her along. I thought she needed some entertainment – not that she's going to get any here,' said Annya querulously.

'We must entertain you then, Natalie,' retorted Pyotr. 'Annya, we can go and see Yuri and Slava another night, there is no hurry.' He spoke in a slow, lazy voice but Annya was not going to be put off.

'Pyotr, you promised to take me tonight. You're as slippery as a fucking eel, I know how difficult it is to pin you down. Anyhow I want to discuss my fucking exhibition with you.' She looked quite cross. I didn't like being argued over, it made me feel like a parcel. I stammered out that I'd be fine, honestly, perfectly fine, there was no problem.

Pyotr put his hand on my shoulder and turned to Nikita, 'Look after her Nikita, but don't look after her too well.' He looked at me. 'You'll be OK, Nikita will take care of you,' he said, turning to follow Annya who was plucking impatiently at his elbow.

I watched them leave, Pyotr walking in a long roll and Annya in short, determined steps. Nikita grinned at me. 'Annya, the little English militant. She's right, this is boring, not like Tornikov's last opening. You should have been there, that was crazy. Tornikov body-painted a troupe of dancers, they all had faces on their bellies and snakes crawling up their legs. Anyhow, as I am in charge of your entertainment for the evening I suggest we go to Pushkinskaya.'

I agreed enthusiastically. I didn't want to have to go back

to my room, that would have been such an anticlimax. I felt a touch of vertigo, the same kind of feeling that I'd had in London months before, when I had sat in front of the newspaper and dared myself to go to Russia.

Pushkinskaya is a block of condemned buildings on Ulitsa Pushkinskaya that is squatted by painters, film makers and anybody else who feels like it. Lots of the underground artists have studios there but the authorities seem to ignore it. Annya was always talking about it and it was very satisfactory to be going to see it without her.

The snow had started falling while we had been inside and now it was coming down in fat, fast flakes, so thick that I couldn't see the far side of the square.

We paused at the exit while I pushed my fur hat on and looped a red scarf over the top of it to stop the snow going down my neck. Nikita thrust his hands deep into the pockets of a moth-eaten duffle jacket. While we were standing there a large man, without even a coat to protect him from the cold, barged past us and scudded down the flight of stone steps to the pavement. He turned right and ran shambolically, limbs flaying, towards the Russian Museum. It was Tornikov. I pulled on my gloves and shivered. 'My God, he'll die of cold.'

'Who knows, the man's cracked,' said Nikita, shrugging and pushing his hands deep down into his pockets. 'I don't understand what he's on at all.' We set off across the square to Nevsky.

In the courtyard at Pushkinskaya, shapes were etched and highlighted by the snow. Animals and mountains and things that weren't either lay unlabelled in the snow-light. This moonscape was created from frozen mud, wrecked machinery and rubble. We picked our way across it and, in the far corner, stepped through a door into blackness. I felt Nikita's hand patting my arm, searching for mine. His palms were hot through the wool of my gloves, almost feverish. He led me up some stairs to a landing where a glassless window was letting in the mute light from outside.

I could just make out patterns on the walls, doodles, graffiti, paintings on top of other paintings. Large double doors led off either side of the landing; their size and style suggested that they must have once had prosperous tenants. The stone staircase went on curling upwards. The steps were shallow, and many of them were crumbling and broken. It was very quiet. Shattered glass and frozen leaves gathered at the edges of the steps, giving off a flat, dead smell. Nikita ran on ahead of me, taking two steps at a time. 'We're going to visit my neighbours,' he called out over his shoulder and his voice echoed and repeated down the stairwell.

Nikita knocked at a set of double doors on the top floor which were opened by a dark-haired man with high cheekbones and fleshy lips. We followed him down a corridor to a small back room where a girl sat at a table.

Nikita didn't explain about me but with exaggerated jerky actions he began to tell his friend about Tornikov's tantrum. I stood in the middle of the room feeling awkward. I removed my hat, scarf and gloves. My hair was sweaty and stuck across my forehead. I unbuttoned my coat and perched on the bench beside the girl, my hat on my lap. She turned and examined me, quite carefully. She was blonde and pretty but she had a terrible black eye, bruised and puffy with a painful red mark across the bridge of her nose. I glanced at Nikita but he was engrossed in his story, shaking his fists in an imitation of Tornikov.

I thought I'd better introduce myself. 'Hello,' I ventured, holding out my hand towards the girl, 'my name's Natalie.'

The man stopped laughing with Nikita and turned to me, 'And I'm Arkady,' he said.

The handshake, I realised too late, was out of place, it was too English and formal. The girl returned it in a long loopy shake like a child's. 'I'm Yelena,' and she passed me a joint. It surprised me, I hadn't expected grass to turn up in Russia, but these were hardly clean-living Young Communists. I took a small puff and handed it back.

The grass made me feel fuzzy around the edges. I sat there, happy to let the others talk around me. Later on Nikita chivvied me out on a vodka run. Outside it was still snowing hard and most of the shapes in the courtyard were covered. I was less careful this time and I slipped over onto my bum, jarring my spine on a hillock of frozen rubbish.

Nikita giggled and began frenetically gathering snow from the top of a cement mixer. I didn't sit down long enough for him to take aim so, armed with a snowball, he chased me out under the arch and into the street.

If I was to leave this little room now and go down to the Metro, every one of the kiosks that cluster around it would have three or four different kinds of vodka or multicoloured liquors stacked up in its window. It's amazing how much things have changed; back then vodka was incredibly difficult to find. You had to hustle for it, know your area and know where the vodka sellers hung out. Gorbachev only stepped down at New Year so we were still under virtual prohibition. Even if you did succeed in finding vodka in the shops, which was rare, you had to have ration tickets to buy it. I used to enjoy getting vodka, it was an adventure. You had to go out and track it down. Nikita said he knew a place where you could always find some and we headed off through the quietened streets.

We came across five men, dusted with snow, loitering on a corner behind Moscovsky Station. Nikita insisted that I do the bargaining, I don't think he had any money. As we slowed down they hissed numbers at me. I settled at eighty roubles, Nikita giggled, stepped in and talked him down to fifty. I paid for the bottle, fumbling around for my money, my fingers fat and clumsy with gloves. The outer layer of my face was numb with cold.

We ran back, skidding on the patches of black ice that the children had made. We took them at speed, positioning our feet sideways. I lost my balance twice, but although the back of my coat was covered in snow I miraculously managed to keep the vodka bottle intact.

We stamped back into Arkady's studio, brushing down our coats and chattering. The atmosphere in the little back room had changed completely. Arkady was now sitting on the windowsill, hunched over his knees and sucking viciously on a cigarette. Yelena was gouging grooves in the wooden table with a Biro. The small top window had been opened and a stream of freezing air elbowed its way through the cigarette smoke.

I stood next to Nikita, dangling the vodka bottle.

'He's dead,' said Arkady breaking from his cigarette.

'Who?' asked Nikita.

I stepped forward, put the vodka bottle on the table and quickly returned to the doorway.

'Tornikov,' spat Yelena.

'No, he's not,' I told them, and I remember my voice sounding too loud and jarring. 'We've only just seen him, we were at his exhibition earlier on. He ran down the steps just as we were leaving. You already told them about the shouting match, didn't you?' I said, appealing to Nikita for support.

Yelena shook her head. 'He's dead,' she repeated in a flat voice and then she went back to digging grooves in the table. 'You saw him before he died. They shot him in the square outside the museum an hour ago.' It was just past eleven o'clock.

Arkady got down from the windowsill, took a stack of glasses from an empty bookcase, and placed them on the table. Nikita stepped forward and, picking up the bottle, tore the metal foil cap off with his teeth.

'Who?' I asked and they all looked at me, not understanding what I meant. 'Who shot him? Who is "they"? Who told you?' I persisted. They looked away, guarded and embarrassed. Nikita pushed a glass at me with two inches of vodka in it, which in effect was a 'shut up' and the only answer I was going to get. I drank the vodka.

They didn't talk to each other, they just drank. The mood in the room was sullen and miserable. I watched the cigarette smoke being sucked in coils out of the window and thought of Tornikov. I wanted to talk to them about it, because we had just seen him. Four hours ago he'd been angry and very much alive. But they didn't want to talk, they wanted to drink. For me it was stunning, I couldn't get my head around the fact that he was dead, yet I had seen him only four hours earlier.

I wondered what he'd been so angry about? Who had wanted to kill him? All I knew about him was that he had a reputation for fighting with critics and that he'd only just come back from the West. I didn't even like his paintings. I told myself off for that, it was disrespectful. Why shoot a bad Russian artist? There had to be a reason, no one died without a reason.

I accepted another vodka from Nikita. 'Last one. I ought to be getting back. I have to teach tomorrow.' As I put on my coat Yelena thrust a pile of sketches into my hand. 'No, no, no thank you, it's very kind of you, but . . .' She thrust them at me again, insistent, her black eye bulbous in the shadows thrown by the lamp. I accepted them, Nikita offered to walk me to the Metro, I shoved on my outdoor clothes and he ushered me out of the door.

Nikita stalled me under the arch at the entrance to the courtyard. 'Natalie, it doesn't matter who shot Tornikov. He's dead now. Last year it would have been the KGB, now it might be mafya, but it's the same hitmen, the same people. Do you understand?' He was gripping my arm so tightly that it hurt. I can understand what he was getting at now, but at the time I couldn't see it. His fierceness embarrassed me. It was my turn not to want to talk about it.

It was still snowing hard, we had to move slowly, sliding our feet along the pavement, not picking them up between steps so that we wouldn't slip over. We walked in silence. Cars were crawling down Nevsky. Through the flakes everything moved in slow motion, as if we were all caught in a strobe light.

On the marble walls inside the Metro station there was a bronze relief of a square-chinned boy with a torch. The slogan 'Youth of the world unite' was written underneath it in Russian and English. Nikita wrote down my address in a small plastic notebook.

At the barrier he leant forward and kissed me goodbye lightly on the lips. As the escalator carried me downwards I remember wondering whether that was a Russian custom.

3

Tornikov's death disturbed me. Nikita, Arkady and Yelena were secretive about it. They knew or suspected something but they weren't going to tell me. I sensed a taboo against asking questions and after the night of his death I didn't try again. I hadn't known Tornikov, so I wasn't sad. I wasn't thinking of a man or a life; this was a murder and it shocked me deeply that murder could happen so close to me.

I felt the need to keep it a secret as well; I didn't tell anybody at school and I was relieved when Annya didn't turn up to teach the following Wednesday. I knew that she would have strong opinions about Tornikov and the way he had died, and I dreaded hearing them while my own feelings were so confused and uneasy.

Overnight the city seemed to have grown dangerous and the alleyways dark. I found myself clutching my bag tightly as I stood on the crowded trams and buses. Then gradually, lulled by the familiar routine of lessons and the life around our courtyard, I began to forget about Tornikov and his violent death. I started to take short cuts again and I stopped scowling quite so fiercely at anybody who jostled me on the Metro.

Arkady might well be right in maintaining that everything began with Tornikov's murder, but for me it started the night that Pyotr came around to my flat. He must have got my address from Nikita; they were old friends. The only other person who could have told him was Annya and I can't imagine him asking her.

It was nearly midnight when the doorbell went. Babba Lenna was spending a fortnight with her brother in the countryside so I was alone and uncertain whether I should open the door. Then I thought it might be Annya, who has never been a respecter of time, and I undid the latch.

Pyotr was standing in the hall with his bright red and yellow scarf wrapped around his neck. 'May I come in?' he asked in heavily-accented English. It sounded like he had been rehearsing the phrase, he certainly never spoke English again after that.

'Da, da, da, da, yes, yes, yes,' I stuttered. 'Let me make you a cup of tea.' He came into the kitchen and talked to me while I boiled the kettle. He took off his boots and, clearing off a cockroach, unfolded his whole length onto a chair by my worksurface. He rolled a cigarette using a rolling machine on his thigh. He asked me questions about my school and about home, and I told him about my mother who's a teacher, and how I didn't really like the idea that I was doing the same thing as her. He laughed and said that he reckoned that St Petersburg was probably very different from South London, so I wasn't really doing the same. There were, he said ironically, slight variations.

I carried my kettle back to my room and began to make tea at the table. He checked out the chairs and settled himself down on one of the strongest.

'Do you know about gnus?' he asked and we had to look it up in the dictionary because it was too exotic for my Russian. 'Gnus,' he told me, 'like to sniff ants. If you are a gnu, ants are a great delicacy. In the deserts of Namibia there is a specific breed of ant that bores into the brain of a gnu and destroys its sense of direction. It's quite easy to recognise these gnus because the poor bastards keep on wandering around in circles. Apparently all over the Kalahari Desert there are gnus wandering around in circles, not knowing which way they are going because they have sniffed the wrong kind of ant.'

I laughed. Pyotr was very easy to listen to, his Russian was languorous and a fine gravel of irony ran under everything he said. I think Pyotr believed it was dangerous to take anything too seriously. It would end up doing your head in.

He talked about Nikita. They had grown up together near Lvov in the Western Ukraine. They had both dodged National Service and at twenty-six had come to St Petersburg together, lured by the existence of an underground where it was possible, although precarious, to live outside the grip of the authorities.

Next he told me about the mental hospital that he and Nikita had been to in order to avoid National Service. He said he had convinced the doctor he was mad by staring at him with what he called a 'death stare'. 'The poor bastard was terrified,' he said with his quick laugh. 'Nobody in the Soviet Union ever looks anybody straight in the eye. So if you insist on doing so you are obviously crazy.'

He told me about some of the sadistic nurses and the crazy people being treated in the hospital. 'I never knew which poor bastard was mad and which was sane. I used to act mad all the time, because I never knew when they were watching us. I tell you, I couldn't tell the difference between madness and sanity by the time I came out.'

He seemed to occupy a large amount of space: every time I changed position I found myself brushing against his legs. I was transfixed by what he was telling me. It was so awful, so horrific, but he had a knack, especially when he was talking about the other inmates, of making it very funny. In fact the more awful it was the funnier he made it. 'In Russia,' he said, 'if you're mad you are free.'

As he was talking I was aware of his eyes resting on me. Eventually he settled on a pause, but continued looking at me through the silence. I fought to try and behave naturally, in the way that you do when a camera is focussed on you, but I was too aware of him blatantly absorbing me.

His hair was short and spikey and old-blond in colour. There was a suspicion of summer freckles across his cheek-bones but it was his eyes that I really noticed. They were an extraordinary colour, burnished green shot through with yellow. His gold tooth flashed from the left-hand side of his mouth as it relaxed into a long smile. He coaxed a nervous return smile out of me until the tension became too much and I had to break it. I dropped my eyes down to my tea and circled the glass in my hands. I didn't know what to do, I didn't know what was the best thing to say.

I came out with an inane and flustered excuse about having an early lesson the next day and needing to go to bed. I don't really know why I did that. I think I just felt a bit overwhelmed and I wanted some time.

'I'll come back tomorrow,' he said and he laced up his workmen's boots and put his beret back on his head.

When he was halfway down the staircase I shouted out of the door, 'I'll be here at six o'clock. Come then, I'll be expecting you. *Paka!*' He waved from the staircase and shouted something in return. I tried to carry everything back to the kitchen in one journey and dropped one of the glasses. It didn't break because it was Pyrex, but it sprayed tea leaves across the floorboards in the kitchen. It was a good thing that Babba Lenna wasn't there, the noise would have woken her up.

The next day was torture. I tidied up my room even though Pyotr was obviously not the kind of man to notice or care whether or not a room was tidy. I couldn't be still. I felt slightly sick. I tried not to listen to the footsteps in the courtyard. I pretended to myself that I wasn't really waiting for him at all and I would be surprised if he turned up. I began sewing an inside pocket into my winter coat. Babba Lenna covers all the cutlery and plates in our kitchen with patches from old sheets to protect them against the cockroaches. I nicked one of these and made a pocket big enough to hold a book, so that I could read in queues. By half past six I was imagining that every sound was the doorbell or a footstep. What if he doesn't come? I turned my body into an ear and listened so hard I could practically hear falling skin cells. By that point I was convinced he wasn't going to come. It was my fault, I had given him the wrong impression.

I set him a deadline of seven-thirty but by a quarter to eight he still hadn't shown up. Damn him, damn him, why should I wait for him any longer, making a fool of myself? If he was really interested in me he would have been here on time. Well if he turned up now he could stuff it. Who did he think I was, that I would wait this long for him?

I patrolled my room, wheeling around on the parquet floor at the window and at the door. Then I had to get out, it didn't matter where I went. If I met him in the courtyard full of excuses that would be awful, almost worse. Instead of going straight out onto the street I went through an arch into the next door courtyard and, forgetting all my caution, made my way to the Metro along the back routes.

I emerged in the narrow street running into the main road by the Metro and slunk into the station. As I stood on the escalator I imagined what would happen if Pyotr was coming in the opposite direction. I'd be helpless, the clockwork machinery would draw us together and then, inexorably, draw us apart.

Damn him, I'd been so stupid but I had honestly believed that he wanted to see me again. I had never known myself so sure. So why had he stood me up? It just showed that you should never trust your judgement.

In the train I held onto a pole. Nothing made sense to me here. In England I would have known that I was right, but in Russia it was more complicated. I didn't understand the rules; every time I thought I had them worked out they seemed to change. The train swung around a corner and I lurched forward. A woman, her hands held primly in her lap, glared at me. She thought I was drunk.

I went to see Annya because she was English. She blithered on about a Polish businessman called Leszek who was going to help her with the exhibition and she was too engrossed in the prospect of Leszek to notice my mood. 'He's quite attractive, I think we will have an affair,' she said confidently. It is the kind of comment that only Annya could have made. She is extremely upfront about sex, and although she is quite ugly she has a lot of affairs and talks about sex with a relish that I used to find alarming.

It is sometimes a relief to be able to speak English and at least with Annya I can just sit and listen. I don't have to explain everything I say, she understands. She cooked me some supper and we drank a couple of beers that she had found. I left her flat at about midnight feeling slightly happier.

A week later I was having a lie-in when my doorbell woke me. I stumbled down the corridor without my slippers, asked who it was, couldn't decipher the name and opened the door anyway. Pyotr stood there in the clothes I had said goodbye to him in. His skin looked blue, as if a bruise was developing or fading. I was sleepy and confused and for a moment I questioned whether I was actually conscious or whether this was some early-morning waking dream. When I decided that it wasn't I was still too amazed to say anything. I waved him in mutely.

He stood in the hallway with his arms held a couple of inches away from his body and his hands at an angle like a child's. 'I'm sorry I didn't come, I was in prison,' he announced, 'yes, prison,' he repeated. 'I kept on thinking, she will have gone, I have missed her appointment.'

'Oh God,' I said, stepping forward to hug him. His leather coat crackled under my arms, it felt cold and hard against my face. He stroked my back from my shoulder blades to the hollow of my spine, smoothing down my pyjama tops.

When I looked up at him he was laughing. 'It's all right, I'm out now.'

I dressed and began to make porridge and tea. I measured out the oats and the water in a trance. I felt as if I'd been koshed on the head. Prison, prison, I kept on repeating the word to myself. The trim little life that I had set up for myself in St Petersburg was cracking and moving. I was alarmed but I don't actually think I was sorry. I had the image of my life being like the Neva ice in a thaw, splitting, moving slowly away from the banks and out of my control.

Pyotr sat at my table and placed a small, green, military rucksack by the door and laughed. Everything he looked at seemed to make him laugh; I think he was slightly crazy with relief. 'They gave me porridge in prison. Not porridge like this, of course. This is royal porridge, this is . . .'

'What happened, Pyotr?' I asked anxiously. He hesitated. I noticed his eyes had grown yellower. 'Why prison?' I prompted.

He inhaled through his teeth and put down his spoon. 'When I came to visit you I was carrying grass on me, three glasses of it. I'd just come from Alexey Andreev's birthday party. I don't know what time it was when I left here, but it must have been late and the streets were deserted. It was an empty night, very quiet and clear. I walked along thinking about you, thinking how pretty you were and wondering how it would be the next time I saw you.' I bit my lip and tugged a loose piece of hair firmly behind my ear.

Pyotr continued, 'I saw the police when they were about

a hundred yards off. They had already seen me and they were making their way towards me in that dumb, determined way that policemen always have, as if they are having to think about it very hard. There was nowhere I could go and there was no one else on the street. I thought, I am going to make their day, they are going to be so happy when they stop me.' He gave another quick laugh. 'It was just me, the stars and the policemen – and the only ones who were happy about the situation were the policemen. I could see their little piggy eyes all excited and glittering. They stopped me and asked a lot of stupid questions, and when they sussed out that I didn't have a *prepuska*, a permit for the city, they almost clapped. But you should have seen the poor bastards when they found my grass.' He threw up his hands and rolled his eyeballs. 'It was as if they had found bloody treasure.'

He pushed his porridge bowl away from him. 'OK, enough Natalie,' he said dismissing the matter. 'I have bought us a treat.' He pulled two grapefruit out of his little rucksack. They came from Cuba or as Pyotr put it 'a present from our Latin Comrades'. Apart from a few pathetic withered apples they were the first fruit that I had seen since arriving here.

He cupped a grapefruit in both his hands and dug the fingers of his right hand into the yellow plastic skin, making five small wounds. He plucked at one of these, tearing through the thick pith. When he had peeled it he pushed his thumb down into the core of the fruit, separated it into two parts and handed me one. I lay a segment on my tongue, then slowly crushed it and felt the acid capsules popping against the roof of my mouth.

I saw a flash of pink on his wrist as he tore himself off a second segment. 'What is it?' I asked, although I think I already knew the answer. I was horrified that anyone could do that to themselves. I felt the skin around my wisdom teeth pucker as if the grapefruit juice had turned to caustic soda.

'Nothing, Natalie, it's not important.' He retracted his hand inside his sleeve. 'It's just silliness, it's nothing at all.'

There was a pause. He looked straight at me but this time I was not going to drop my gaze and slowly, without his face moving, he held out his hands towards me. When they were fully outstretched I looked down. Across the thinnest part of his left wrist four ridges showed bubblegum pink on his fine skin. The cuts had been made a couple of days ago. Whatever had caused them had been very blunt, but it was hard to tell how deep they were because of the swelling. I felt guilty at having been so bossy and making him show me this. I rustled around in my bedside cabinet for my First Aid Kit. I emptied out the contents on the table in front of me. The wounds were too deep for Germoline but the only other disinfectant I had was Mercurichrome. 'It's going to sting,' I warned.

'I suspect I can probably take it,' he said. I held his forearm and applied the Mercurichrome with a piece of cotton wool. He didn't even wince. When I had finished, the four pink lines were stained an angry red. 'That looks much worse,' he said with satisfaction and grinned. The gold tooth was back. I think he rather liked the attention.

'How did you do it?' I asked.

He tapped ruefully at the wall. 'Plaster; honestly Natalie you don't need to worry, it isn't very serious. I did it twice. The first time was because I was just so angry. They told me that I might have to stay in prison for two years and I just couldn't imagine it. I hate prisons, I really hate them, they make me go mad and I was in a bum cell with hardly any light, just this . . .' He held up his forefinger and thumb, making a circle about the size of a fifty pence piece. 'A hole in the door and a lightbulb in a cage. On my second day they took me to another place, same sort of thing, a bucket and three wooden racks. There was an old intellectual in there, one of the Sixties' dissidents. He was OK, quite a good sort of man. They were just about to let the poor bastard out. We weren't allowed to talk so I opened up one of the cuts and wrote Alexey's address in blood on the floor.'

I couldn't believe what I was hearing.

Pyotr laughed. 'Well it worked,' he said. 'The old intellectual found Alexey and told him where I was. I don't know what Alexey did but he managed to get me out. I met him on the stairs. I tell you, I've never been more happy to see anyone. I hugged him, just like you hugged me. I wasn't very clean after eight days in prison so I went to my studio first and washed, then I came here, as you can see.'

I'd been so angry when he hadn't turned up the week before. Now he was there, sitting in front of me with grapefruit peel scattered around him like confetti, fresh out of prison and laughing at it so that it wouldn't hurt him. I had no guidelines for something like this. I knew that I would go along with whatever he decided. I felt weightless with fatalism.

Looking back on it now I am amazed by how happily I let myself go, how I assumed that I would be safe, that whatever happened, whatever dangers Pyotr was involved in, I would be OK.

'Shall we go to my studio?' he asked. I locked up my room and we left together. I don't know how long we spent over breakfast or what time of day it was when we left Babba Lenna's. Time became elastic, expanding or contracting to the importance of the moment. Space too became unpredictable. My room had been very small, kernelled around us. The street was huge; a whole city poured between the double lines of shops, houses and tramlines. Then the street shrank and Pyotr's studio opened up in front of us like a system of limestone caves.

4

Pyotr had his studio in an archæological storeroom that the University had forgotten about. It consisted of four basement rooms and Pyotr lived in the largest.

He flung open the door of the main room, strode across it and flicked back one of the curtains. Behind it on a windowsill fingernail-deep with dust was a crystal radio set which he thumped energetically; a buzzing sound followed and Radio Europa Plus lurched its way into the room.

I was still hovering in the doorway. He turned to me, held out his arms and grinned, 'My atelier!' he announced with pride. The plaster was crumbling and the ceiling was curved, the walls were spotted with rusting nails and directly on them Pyotr had drawn sketches and lines and sayings that he wanted to remember. 'Better Dead than Red' was painted in English across an easel that was doubling up as a coatstand. There were two tables: one large rectangular work table by the door with an electric-blue barrage balloon suspended above it, and another round table on the far side of the room between two tall windows whose grimy white curtains were closed. There was a light-blue, tin, wood-burning stove in one corner; next to it was a chest of drawers and a mattress made up with blankets but no sheets.

I took a few hesitant steps into the room towards the

round table. Four metal tube and cardboard chairs crowded around a bigger chair that had been hand made from planks and bits of plywood. 'Sit, sit!' insisted Pyotr, waving grandiosely at the big chair, 'this is the Captain's Chair.'

He left me perched warily on the edge of the chair, while he went to boil a kettle. In front of me, leaning against the wardrobe was a big green canvas with shadows curling out from underneath a black, stencilled, geometric figure. I hadn't spoken a word since I had arrived. I looked around me. I had never seen a room like this before, it was like a fugitive's cave. The sort of place where desperately poor students sit around and plot the fall of the evil bourgeoisie.

Time was expanding again and great gaps of it passed before he returned. I leaned forward, my hands, palms flat together, inserted between my knees. He put the two glasses of tea down on the table, knelt beside me and kissed me on the mouth. A sip of tea later and the caress developed until I had forgotten to feel nervous at all.

We were so close to the window that the knocking seemed to be actually in my ear. Four rough and heavy knocks that jolted me and flooded my muscles with adrenalin. Pyotr swore and got up, knocking over a glass of tea that pooled and dripped off the table. The knocks were repeated, more this time and very demanding. He smoothed the palm of his hand across my forehead, pushing back my fringe, and kissed my hairline. 'I am sorry about this, Natalie.'

He twitched the curtain, to see who it was, stiffened his back and gave a terse wave. He went out into the corridor to open the door and returned escorting two men in tracksuits.

'Natalie, these are my very good friends Yuri and Slava.' Yuri had a big belly and a story-book laugh, as if I was a very good joke and possibly one that he could eat. He had too much flesh on his hands which sat like bread and butter pudding on his finger bones, separating out the hair follicles across the top of his wrists. Slava was his antithesis, small, whip-limbed and sporting a long, groomed moustache over a constant high giggle.

'This is Natalie, my English friend,' introduced Pyotr, 'now sit down and have tea.'

But Yuri did not want tea. He slammed the flat of his hand on the round table so that it shook and wobbled on its stand, disturbing the pool of spilt tea. 'Where have you been, Pyotr?' he demanded.

'Where have I been, where have I been, well obviously I've been visiting Natalie,' he replied in a sing-song, cheeky boy to teacher voice. Yuri and Slava turned in perfect synchronisation and looked me up and down. Their colouring was dark; they looked like they came from somewhere in the South. Pyotr winked at me from behind their backs and I blushed.

'Six days is a long time to be visiting "your English friend" Pyotr,' commented Yuri in a voice heavy with sour innuendo.

'It's not what we heard,' sniggered Slava. 'Were you with Natalie all that time?' The end of his sentence disintegrated as he was overcome by his own humour.

'Not quite all the time,' began Pyotr, enunciating each word separately. He clicked his tongue on the roof of his mouth and then smiled wide enough for us to see his gold tooth. Despite the smile I could tell that he was being cautious. 'No, not quite, I had a little bit of trouble last week.'

'Why don't we forget about the tea and go for a drive in Slava's car and then you can tell us all about your troubles,' said Yuri.

'But it would be too rude. I have a guest. I can't possibly leave Natalie.'

'Bring her along too,' interrupted Slava and he smirked stupidly at me. 'We can show her the sights.'

Driving around the city with two slime balls was low on my list of enjoyable things to do that afternoon but I was happy to drift along with Pyotr wherever he needed to go.

Slava's car, the one I was meant to get so excited about, was a beige Lada with crocheted doilies across the back seat. Pyotr opened the back door for me and then got in after me.

It was a freak day; a day out of season. The sky was Wedgwood blue with silly little white clouds floating about in it. The temperature had drifted just above zero and the roofs were dripping like old men's noses. Yuri swore as he put a foot in a gutter shin-deep in melting sludge.

After a few minutes' encouragement the car started and we jerked off towards Tuchkov Bridge and Petrogradsky Island. Slava concentrated on the driving, emitting little squeals of hysteria as we thumped over the potholes. As we reached the bridge Yuri twisted his thick neck around and started on Pyotr. 'Your trouble, Pyotr Sergeivich?' He was openly threatening now and I began to get nervous; this was Pyotr's world but it was not yet mine.

Pyotr had arranged himself, lounging with one arm along the top of the back seat and the other holding the handle above the left door to steady himself. He slid his arm down from the top of the seat around my shoulders and pulled me in towards him. The rest of him remained studiously casual.

'The police picked me up and I had to spend a couple of nights in the cells, that's all.' A throw-away line.

'What have you been playing at, for fuck's sake, Pyotr? Where did they pick you up? Were they waiting for you? What were you carrying? What address did you give? This isn't a game. Fucking artists don't know their pricks from their arseholes, I don't know why we bother with them, Slava.' Slava giggled and lit a fake American cigarette.

I wanted to vaporise. I had a uneasy feeling that Pyotr

was using me as a shield. In those days a foreigner still had some kind of status, and I suspected he was gambling on them not really letting go while I was there.

Pyotr responded sulkily. 'It was not important. It was two o'clock in the morning and I was on my way home. The police were bored so they picked me up. I had a bit of grass on me. Not enough to get excited about. You needn't worry, your little necks are safe. I said I bought it on the street at Ploschad Mira. They were much more excited by my lack of *prepuska*. At least you're legal here.'

We were driving past the old arsenal. Defunct canons lay like fat sows in a row on the snowy verge. A little boy sat astride the mouth of one whilst his friend loaded it up with pretend gunpowder at the back. 'Aim, Fire.' The sound of the child's voice came muffled into the car and then returned as it echoed off the red brick walls.

'You fool,' shouted Yuri, 'what the hell were you doing walking around the city carrying grass in the middle of the night. Were the fuckers waiting for you? That's what I want to know.'

'Yuri. How many times do you want me to repeat it? It was not important. I was an unlucky bastard, sometimes people are. As far as they are concerned I am a bum artist, dregs of society type who is staying with more of the same in Pushkinskaya. End of bloody story. OK?'

For about thirty seconds we all stared stolidly out of the window. It was like a rest between boxing rounds. Suddenly we skidded and juddered to a stop. I hit my nose on the back of Yuri's meaty neck and then bounced back to Pyotr's armpit. 'Taxi,' squealed Slava with excitement, then he crashed the gears, turned right and raced towards Troitsky Bridge and the mainland.

Pyotr started up again. 'You guys are out of date. You're still stuck in the old times. We don't have to worry about the police any more, we can do what we want, this is a democracy now. Isn't that right Natalie?' I nodded hastily. 'The police are not going to be worried by a couple of part-time marijuana sellers. The poor bastards have got lousy pay, inflation and a future to look after.'

The argument, the words, were only half of it with Pyotr. There was an undertone, a lilt of amusement and irony that ran beneath his words. It's all so funny, can't you see the whole world's a joke, why are you taking it so seriously?

Yuri, however, was too angry for the spell to work on him. 'You're too much fucking risk. You're not going to stroll around in the middle of the night with our stuff on you any longer. If the *Mintey* have found out where you live then you can suck their dicks but we're not going to protect you any longer. The world hasn't changed as much as you think it has. Fucking artist scum.' His voice rebounded around the little car, so that I thought that if I opened my mouth I would get a gulp of his abuse. I hadn't heard the term *Mintey* before but I realised Yuri must mean the police. I shrank closer into Pyotr's side.

We were running down the embankment by the Winter Palace now, the melted slush splatting up onto the windows, the tin-can car buck-jumping over the potholes. 'Well Yuri, you've never been much protection anyhow,' said Pyotr silkily, 'and if that's the way you feel that's fine. I might buy your grass, but I do what I want and I go where I like, I'm not your bloody puppy. Slava, comrade, drop me and my English friend on the Fontanka outside Alexey Andreev's place please.'

Yuri snorted in disgust and Slava gave a little nod. We swung out of the traffic in front of the gloomy façade of St Isaac's Cathedral and headed south down Ulitsa Dzerzhinskova. With his arm around my shoulders Pyotr rested triumphantly on the crochet-covered back of the small beige Lada.

We got out at the Fontanka, Pyotr slammed the car

door behind us with childish force and Slava drove off, splattering us with slush as they went. I breathed in the placid air coming off the canal, relieved to be out of the crudely violent atmosphere of the little car. I had found Yuri and Slava intimidating. My hands were still trembling.

Pyotr let a peal of laughter stream out onto the breeze and, still laughing, with his mouth wide open, he lifted me up in a hug and whirled me round. 'I'm glad that's over. I'm sorry Natalie, you shouldn't have had to meet those punks – I knew that was going to be difficult.'

'Is it serious?' I was concerned.

'It's not important. I had had enough of them anyhow. I am going to buy from Alexey, it's easier. We will go and see him now. I haven't thanked him properly for getting me out yet.'

I recalled the ringmaster figure from Tornikov's exhibition. That night seemed a very long time ago. I almost felt that it could have been somebody else there with Nikita, someone who had told me all about it.

We walked a little way down the embankment of the Fontanka Canal until we had almost reached the Egyptian bridge and the concrete bunker of the Sovietskaya Hotel. We entered a crumbling baroque house opposite the hotel. Pyotr was still ridiculing Yuri and Slava for taking his prison visit so seriously. 'Poor bastards, they are never going to get anywhere. Yuri is Azerii and Slava is Armenian. If they go home they have to fight each other so they stay in Petersburg and sell drugs grown in Yuri's uncle's dacha.' I laughed with him as we climbed the stairs: he made them sound so silly.

Alexey Andreev's atelier was on the sixth floor. The lift wasn't working so I was panting and out of breath by the time we got there. A small card on the door read 'The Experimental Laboratory of Life'.

Alexey Andreev himself opened the door. He hugged

Pyotr in a very masculine strong-arm way and scrutinised me over his shoulder with eyes the pale-blue of gas flames. I wheezed on the doorstep.

'Welcome,' he said courteously, 'you must be Natalie, I am honoured to meet you.' His face was as white as wax and his skin was tight against the bones of his face and skull. He was dressed in an ancient English tweed suit. 'Like an English gentleman, Evelyn Waugh, yes?' he said, brushing one shoulder fastidiously with the palm of his hand. He pushed up his sleeve and I noticed a blue tattoo of a spider's web on his forearm. His formal manners took me by surprise but they were a welcome contrast to Yuri's coarse threats.

The flat was enormous and very stylish. Alexey used it as a gallery space as well as a place to live. There were five rooms all painted white with polished wood floors. Large abstract paintings hung on each wall, and amongst the sparse modern furniture were dotted sculptures and bizarre installations. A mask of Goethe peered down at me from one wall. I poked my head around the door of the second room and saw an old televison set with a surgical bandage around it, and cabbages growing out of the top.

We sat in the kitchen at a modern mahogany table under a large Soviet-style chandelier and drank coffee. Alexey pressed us with bright-pink iced cakes and Marlboro cigarettes (you could tell that they were the real thing because they were in soft packs with the customs seal still intact). A pregnant Persian cat, with fur the colour of a milk-chocolate orange and marmalade eyes, sat complacently on the sideboard by the sink.

Alexey probed me carefully. He had that journalist's trick of making you do all the talking. I found myself babbling on, telling him all about how my job had been advertised in the newspaper, my students and the school where I work. He looked shocked when I told him what I earnt. 'Natalie, they are exploiting you, this school. I can arrange private students for you. They will pay much more, maybe even in dollars. It is no problem.' Nothing, I was soon to learn, was ever a problem for Alexey.

'You must excuse my rudeness, Natalie, but we must talk business.' He turned to Pyotr and, plying him with more Malboro, began discussing lawyers. I felt a bit foolish for having talked so much. I played with the cat and hoped that I'd said the right things. For Pyotr's sake it seemed important to impress Alexey. I wondered how he had got Pyotr out of prison but it didn't feel right to ask him directly: it seemed too clumsy, somehow.

When we left Alexey clasped my hand. 'I am pleased to have met you. I hope that you will come and be my guest here again very soon.' As we reached the ground floor hallway I heard his voice rolling down the stairwell, 'Are there reds in your bed? bed? bed? ed, ed, ed,' followed by a dry little laugh.

We decided to walk back. Pyotr's mood had changed very abruptly, he was striding with his shoulders high and his head poked forward. 'You look like an eagle. What's the problem?' I asked as gently as I could.

'Nothing, it's in the atmosphere.' A pause hung between us like a reproach. On Letyeny Bridge we stopped and looked over the edge into the river. The ice packs were loose. I could see bitter, black water in the cracks. 'Natalie, I'm not a very good man for you,' he said. It was a bit late for that, I thought. 'Sometimes there is too much darkness in my head.'

'Don't be silly,' I protested.

'No really, I could still go back to prison, Natalie. Two years.'

'What about Alexey's lawyer?'

'You can't trust a lawyer.'

He was leaning his elbows on the iron balustrade. He turned and looked straight up at me; his face had lost all movement, like a clay mask. I linked my hands around his waist, 'Oh Pyotr!'

'No, Natalie, please,' he said, wriggling away from me, 'don't make a fuss. We will know more tomorrow.' He frowned and retreated from me like a crab.

We'd been back in the studio for about ten minutes when there was another, gentler knock on the window. I can't remember who the first visitor was – about ten people came to see him that night: some had heard that he'd been in prison, some had wondered where he was and some had just seen that the lights were on. He stepped out of his black mood just as quickly as he had stepped into it, and as he opened the door for the first visitor I could hear him laughing again.

Pyotr checked the knocks on the window to see that they were friendly. He conscientiously introduced me to each of his friends as they arrived. We sat around the table joking, discussing, drinking, smoking and eating fried potatoes communally from the pan. This was Pyotr's court. He never sat down and his tall, constantly moving figure dominated the room. We picked up the tails of his jokes, his ideas, his great black philosophies and spun them under licence. It took me a little time to understand the Sam Golod idea: it was a joke on Russia but it was also a way of explaining the changes. Pyotr made Sam Golod sound like a capricious autocrat, a Peter the Great, a Stalin, who was the cause of all the craziness outside. He was our faith that night, and the jokes we made about him became more and more elaborate. Every shortage, every deficit was attributed to Sam Golod and his awful power and every fortunate find – a vodka bottle, some decent potatoes, Pyotr's release from prison and my existence – was attributed to Sam Golod's temporary quirks of good humour. 'Sam Golod gives and Sam Golod takes away,' said Pyotr.

Yelena turned up. The swelling and bruising around her

eye had gone down, leaving a yellow nicotine stain on her skin. I heard her tell Pyotr that she was going back to live with Alexey. She pulled a bag of clothes from the chest of drawers and a suitcase tied up with string. She didn't, I noticed, ask Pyotr why he had been in prison. In fact nobody asked him all night, although to me it seemed the most obvious question.

A girl who appeared to be about thirteen arrived. Her skin was white and her hair was the colour of paprika. She brought a large red tulip with a thin elastic band keeping its petals together. She filled a jar with water, put the tulip in it and snipped the elastic band. The petals swung slowly out, red and glossy with black centres, the colour and texture of Soho underwear.

There was another girl with no eyebrows and a hairstyle like a mediæval monk. 'Crazy Ivan' who, contrary to his name, looked very normal dressed in a Russian made stone-washed jean jacket and blue jumper with a fake crest sewed onto the front, a rather studious Azerii, who apologised for the 'lack of culture'. Next to him stood a mountain of a man with a big black beard and a shattered slab of a laugh who, as he handed me a large vodka, told me he was a necrorealist.

I got dizzy with them all hovering and swirling around the room, with their curiosity about me and with the chatter and the drinking and the smoke. Pyotr appeared beside me, suddenly distinct from the crowd. I hoped that he was proud of me, that his friends approved of me, which I think is very difficult to tell in a foreign language. He squatted down beside the chair so that his head was on a level with my shoulders. 'Shall we go?'

'What about all these people?'

'They can stay, we can go.'

The redhead with the tulip let us out and closed the door behind us. There was a breeze coming off the river into the

dark street, fresh and quiet now. The walk to my room was
no effort at all. I didn't use a muscle. I had a feeling the city
was going soft and quivering; the whole street seemed to
be rising upwards on the back of the river breeze. Even the
sound of the trams rocking in their rails seemed to have
bubbles in it.

5

It was a black and white world that we woke to in the morning. There had been a heavy fall of snow and the sky was still white and turgid with it. I stood barefoot in a shirt in the kitchen, stirring porridge and waiting for the kettle to boil. Pyotr came in patting his feet down lightly on the wooden boards and, hugging me from behind, rolled me from side to side until, giggling and protesting, I dropped the wooden spoon I had been stirring the porridge with.

Our breakfast was as lazy and stretched as a cat in the sun. At midday reality intruded and Pyotr dressed himself, kissed me quickly and went off to meet the lawyer. I lay on the still body-warm bed and thought of my love affair. I wallowed in the idea of it.

I had tried the night before, with a sheet knotted around me, to explain about how inexperienced I was. Pyotr had laughed and been unimpressed. 'It is not,' he'd said, 'important.' When I remembered that he had come out of prison that morning and he might still go back, I too had thought it wasn't very important. That gave me a freedom; it cancelled all my doubts and made the situation simple. In London I would never have slept with somebody quite so quickly, but in the circumstances it would have been inhuman to wait.

He hugged me so tightly that I felt his muscles strain

against my arm bones. He kissed my eyelids and as I lowered my head he pushed it into the curve where his neck sloped into his shoulder. I felt the welts on his wrist rough across the soft skin of my lower back and I twisted my head up to kiss the underside of his jaw.

I had two lessons in the afternoon but I hadn't prepared anything for either of them. I set the students long exercises, and then a role play. All I could think of as I watched them pretend to buy tickets for a second-class sleeper to Vienna was the lawyer. I was confident that Alexey would have found him the best possible lawyer and yet Pyotr had said he didn't trust any lawyers. I didn't know enough about the Russian legal system to judge whether he was right. Normally after a lesson I talk to my students, who are mostly teenagers, or I go up to the office and chat with the other English teachers about the problems they're having with their parents-in-law or their children. That day I left straight away, I didn't even wait for a tram, but walked instead.

'How did it go?' I asked Pyotr as he opened the door. Annya was there, I could hear her voice in the main room.

'OK,' he said noncommittally. He ruffled my hair. He wasn't going to tell me then, he had visitors, I would have to wait until later. His manner was flippant and light; I wondered if it was because of good news or whether he was stoned.

Annya and Nikita were sitting on either side of the round table. Standing in the middle were three glasses and two vodka bottles. One bottle was empty and the other was about three-quarters full. Nikita, looking like a large skinny rabbit with his big red nose, flapped his arms at me in pleasure and kissed me sturdily on the lips. Annya, irritatingly, gave me a big stage wink. Annya likes to be involved in everything and she will steamroller herself in wherever she wants to go. She was obviously very pleased with herself for having introduced me to Pyotr, but I really did not want her attaching herself to us like an advisory third force.

Pyotr helped me out of my coat and hung it on the easel. 'Nikita is going to Berlin,' Annya announced.

'To your health,' said Nikita, handing me a glass of vodka. It is a Russian tradition to toast your health when you are about to do something really unhealthy. Pyotr insisted I sit down in the Captain's Chair. Behind me he began rolling a joint. He was strolling around the room mixing up the grass and tobacco, using the palm of his hand and one thumb as a mortar and pestle. From time to time he would carefully funnel some of this mixture through the dip between his thumb and the edge of his hand into an empty *papeross*. When he had finished, he screwed up one end to stop the contents falling out, lit it and inhaled hard. He slowly let his breath out and handed on the joint to Annya.

'Berlin, how come?' I asked Nikita.

'There is a Fräulein,' he explained. 'She has given me an invitation so now I can get a visa.'

'How long for?'

He shrugged, 'Who knows? Alexey Andreev has friends with a gallery in Berlin, maybe I can get a show there and then I can stay for longer.'

Nikita is incorrigible, he drinks and smokes too much and has had more lovers than anyone else I have ever met. He claims he loves them all, including his wife and baby girl in Lvov, and I haven't yet met a girlfriend of his who doesn't forgive him. I don't think Nikita has morals. He gets through, he plays, he swindles, he parties but there is no point in worrying about him because you know he's going to be OK, he has that lucky air about him. He never has any money and he's permanently thin and unhealthy, but Nikita is one of those people who somehow or other manage to end up on the right side of the battle lines.

Pyotr put his arms possessively around my neck and tipped the Captain's Chair so that it was balancing precariously on its shaky back legs. 'Berlin, how about that? Nikita makes a break for freedom, eh! Leaving us poor bastards behind.'

'But how will you get there?' I asked once Pyotr had let me go.

'Don't know yet.'

'You know they are now charging hard currency for all international train tickets?'

'I'll find a way,' he said confidently.

We all left the studio together. Annya and Nikita took a tram back to the mainland and Pyotr and I walked to my room. The sky had cleared, there was a full moon and it was freezing hard. We walked to the quay where the cruise boats dock in the summer. The ice on this leg of the river had melted the previous day but the surface had a stiffness that suggested that it was already returning.

We continued up Maly Prospect. Soon after the *molochnik* we slipped off the main street and meandered through the cells and courtyards, arches and tunnels of the back routes.

'Look,' said Pyotr as we came out from the darkness of an archway. 'It's a stone sun.' He pointed at the moon and, putting his arm through mine, pulled me abruptly against him. It was past two o'clock and the bruised streets were empty, ringing in the cold. The streets must have looked very similar when he was arrested: a week before there had been policemen standing and waiting for him like the shadows on the corner.

The hallway of my staircase was darker than outside because the *hooliganchiki* who live on the ground floor had nicked the lightbulb. The day before they had also stuck burning pieces of paper into the metal postboxes and a chemical smell of scorched paint still lingered in the air, hurting my nose but masking the more usual aroma of cats' piss. We stumbled up the staircase in the dark, Pyotr's steel toecaps clanging against the stone.

I went to the kitchen to boil a kettle for some tea. As I turned on the light the cockroaches scuttled under the cabinets. I left them in peace again and carried the kettle back to my room, two glasses held precariously by my fingers.

Pyotr had settled himself on the windowsill with his feet on the radiator, an old can of condensed milk balanced on his knee, acting as an ash tray. The curtain wasn't drawn and he had opened the small top window known as a *fortochka* to let the smoke out. Putting the kettle on the table, I turned and kissed him. His lips curled up in a smile under mine. I felt as stilled as the night air; we had left Annya and Nikita behind and the walk had cleaned me of the smoke from the studio. Ours was the only light on in the courtyard.

'What happened with the lawyer?' I wasn't prying, I just wanted to know.

'There are some difficulties. He wants $300.'

'Jesus. I thought he was state.'

'He is Natalie, but he is crooked as well and if I give him $300 I probably won't have to go to prison. It is a question of how generous he is feeling. I don't think I could manage two years in prison.' Very gently he drew the edge of his hand across his throat; he could almost have been caressing it. His lips were closed and lightly curled at the edges with the patient expression of someone who is explaining an unpleasant fact of life to a child. Pyotr used to enjoy teasing me like that.

I couldn't look at that face. I turned back to the table and opened a tin of tea. As I poured hot water from the kettle into each glass I watched the tea leaves mill around the centre, staining the water. I touched the surface in each glass with a cold teaspoon and the leaves began to sink to the bottom.

'You know, Pyotr,' I said, not looking up from my tea-making. 'I have some money that you can have.'

He gave me an indulgent smile: he wasn't going to take my offer seriously. 'Don't worry. My sponsor will lend it to me. Oleg's much richer than you Natalie, it's better that way.'

'What is a sponsor?'

'Suspicious?'

'Is he mafya?'

'What do you mean by mafya, eh?'

'I don't like the sound of it. Pyotr, be careful who you borrow money from.'

'You think it would be safe to borrow money from you?'

'Don't tease, this is serious. Of course it is safe to borrow money from me. I'm not a spy you know.'

'How do you know that I'm not.'

'Don't be silly Pyotr.'

'Natalie, I am being serious. You have such convenient categories. What do you mean by mafya? There are all sorts of different kinds of mafya: the Chechens are mafya, the artists from Pushkinskaya and Alexey Andreev are a kind of mafya and the Party is still the biggest mafya of all. Do you really think that one kind of mafya is better than another?'

'No, well, yes I do. Look what happened to Tornikov. It could happen to you.'

He gave a short laugh. 'No, this is something different. You don't understand, Natalie. Oleg buys my paintings because he likes them. It's that simple. He is also a friend and sometimes he lends me money, but it works both ways, I help him out too. Sometimes I do a bit of work for him. Anyhow, he owes me at the moment; he has got two paintings that he hasn't even paid for.

'How are you going to get back to Granny England if you don't have any money? You should keep your money in case of an emergency – like Babba Lenna's crusts in the kitchen – something might happen here, there could easily be another coup. Don't go throwing your money away on no-good bastards like me. This is a hard place for you. I know. I know.'

He had come up behind me and was holding me very tightly, laughing and lifting me off the ground with every 'I know'. I laughed with him: it couldn't be that dangerous, he must know what he was doing. Now, I am not so sure that he really did know what he was doing, but at the time I was prepared to believe him. We were alone together: right then that was all that mattered, and although I knew I was being fobbed off with half-truths I thought I would worry about that later.

I felt a side draught under the sheets as Pyotr got out of bed in the morning. I wasn't officially awake. I didn't move and I didn't lift my eyelids. I lay there pretending that instead of a collapsed sheet the long, warm flesh bolster of his body was still there beside me.

The door of my room clicked open and I rolled onto my tummy, pushed my arms out and stretched, curling upwards like a fish. I yawned and collapsed back onto the pillow. Slowly I became aware of the hot damp steam from a glass of coffee and condensed milk that was being held in front of me.

'Good morning, Natalie.' I grunted in reply and he came around to the side of the bed and sat down, put the two glasses on the floor and began to roll a joint. I shuffled over, bringing the sheets and blankets with me, twisting them around my legs, curling up and putting my head on

his lap, feeling the toughness of denim under my cheek. I
groaned again.

'Come on Natalie, wake up, there is life.'

'But bed is so nice,' I mumbled into his thigh.

'You're nearly there, sip some coffee,' he coaxed. I
dropped my head and one arm over the edge of the bed
and sipped hot coffee through my hair, then returned my
head to his lap. Pyotr put the end of the joint in my mouth.
I took a puff and thought about getting up and letting the
day drift in.

February and most of March rolled by. Pyotr and I jaunted
around the city as if it were a playground. Everything was
a joke, every gathering became a party and while I slept
he painted. He was working on a series of Sam Golod
paintings for Annya's exhibition, using brightly coloured
ship paints that he got from a friend who worked in
the docks. The only thing that marred it were the black
moods that Pyotr periodically suffered from, during which
he worked incessantly and the symbols in his paintings grew
more mechanical. At one point he gave up paintbrushes and
palette knives altogether and started using only stencils that
he cut out with razor blades. He said the moods were *tosca*;
spleen or depression which, according to Pyotr, were caused
by the atmosphere. I dreaded these moods because nothing
I tried seemed to help him, but luckily they were rare and
once we were laughing again we soon forgot them.

I scaled down my work until I was only teaching four
lessons a week. Alexey put me in contact with some private
pupils: two wives of black marketeers who lived a block
apart from each other near the Summer Gardens. They
had bleached hair, newly fitted kitchens and they bought
all their food for dollars from the *berioska* shop under the
Alexander Nevsky Hotel. They weren't very good pupils. I
was more of a status symbol than someone to learn from.

They were both rather spoilt and bored and I don't think they knew what to do in the time they had previously spent queuing. At the end of each lesson they paid me from little wads of money left by their husbands in the hallway but never, as Alexey had so tantalisingly promised, in dollars.

Inflation began to go crazy: in the *molochnik* they stopped serving at eleven o'clock each day in order to put the prices up. It made us reckless. We spent all our cash the moment we got it, because there was no point in keeping hold of it. As I was teaching less I was poorer than I ever had been, but I didn't care. My life was spinning very fast, I ate and slept erratically. My days were filled with a jumble of lessons, Pyotr's moods, vodka, grass and guests.

Our love-making was as unpredictable as everything else. Mostly we laughed in bed and gasped at our good luck but sometimes Pyotr's mood would be different, and when I held him inside me I sensed an emotional pain in him that worried me. Afterwards as we lay together, breathing deeply in the dark, I would stroke the length of his back and his long limbs to try and soothe it away.

Guests came knocking on the studio window around the clock and there were always two or three people sprawled over the table, even while Pyotr was working. If they were sleepy they simply lay down on the bed or on a hard old plastic couch that stood behind the door. There were deposits on all the bottles, so we used to sell the empties that our guests left behind and spend the proceeds on bread and cigarettes.

When we got tired of the crowds in the studio Pyotr would hide the key in a pipe by the staircase, or hand it to someone he trusted, and we would go off visiting ourselves or retire to my place. Babba Lenna came back in the middle of February. She seemed to accept Pyotr's presence. I never gave out the address of my room, which became our sanctuary, the only place we were ever alone.

The influence of Granny England moved further and further away. I made love in Russian, lived in Russian, thought in it and dreamed in it.

The streets were changing, goods were coming back into the shops and the three flowers sellers and single cabbage stall outside the Metro developed into a whole market. The steps up to the glass doors became crowded with old ladies thrusting one pathetic packet of cigarettes in your face, and with opaque-skinned children as young as seven selling bottles of medical spirit for those desperate for a drink. Behind the stalls mafya men patrolled in imitation Western clothes.

An ice-cream bar opened on Sredny Prospect. It was one of the new co-operatives. They painted the windows so that the light couldn't get in, the walls were panelled with tongue and groove planks and a stroppy girl stood behind the counter, her eyelids pasted with blue eyeshadow. Pyotr made me sit at a little table while he brought over two glasses of plum juice and a metal bowl containing three balls of ice-cream decorated with jam and nuts. We shared the ice-cream and struggled to drink the thick plum juice through straws.

'In Pushkinskaya they're saying that Tornikov had a habit.'

'What, drugs?'

'That's what they're saying. Apparently the poor bastard was a junkie. That's why they shot him.'

'Why would anybody shoot him because he was a junkie?'

'Wakey, wakey Natalie. He probably borrowed too much money off the wrong kind of people and spent it on the wrong kind of things. It happens, even to people as well known as Tornikov.'

Nikita's German visa came through in the middle of March. We went along with Alexey to see him in his studio in Pushkinskaya. Alexey provided us with supplies of Marlboro, bread, sausage, cheese, ginger biscuits and bottles of vodka and champagne; a mixture that Pyotr referred to as *Ngorny Karabak* because it caused civil war in your stomach.

The door to Nikita's studio had plywood tacked across it. Pyotr had kicked through it one day when no one was sober enough to let him in. The main room of the studio was large, three tall sash windows ran along one wall. There was a worrying patch in the centre of the room that didn't have floorboards, and at the far end there were five milk crates. A red crate was the kitchen and the blue crates were for chairs.

Alexey fussily arranged the feast that he had provided on a canvas on the floor. Nikita offered us tea, which he brewed on a hotplate with a dangerously loose connection and frayed wires. 'I'm afraid I don't have any sugar,' he said pulling a face. He didn't have a lot of things, I noticed. The red crate contained four dried biscuits, a packet of tea and some salt in a screw of newspaper.

Nikita was very fidgety that day. He couldn't sit still. He questioned me about Germany but as I had never been there I couldn't help him much.

'So where have you been then?'

'Well, I've been to France on family holidays and we once went to Canada because my aunt, my mum's sister, lives there.'

'I always liked the look of Canada.'

'Yeah, we went over to the west coast, it was really beautiful.'

'It always looks such a nice shape on the map.'

He jumped up from the milk crate and rolled around the room with his hands shoved deep inside the pockets of his thin duffel jacket. I think it was impatience; now that the visa had come through he wanted to be in Berlin and nothing would satisfy him until he was there.

'You're making me dizzy moving around like that,' I complained. He grinned apologetically and squatted against the wall. He rummaged around behind a pile of canvases and unearthed an old radio set and a minute later we were tuned into Radio Europa Plus.

'I phoned my wife and little girl today and told them I was going.'

'Jesus, how did that go down?' asked Pyotr.

'Not too badly. I'd like to see them before I leave but I don't know if I've got time to go down to Lvov.'

'When are you going?' I asked.

Nikita gave a deep bow to Alexey, who had now finished cutting up the bread and had placed a small piece of cheese or sausage on each square. 'Eat, eat,' he insisted munificently, instructing Pyotr to open the champagne and vodka. Nikita emptied the tea leaves from our glasses onto the floorboards and placed them next to Pyotr.

'I have some Italian friends in Berlin,' said Alexey in his measured, slightly twanging voice as he handed me one of his canapés, 'and Nikita has very kindly agreed to deliver some paintings to their gallery.' Which, roughly translated, meant that Alexey was paying for Nikita's train ticket. It used to worry me that we all took so much advantage of Alexey's generosity. I know that I was guilty of it as well. The problem was that he was so correct and polite, you knew that he would never say no.

'Oh that's wonderful!' I enthused, 'what a lucky coincidence.'

'There is a lot of interest in Russian artists in the West at the moment. Their paintings are selling for many thousands of dollars now.'

'And,' said Nikita, 'we are hoping that Alexey's friends

might want to put on a show of my work in their gallery.'
Alexey smiled and looked slightly smug.

We slept at the studio that night because Pyotr said he
wanted to work. I'd gentrified the mattress with some of my
sheets, which made staying there much more comfortable.
I lay watching him and listening to the radio. He took out
one of the lightbulbs using the sleeve of his jumper, so
that the glare wouldn't keep me awake. He stood under
the remaining light leaning over the rectangular table, his
arms straight, his elbows locked and his back hunched. He
was staring at a picture on the table. There was a cigarette
gripped between the first and second finger of his right
hand. From time to time he would turn his head sideways
and take a deep drag on the cigarette.

6

'So where are we going?' I asked Pyotr as we stepped from the studio into the dark street.

He paused on the kerb of the pavement. 'Natalie, remember I told you my sponsor wasn't mafya.'

'I didn't believe you,' I told him. Pyotr frowned.

'I don't want to lie to you, Natalie. Maybe he is mafya, everything here is mafya, but he is not bad mafya. He is a good friend and he is very kind.'

'And we are going there now?'

'Yes we are going there now.' He squeezed my hand hard enough to push my little finger painfully underneath the others. Pyotr never told me the whole truth of any situation. I found it frustrating but I knew that his wariness was instinctive, that it was the accumulated caution of years of never dealing in facts because facts were dangerous and of never trusting anyone, not even the people you loved. It must have been difficult for Pyotr, who had lost the facility for trust, to love anybody – let alone a foreigner like me.

A tram was rattling to a stop on the other side of the street. He jerked at my arm and we ran across the road dodging the cars. The doors had already closed by the time we got there, but the driver saw us running and as we reached the tram he reopened the last door and we jumped in breathing hard. Oh God, I thought as I swung myself breathlessly into a seat, mafya – what am I getting myself into?

We took the Metro out to a station in the northern suburbs. There was a futuristic monument to the glory of the workers standing in the middle of the station platform. We walked up a hill from the Metro and at the top turned off the main prospect into a tree-lined side street.

The lady who opened the door to the flat was dark and glossy. She greeted Pyotr and kissed him on both cheeks. 'You must be Natalie, I'm Allia,' she said, smiling to me over Pyotr's shoulder. 'I'm so pleased to meet you. Oleg isn't back yet but we won't wait for him.' She turned back to Pyotr and added, 'I'm so glad you could bring her.'

The furniture in the kitchen wasn't new, but the frying pan was and the cupboards were full of food, flashing like an amusement arcade of Western labels. She brought two glasses over to the table and then a large two-litre bottle of Bacardi and a bumper plastic bottle of Coke (both of which I knew you could only get in *berioska* shops). 'There you go Pyotr. We remembered that you like rum. Now Natalie, what would you like to drink?' I said that Bacardi and Coke was fine, thank you very much.

A little girl hovered at the doorway to the kitchen. I'm not very good at the ages of children, but I'd guess she was about eight. She had long seaweed-type hair. She stopped singing when she saw us. Allia called her in and she stuck her thumb in her mouth and shuffled awkwardly forward. 'This is Olga,' introduced Allia. 'Olga, say hello to Pyotr and Natalie.' The little girl stared at us and refused to say anything. Eventually she crab-walked out of the room and a minute or so later I heard her singing next door.

Allia talked to us over her shoulder as she made a salad and fried two steaks. She angled herself around, holding her frying pan like a cocktail waitress's tray. 'Oleg tells me that Alexey has paid for Nikita's ticket to Berlin. Silly boy, he should have asked Oleg.'

'He's going this Sunday,' said Pyotr.

'I think he might come and see us tonight. He's not the only one going West, you know. I've decided to take Olga to Germany, Pyotr.'

'Really? To Berlin?'

'Not yet. At the moment we have only got visas for a refugee camp in Eastern Germany.'

'But what about Oleg?'

'We're leaving him behind, but I hope that he'll be able to follow us later on. I want to get Olga out now, I don't like her growing up surrounded by all this.' She gave a vague wave in the direction of the window and the street. 'It isn't a place for a child.'

Allia served us with two enormous plates of steak, fried potatoes and salad. 'What about you?' I protested.

'I'll wait for Oleg, you eat now. Look at you Pyotr, you are too thin, you are all cavities, there is nothing left of you.'

I pressed my knife into the steak and a little clear fat tinged with pink oozed out under the pressure.

Oleg arrived as I was wiping up my plate with a piece of bread. Pyotr, always a faster eater, had finished and was ogling me like a famished dog as I finished off the last scraps of lettuce and potato.

'Pyotr, how are you doing?' said Oleg, walking straight up to Allia and kissing her. He took his outdoor clothes off, a stream of talk reaching us from the hall. 'Crazy day, what a crazy day, I've got a new plan to talk to you about Pyotr, I've just come back from Riga. It's crazy, crazy there, though maybe not quite as crazy as here.' He came back into the kitchen, 'Have you eaten, I'm starving, is there anything left for me, *milaya*?' Allia was already frying another steak.

He hadn't put any slippers on and he stood in dark-blue socks leaning on the side with one foot resting on the knee of his other leg, treating us to a continuous string of impressions, opinions and plans. He didn't look like my idea of a mafya man at all. I'd been expecting a big gun-toting ape wearing lots of flashy gold jewellery, not this dark, garrulous, weather-beaten little man.

He ate standing up while he lectured us on the opportunities to be had in Riga, using his fork as a baton. 'In Riga there is more food than here, much more food.' He stuffed another potato into his mouth and I watched it appear as a lump in his cheek. 'I tell you there are fortunes to be made in Riga. They are much more advanced than we are here. Last week they had to stop the Petersburg–Riga train for two days because somebody took down all the wires and sold them for metal. It was, I think, a neat little operation.' He wagged his head to underline his admiration and carried on talking through the churning food in his mouth. 'But I tell you the ones to watch out for are the Army. Absolutely without question they are the worst of the lot; they are selling hardware wholesale at the barrack gates.'

In went another potato and the lecture carried on. 'Much less violence in Riga, hardly any murders at all. But then they have it well-organised, there aren't so many people in charge, they are all very strong but they talk to each other like normal human beings. Not like here. So it's more peaceful and they make more money. They told me that this is an American method, but then Riga is civilised. Seriously, I think Petersburg has a lot to learn.'

Pyotr winked at me. He was trying hard to suppress a smile; this earnest contemplation on how best to organise mafya gangs appealed to his sense of humour.

Oleg changed the subject. 'Has Allia told you that she is going to the West to escape me? Oh, before I forget, I bought some gin on the way home.' He unhitched his leg and strolled out into the hall. He came back waving a bottle of Gordons (the clear bottle with the yellow label

that you only get abroad) and a plastic bottle of Schweppes
Diet Tonic Water. 'There you go, Natalie, gin and tonic for
a proper English lady.'

When Oleg had finished eating we moved into the sitting
room. There was an old tapestry hanging along one wall, in
the corner stood a modern Japanese television and video,
the rest of the furniture was standard Soviet issue. Olga
was doing her homework at a table. 'Did you have a good
day?' asked Oleg. She inserted her thumb into her mouth.
Once it was all in she smiled at him and wriggled on the
chair. 'Why don't you go to your room, we have to talk in
here,' he said gently. She slid off the chair sideways, picked
up her exercise book and a pencil and scuttled out.

'She's very shy,' said Oleg. I noticed that instead of going
to her room she had gone into the kitchen where Allia was
doing the washing up. 'I think she will have a better life
if she grows up in Germany.' He sighed: either he didn't
believe it or he wished it weren't true.

I joined Allia and Olga because I knew that Pyotr and
Oleg wanted to talk business. It took a lot of self-control:
the last place I wanted to be in was the kitchen. I was itching
to know what they were discussing and, while Allia was
asking me questions about how much secretaries got paid
in London, I strained to try and pick out individual words
from the hum drifting across the hallway. I liked Allia.
She seemed independent and sophisticated and I thought
it was very brave of her to go to Germany with Olga,
not knowing what she would find when she got there. I
liked Oleg as well but I wouldn't want to double-cross
him: beneath the chatter he gave the impression of being
quite tough. As I dried the plates from the rack and
handed them to little Olga to put away my curiosity
increased, and I worried about what Pyotr would have
to do or promise before Oleg gave him $300 for the
lawyer.

Later on, some other people turned up and the gathering turned into a party. It was the usual Pushkinskaya crowd: the girl with the monk's haircut and no eyebrows, the necrorealist with the big black beard, a guy called Sasha whose face was familiar but I couldn't think where from, the childlike redhead who brought the tulip the day Pyotr got out of prison, Nikita and Arkady. The only people who weren't there were Yelena and Alexey.

We all sat on the floor, drinking and smoking. Oleg showed Pyotr how to prepare marijuana pollen by wrapping it up in silk, steaming it over a kettle and compressing it with a heavy weight. The heavy weight in this case was the leg of the sofa. Four of us were commandeered to bounce on it in order to increase the pressure.

I positioned myself beside Nikita, who was leaning up against the sofa and daydreaming – I think part of him was already in Berlin. 'So it's Sunday, Nikita, I didn't realise it was so soon.' He grinned in anticipation.

'The Italian gallery say they want the paintings delivered straight away,' he said happily.

'Are you going to try and get your wife and little girl out too?' I asked. I could never get used to the idea of Nikita being married.

He flipped my knee with the back of his hand and looked bashful. 'It's complicated, I don't know how long I will stay. Maybe I will go to America. Also there is the German Fräulein, you see.' I did see. Nikita's life is always very complicated.

'We will have to see you off in style, have to have a party.'

'But of course. We will have the biggest party ever. Oh I can't wait, I want to be there now. I can't imagine what it must be like. To be in Germany. I'm tired of Petersburg, we've had no heating at Pushkinskaya for the last three days. There is a girl out at Ozerki whom I have been staying with, but . . .' His sentence trailed off and then rather limply he added, 'I want to be in Berlin.'

Pyotr was picking his way carefully across the room, avoiding ashtrays, people, hands, glasses. He stood by Nikita, facing me, 'Will you be OK, Natalie? I have to go somewhere with Oleg for a couple of hours. Nikita, you take care of her, OK?'

I was uneasy. 'It's nearly eleven o'clock,' I protested, 'what kind of job are you going to do at this time of night?'

'I'm a werewolf, I do my work at the midnight.' He gave me a fake snarl and a laugh. He was excited, the skin around his eyes had creased up and his gold tooth was flashing from the side of his mouth.

'You'll be OK. I'll be back soon and Nikita will take care of you.'

'I don't need taking care of,' I snapped, not very crossly, 'you do. Pyotr, please don't do anything silly.'

'Trust me little *feministka*.' He ruffled my hair and said to Nikita, 'Hey Rabbit, you take care of my *feministka*, my little English lady.'

'My pleasure,' grinned Nikita. Pyotr nodded and walked back across the room. I noticed that people moved slightly aside to let him pass, unconsciously, without stopping their conversations or looking at him. Oleg was standing in the hallway wearing his outdoor clothes, but he was out of the light so I couldn't see his expression.

I didn't ask Nikita what was going on because I knew he wouldn't tell me. I got up to find a drink. I'd been sitting on my legs and they had gone numb and prickly. I went out into the hall, fished around in the pocket of my coat for a new packet of cigarettes and found the gin in the kitchen.

How out of place all those people looked. It was as if Allia had decided to hold a theme party. She sat gracefully on the sofa while all of the rest of them were crammed into the space of a Persian carpet, as if they were aware that they needed to be contained. Columbus clouds of sweet smoke hung above the crowd. The guy called Sasha, who had joined Nikita now, had spiky black hair and heavy bull shoulders. I handed a drink to Nikita and put mine on the ground, and Sasha moved aside to give me room to sit down.

Sasha flirted with me. He drew sketches of nudes on the back of three old New Year cards and signed them in shaky Latin script, 'Dear Natalie, love from Alexander'. He had a home-made tattoo of a triangle on the back of his hand. The thin bones of the back of his hand made it ripple as he sketched. He filled up my glass and tried to persuade me to drink some double-strength vodka, and implied that he thought I was rather quaint when I demurred. He was attractive, with blue eyes and a boxer's broken nose, and I quite enjoyed the attention. I was cross with Pyotr because I was worried about him: whatever it was he was doing, it was certainly not legal. If Nikita could live it up with three different women simultaneously then I could have a light flirtation with Sasha, but as he grew drunker I got tired of him. It began to get late and Pyotr and Oleg had still not returned. The room started to clear at half-past one in the morning. The last Metro was at two and most people lived in the centre. I had given one of my private lessons that morning so I had enough money for a taxi. I kept on looking over towards the door to check that nobody had come in.

At last Pyotr returned and he laughed as I hugged him. He was pink but his cheekbones and the rims of his eyes and mouth were tinged with white. He looked tired but very happy. He put his hand around my waist. 'You see I came back and all of me is here. Were you all right without me, little one?'

I said that I was fine, and that never mind what he thought, the world could function without him and would he mind not making rude comments about my height. I said it lazily and with a smile. Sasha was still there but quite drunk by that point; I could feel him looking at us.

'Do you want to go home soon?' I asked hopefully.

'Yes, OK, I'll just have one joint with Oleg and then we'll go. Can you hang in there for just a bit longer?'

I was still holding Sasha's sketches in my hand. 'That's fine,' I answered and oozing myself out from his arm I walked into the hall and put the sketches into my coat pocket, folding them a bit so that they didn't poke out of the top. Then I went back and joined Allia on the sofa and waited.

We caught a taxi, so I couldn't ask him what he had been up to immediately. The taxi had amazing suspension, swinging over the holes in the road like a cradle. We slipped down the side of the Neva, where the ice had melted and shone a dull pewter, past the Winter Palace with its ornate crusting and then over the bridge to Vasilievsky Island. By the time we drew up outside the archway of my block the car was driving through my sleep. Pyotr had to shake me awake and pull me to my unwilling feet.

We drank some tea before going to bed. 'What have you been up to, then?' I asked, sitting cross-legged on the seat of my chair and blowing on the surface of my tea.

'Nosey Natalie.'

'Tell me.'

'All right, I've been loading nickel.' He was so delighted with himself, he reminded me of a schoolboy who has managed to sneak out to the newsagent for sweets in between lessons. He dangled a triumphant pause and I sipped my tea and waited for him to carry on.

'Apparently there are these nickel mines behind the Urals that are completely staffed with black labour, not state, it's all unofficial. I think quite a few of them come from Vietnam. They get the nickel out of the mines and load it onto the floor of train carriages and then put another, fake, floor on top of the nickel. Eventually these trains come to Petersburg. Oleg and his associates pay five dollars an hour to unload the nickel and put it into lorries. These go to Latvia, where there is no export duty and from there they sell the nickel to the West. Latvia is now one of the world's largest exporters of nickel but there isn't a nickel mine in the place. It's amazing isn't it? Five dollars an hour.' He made it sound like all the riches in the world.

He pulled some little bobbly bits of nickel out of his pocket and then some flat square scraps of nickel sheet. He handed them to me. They were warm from being in his pocket, dry and very light in weight. The bobbly bits rolled around the creases in my palm and got lodged in the cracks between my fingers. 'A present for you, Natalie, a souvenir.'

7

Nikita had friends playing in a band at the Tam Tam Club on the day before he left for Berlin. The Tam Tam is an occasional club in the old Komsomol, on the corner of Maly Prospect and the Seventeenth Line before you get to the stray factory blocks that surround the port. The ground-floor windows were all boarded up when, at nine-thirty in the evening, Pyotr and I swung through a pair of double doors into what had once been a relatively smart reception area. Pyotr bounded up the stairs. On the top step two well-worn youths sat facing each other and, for a charge of five roubles each, they paused in their conversation long enough to rubberstamp the back of our hands and let us through.

Upstairs had the atmosphere of an underfunded secondary school. The walls were painted in two tones, turquoise to hip height and above that a light peppermint green. Pyotr said that his mental home had been exactly the same, so it was probably a state decorating standard. In one room the walls and ceiling had been painted with a single thin layer of black, and you could see the peppermint green through the chips. On a stage where well-washed Komsomolets had once demonstrated their folk dancing, there was a drum kit, microphone set and a couple of big amps. Two guys in tight black jeans and sleeveless denim jackets were sniffing around the equipment. Yelena and Arkady were sitting on a Formica table, swinging their legs, idly smoking and waiting for something to happen.

The corner of Yelena's mouth was puffy and badly cut, the scabs newly cracking. I remembered the black eye that she had the night that Tornikov was shot. I felt slightly sick: somebody was obviously making a habit of hitting her. I wondered if Pyotr knew anything more about it or if he would tell me if I asked him. Not asking questions was becoming a habit.

Pyotr said hello and we both lit cigarettes. 'When are the band meant to be coming on?' I asked.

'Nikita said ten but don't hold your breath. There's a café downstairs, why don't we get some coffee there until they show?' said Yelena. Her voice was forced and I heard a note of fragile defiance in it. I think she knew I was trying not to look at her mouth.

'How's Kolya?' asked Pyotr.

'He's gone back to be spoiled by his grandmother. I'll miss him, but Alexey doesn't like him hanging around, so it's better this way.' She cracked a taut little smile.

The café was through a door under the stairs. Smoke was knitted tight into the air. Annya was there with a bulky, bearded man whom I took to be her new Polish lover and the reason she had been out of circulation for a while. She had told me about him at school, which was the only place that I had seen her. They were sitting very close together in a cubicle lit only by a green-fringed lamp. We squashed in beside them.

'Good to see you Natalie, Pyotr. Here, I want you to meet Leszek. Leszek this is the other *Anglichanka* I was telling you about from the school, and this is Pyotr, and Yelena and Arkady.'

Leszek was drunk and friendly in a 'You *will* be happy' kind of way. He frowned hard and tipped his face down

towards his lap, until it flashed with recognition like someone sweeping a torch underneath a sheet. 'Yes,' he said in
English, thickly filtered through Polish, 'Strawberry fields
forever'. I grinned and Annya gently patted his forearm
and beamed as if she had just hatched him.

'Cognac?' he asked.

This time I was more positive. 'Yes please,' I said, nodding
to make sure he understood.

He extracted a half bottle from his coat pocket with a label
advertising 'STRAN' in Latin script. He unscrewed the top,
filled it with cognac, and threw the contents of the bottle
top into his mouth like a little hole above his beard. He
refilled it and passed it to me.

I wasn't aware, until then, that your throat has hairs in
it. But as I swallowed the Stran I felt them stand up on end
and bristle like the back of a dog when it sniffs trouble.

As I tossed back my second cap, Nikita emerged through
the dry ice of Bulgarksy smoke, accompanied by Arkady
who'd been off to buy some coffees. 'Ah cognac!' cried
Nikita joyously as he caught sight of the bottle inefficiently
hidden in Leszek's lap.

He put down the two coffees he was carrying and,
grabbing the bottle, poured a generous splash into each.
'Irish,' he said.

'Medicinal,' I coughed.

When it came on, the band was like a student band,
loud and enthusiastic. A Paul Weller look-alike and a
Robert Smith clone thrashed out Aquarium cover versions,
'Anarchy in the UK' and some heavy rap. The crowd loved
them and roared when they did three dedications to Nikita.
The black room was crowded and a hard core around the
stage were dancing manically.

Pyotr hated dancing so I left him by the windowsill
talking to Yelena. Nikita, on the other hand, moves like
a strung-out puppet and I love it too, so we hit the floor

with Annya, Leszek and Arkady and didn't stop until the band came off.

When we made our way back to the peppermint green foyer I was panting hard and my T-shirt was dripping with sweat. Nikita wheedled the Stran from Leszek and we swigged it in turn.

'So what's next?' I demanded.

'There is a backstage party but we've got to wait until Alexey arrives first. Are you on for it?'

'Sure, count me in. I'm on for anything.'

We were cooling off on the stairs when Alexey showed up, looking dapper in a leopardskin jerkin and brown leather trousers. Only Alexey could wear clothes like that and get away with it: on any other man they would look camp, but on Alexey they just looked slightly self-consciously weird. He greeted everyone and, bending stiffly, kissed Yelena on her poor damaged mouth in a way that was both gallant and slightly territorial. I winced and wondered if he was responsible, but then I dismissed the idea; I couldn't imagine him hitting anyone.

We went backstage through some curtains in the wings. There was a staircase, a couple of dressing rooms and a hallway leading to a back door where supplies were delivered. It was already crowded and smoky when we arrived. A cheer went up for Nikita. 'To success,' shouted someone. 'To the West,' came another. 'Lucky German girls,' hooted a third, followed by a roar of laughter.

I was jostled by the crowd to the head of the stairs and found myself standing next to a dancer. 'Ballet?' I asked, remembering afternoons with my granny watching *Swan Lake* on TV. I used to make earnest seven-year-old promises to her that I would become a ballet dancer when I grew up, and in my room I would secretly practise balancing on the points of my toes in a pair of clogs.

'*Nyet*,' she replied, 'avant garde.'

'Oh,' I said, a bit deflated. After that I didn't feel inclined to tell her I was a teacher. She said that she was going to the West soon. An Australian opera director had invited a group of them to New York. He was going to pay. 'How amazing,' I said politely. I didn't really believe her, it sounded very unlikely to me. It seemed that everyone was trying to go West. I had an image of Pyotr and I being the only ones left in St Petersburg, wandering around a beautiful but empty city.

She was a friend of Annya's so we gossiped about her and Leszek for a bit, whether it was a good thing or a bad thing, what would come of it and whether we liked him or not. The dancer said that I must come and visit her one day. I agreed and knew that I never would.

I extricated myself and paused at the top of the stairs, wondering whether anything exciting was happening on the ground floor. I had just started picking my way down the crowded steps when there was a knock on the back door.

The drummer from the band opened the door. There was a smack as his head hit the wall and four heavies barged in. Downstairs everything went quiet. I heard the dancer's conversation voice from the dressing room – jangling and light and dangerously out of place. There was a patter, a group whisper as the inhabitants of the two little dressing rooms pushed out onto the stairhead to see what was happening. I looked around but I couldn't make out where Pyotr was.

From where I stood, I had a view of the four men from the chest down, but for the moment the angle of the stairs hid their heads and shoulders. They were wearing stone-washed jeans and bright acrylic jumpers. One of them held a gun. He swung it out of view and fired it into the ceiling, so close the noise stunned me, ringing around my inner ear. Shards of plaster shattered from the ceiling, the scorched smell of the shot mixing with fine plaster dust.

One of the men started to give out orders and directions: I couldn't make out the exact words, but it seemed that they were after protection money from the band. The intruders worked the crowd. The one with the gun came to the base of the stairs. As his face came slowly into view I went rigid. I knew him. It was Sasha. He didn't see me immediately, he was brandishing his revolver, pushing it between people, directing them this way or that with it. I recognised the smudged blue home-made tattoo on the back of his hand.

He looked up and saw me, then he smiled, a warm, sociable, completely incongruous cocktail party smile. I felt a deep flush as my blood flooded to the surface of my skin. I stared at him in horror but I was too terrified to respond. He shrugged mutely and I wondered guiltily if anyone had noticed our dumb play. He shouted four names up the stairs and then turned away. He wasn't going to acknowledge me. I was relieved, really relieved. I felt my hands shiver against my side.

There was a grunt, followed by the sound of a revolver against bone. We all held ourselves as still as we possibly could. Where, I fretted, was Pyotr? A man's voice begged. One of the intruders said: 'That will teach you to pay your dues.' There was another harder hit and a scream of pain.

Suddenly Annya was screaming at them as well. Swearing at them in filthy gutter Russian, taunting them. 'Get out, get out, pricks, thugs, bullies! Fuck off back to the shitholes you came from!' Leszek was hysterically begging her to be quiet, to leave it alone. I heard a slap followed by Annya's surprised, gagged cry. Then the door slammed quickly behind the four men and an engine coughed in the street.

There was a hush, followed, once we realised the intruders had gone, by a surge and a struggle on the staircase as we all tried to push down simultaneously. Everyone was talking. I could hear a girl crying and then thankfully

I heard Pyotr shouting my name. Behind all the noise and commotion was Annya's pained pulse like the cry of a tortured bird.

It seemed to take forever to get down the stairs. They'd beaten up the four members of the band. The girl who had been crying was trying to clean up the face of the lead singer. I could see Yelena leaning over someone else. Annya was close by the door. Leszek, Nikita and Pyotr were crowded around her. She'd been stabbed in the side. Nikita was urging Leszek to go to The Astoria, the most expensive hotel in the city.

'She's got insurance or dollars or something. Get her the best treatment. Go, Leszek, go, you won't have any trouble getting in. You're Polish.'

Pyotr was squatting beside Annya, holding her hand and staunching the blood from her belly with his red and yellow scarf. With his spare arm he hugged me around my calves and pushed his head briefly, despairingly, into my knees. He didn't say anything.

I interrupted Nikita. 'Listen I'll go. There's an English consulate at The Astoria now, I heard about it last week. It's in one of the hotel rooms, maybe they can help. I'll catch a taxi.' I looked down at Annya, 'Hang on in there, you'll be OK girl. I'm going to get help now. You'll be OK.'

From behind us I heard Alexey with more advice, he talked more slowly than the rest of us, or maybe we were all gabbling. He began to take charge.

'Report the matter to the British consulate, Natalie, but you must ensure that they don't inform the city authorities or we will have many more problems on our hands. Meanwhile we will escort Annya to the Lenfinmed Polyclinic on the Fontanka. It is the foremost foreign clinic in St Petersburg and it is where they treat the tourists. I am acquainted with a doctor there. They will ensure that she has the best treatment available. We will rendezvous there. Now come with me and I will hail some taxis.'

I kissed the back of Pyotr's head. 'OK Annya, I'm going to the consulate, be brave.' She nodded and sniffed, the skin around her eyes was stretched tightly from the effort of controlling the pain. The crowd shuffled aside as Alexey opened the back door. I turned and followed him out.

I was right about the British consulate but it had only been open for a month. It consisted of one lady in a hotel suite on the third floor. Her name was Elizabeth Garrett, sensible, in her early forties, with short waved hair. I got her out of bed. She wore a very nice navy blue Viyella dressing gown and red leather slippers. She sat me down and got me a coffee from room service. My hands were still shaking.

I told her what had happened to Annya. I was trembling and confused and I couldn't remember the name of the clinic that Alexey had given to me, but once I remembered that it was on the Fontanka she guessed the name. She didn't seem surprised by what had happened. She seemed to think that all Russians, apart from the trained and civilised restaurant-going variety, were rabid and dangerous. She asked if we had informed the police. I remembered Alexey's words and stammered that I didn't want to get my Russian friends into any trouble. She obviously disapproved but she agreed not to say anything.

I thought of Pyotr standing on my doorstep the morning they had let him out of prison. How his face had had a blue tint as if a bruise had just left. 'There were a lot of people there who didn't have permits for St Petersburg. They're illegal,' I said in explanation.

'Dear, dear,' she tutted. 'You must be careful who you mix with. Maybe you ought to register, that way we can let your family know if something happens.' None of this was very helpful for Annya, though to be fair I don't think there was anything that she could have done. There didn't seem to be a connection between the opulence of The Astoria with its reproduction Louis Quatorze furniture and the back staircase of the Tam Tam. I registered Annya and myself and gave her the name and address of my parents, but I only really did it so that she wouldn't feel that she had been got out of bed for nothing.

'It's been nice to meet you and I hope your friend is not too badly hurt. You will be careful won't you dear, this isn't Fulham.' I shook her hand, apologised for it being so late and left.

The night porter regarded me disapprovingly and ushered me out of the hotel's glittering blond marble hallway into the gloomy shadow of St Isaac's Cathedral. I walked up past the statue of Peter the Great on a bronze horse, rearing over the river with his terrible hand outstretched – calming the people or beating them down, depending on your inclination. On the embankment I flagged down a private car, knowing it would be cheaper than a taxi, and asked the driver to take me to the Fontanka Canal. Definitely not Fulham, I thought.

The clinic was very new, it felt like it had been built and equipped with foreign money, Finnish I guessed. It was just after three in the morning when I arrived. A foreign nurse, speaking English with an accent I couldn't place, led me down a corridor to a waiting room furnished with a yucca plant and dove-grey upholstered seats. Pytor, Nikita, Leszek and Alexey sat around a smoked-glass table loaded with copies of *Vogue*, *Time* and *The Economist*.

'How is she?' I asked.

Pyotr answered me first. 'Asleep at the moment. They've doped her up and stitched the wound. They want to keep her in here for at least a week. She will be OK.'

'The wound is quite extensive but fortunately none of the

major organs have been affected. Did you manage to locate the British consulate?' asked Alexey.

'Yes, but she wasn't much good. She said she couldn't do anything to help us unless we reported it to the authorities.'

'What!' exploded Pyotr, 'that's just crazy.'

'And did you?' enquired Alexey softly.

'Of course not,' I said.

The grey upholstery and the wall-to-wall carpeting were making everybody feel uncomfortable. Even I felt a foreigner. We left, nodding to the yucca plant and the foreign nurse. Outside we stood in a row, leaning over the wrought-iron lace of the canal railing. The ice had melted. The black water looked treacherous and thick.

Alexey invited us back to his place. Pyotr wanted to go but I said that I was done in and all I wanted to do was get some sleep. Nikita said he had to go to Pushkinskaya to finish off his packing. Leszek went back with Alexey. Poor bloke, he looked rough, he must have been feeling awful.

We didn't have enough money left for another taxi so Pyotr and I walked to Nevsky with Nikita, waved him goodbye next to the Red Palace and then trudged silently back through the night city. By the time we climbed up my dark staircase the backs of my calves and the arches of my feet were aching. I couldn't talk to Pyotr, I was dry of emotion and the image of Sasha's smiling face shimmered in front of me and made me ashamed. No one else had mentioned seeing him; even Nikita, who must have recognised him as well, hadn't said anything. It was like a contract in silence. I wondered if Pyotr had noticed him. He massaged the back of my neck but I broke away and went to brush my teeth.

I dreamt that night that I was giving a party and I had hired a clown for the entertainment. I circulated around the gossiping crowds of people, handing out sausages on sticks and glasses of white wine. I kept on looking towards the door but the clown did not turn up. Then I was filled with a sense of foreboding and I shooed my guests away. Some of them were unwilling to leave but I was quite insistent that they must go. When the room was empty I turned around and a tremendously tall clown was silhouetted against the window. In my dream the clown was either Pyotr or my brother Simon but I wasn't sure which. The clown pulled off his hat and then removed his nose. Casually he took my right hand and inserted the tip of a long thin stiletto blade into the web of skin between my thumb and forefinger.

It was a shaky group that saw Nikita off at the station at five o'clock the next day. Eight of us clustered around carriage number fourteen where a sour-faced guard barricaded the doorway. She filled her uniform ferociously, stretching the seams of her suffering official skirt. Her arms were folded in front of her and she wore her guards' cap jammed down over her middle-aged hair.

Pyotr helped Nikita carry Alexey's crate of paintings and his two suitcases into the compartment. Then both of them returned to the platform. Nikita stood in front of the guard in his long thin jeans, pointed brown Chelsea boots and with a red nose.

We'd toasted him one last time in his old studio at Pushkinskaya, as empty now as an orange crate, with its big windows, the holes in the floor and the patches on the walls where the plaster had flaked off and the struts showed through. As a result none of us was particularly sober but the vodka was no protection against the wind, cutting down the platform as disapprovingly as the guard. We stood shivering in the face of it. My eyes felt dry in their sockets.

The sour-faced janitor regarded us. She growled at Nikita to get on the train. 'Or it will go West without you.' She seemed to think that was a better idea.

'Take care of yourself Nikita,' I said. 'Write. I've got the address of the gallery so I'll write to you. Get yourself a nice German girl. I'll miss you.'

'Visit me Natalie, we can have fun. You need a holiday and some good Western food inside you, you're half the girl I met.' He cocked his head and smiled. 'It's only a train ride away for you.' He kissed me on both cheeks, then Alexey and the rest. He hugged Pyotr and they beat each other's backs.

'Go on, you don't want to miss your train, go West comrade.'

The guard was hissing at him to hurry up and the green iron train was flexing its brakes.

He kissed us all again, dropped an Americansky out of his lips onto the platform and with one hand on the rail he swung himself up and squeezed past the guard, who had reluctantly taken a step backwards to allow him in. She bent down after him, her legs planted a foot apart, hauled up the iron steps and slammed the door firmly as if she was afraid that our group of social undesirables would take it at a charge.

Nikita's elongated front half appeared out of the window three-quarters of the way down the carriage. The train pulled away, filling the air with the burning-hair smell of brake fluid. We stood where we were. The stick leaned out of the window and waved, until at the end of the platform the light stopped and the train disappeared into the unknown on its way to Berlin.

8 ∫

About three weeks after Nikita had gone to Berlin Pyotr told me he was meeting the Green Train. I remember that we were just about to go to bed, he had been doing an ink sketch and he was propping it up by the window so that it would dry overnight.

The Green Train is mythical. It travels from the Chu Valley in Kazakhstan to St Petersburg. The Chu Valley is a big grass and opium poppy area and periodically the Green Train brings its produce north. Nikita says that when the Green Train arrives in the summer you can sometimes see addicts making opium tincture in aluminium pots on the roofs of the Pushkinskaya squats.

The organisers pay off the entire Green Train from the driver down, and they say that everybody on board has an enormous party. Some of the stories I've heard about it are fabulous: black caviar, finest export vodka, melon, Western goods that come in from Turkey and of course as much grass as they can smoke.

'What have you got to do with the Green Train?' I asked Pyotr.

'I've got an assignment for Alexey,' he said grinning mysteriously. 'You know how precious he is, he didn't want to go himself so he asked me if I'd go for him.'

'Isn't it a bit dodgy?'

'Shouldn't think so. I've never met it before. Yuri and
Slava always used to go. Apparently they're still furious
with me. Oleg said he bumped into them the other day
and they were cursing me to hell. Poor bastards.'

I moseyed around in a shirt, brushing my hair and
rubbing some Nivea into my face to stop my skin drying
up in the cold. I thought of Annya painfully convalescing
in the foreign clinic on the Fontanka. 'I think it's a bit rich
of Alexey. I mean, I know you owe him a lot, but I don't
see why you should go just because he is too fastidious to
pick up his own sordid deliveries.'

I got into bed. He was standing with his back to the
window and his bottom on the radiator. He gave a short
laugh, turned off the light and joined me. 'I know, I know
Natalie,' he murmured placatingly as he lifted my body over
so that my shoulders rested on his chest. 'You worry too
much about me. You know that, don't you? Look at you,
you're too thin, you are wearing yourself away. I'll be fine,
this is just one of Alexey's foibles. It is not important, and
you mustn't get cross with him. But there is something else
I've got to tell you.'

'What?' I asked, sitting upright. He pulled me firmly back
down onto his chest. 'Well I don't know what to do. I keep
on thinking I am wandering round and round in circles and
I want to know, Dr Natalie, how I can tell if I've been sniffing
the wrong kind of ants.'

I laughed and stretched. 'Sadly, Sir, I am not an expert
in gnu nutrition but I fear there is no cure. You will have
to resign yourself to your fate.'

'Well,' he said, 'this particular gnu has got to go to Lvov.'

'No, why Pyotr?' I protested.

'Boring stuff. I have got to get some papers. I should
have gone ages ago but I've been putting it off. The Green
Train arrives in the morning so I am going to take the
afternoon train.'

'OK,' I said and I tried not to sound grumpy. 'How long will you be deserting me for?'

'It'll only be for a week. I'll come back as soon as I can, I promise.'

'Why don't I come to the station with you?' I suggested.

'To meet the Green Train? No Natalie, I don't think that's a good idea. But I'd love it if you came to see me off to Lvov.'

I wriggled off his chest and on to my side and listened to him breathing. However often he told me not to worry I couldn't stop myself. What were these papers and what was he collecting for Alexey? He told me so little but I had learnt not to pry. Outside in the night a cat screamed, I heard the heavy thud, thud, thud, of a Soviet lorry engine and the cracking of footsteps under the arch before they were swallowed into squeaks by the snow.

I dreamt I was being drowned in dull silver droplets of nickel. I was saved by a fourteen foot Vietnamese giant and put inside his padded prisoner's jacket. I kept perfectly still as he walked out past the guards. I sensed their eyes staring at him and I tried to remember if the giant had tucked in all my blonde hair, or whether some of it could be seen straggling out through the button holes.

I had a lesson in the morning and in the afternoon I took the Metro to Ploschad Mira and went to see Annya. She looked very small in her hospital bed. Leszek had just left. 'How are you feeling?'

'Achy, sore, but I'm still here.'

'Pyotr's going away for a week, why don't I come and stay with you when you come out? You are not going to want to be on your own, and the last thing you need is to have to trudge around for food and stuff.'

'Thanks, but Leszek's going to come and look after me. I don't want him to feel shoved out, he's feeling bad enough as it is.'

'Why?'

'Ach, it's stupid,' she said, pushing herself stiffly up the pillow. 'It's his bloody great Slav male ego coming out. He thinks he should have done more to protect me. But I mean it's my own fucking fault. It's really got nothing to do with him. I should learn to keep my stupid mouth shut.'

She sounded braver than she looked. Her face was yellow against the bed linen and her squinting worse because she was tired. 'You look knackered yourself Natalie, you've lost a hell of a lot of weight recently. Why don't you go down to Lvov with Pyotr? It's supposed to be really beautiful down there. Spring in the Carpathian Mountains. You ought to do it.' I didn't reply. Pyotr had, after all, never invited me to Lvov.

I left Annya to the hushed hygiene of her clinic and went straight to Vitebsky Station. I got there at half-past three, twenty minutes before the train was due to go, and Pyotr was already there, leaning on a painted iron pillar, his legs out at an angle, smoking an Americansky.

'Hello little one,' he said, dropping his half-smoked cigarette and crushing it under his heel. He wrapped an arm around my waist and, bending me towards him, kissed me on my mouth.

'I'm not little – did you meet the train?'

'Yep, it wasn't very exciting. The guys waiting for it with me were much funnier. Yuri and Slava were there, they weren't at all pleased to see me. Business isn't going very well for them. Some trouble with Yuri's uncle apparently, and for some bizarre reason they think it's my fault. Yuri started shouting about it on the platform but I just ignored the poor bastard.'

'Who else was there? What about the guys on the train?' He grinned, flashing his gold tooth. 'They all had two-day hangovers on them, reeling around the platform like gnus with scurfy stubble and bloodshot eyes. It was tricky trying to get any sense out of them at all. It took me a long time to find the man I was meant to be dealing with. It was hysterical, you should have seen it, all these wrecked mafya men desperately trying to see straight and do business. Anyhow I found the right guy in the end and picked up the stuff, so Alexey was happy about that.'

A guard appeared at the carriage door and let down the steps. Pyotr gave him his ticket and got in. We talked to each other out of the window. 'Come back soon, won't you?'

'As soon as I possibly can.' He kissed me again as the train left and I waved him out of the station.

I decided to walk back across the city. It was a long way but I wanted the fresh air, I didn't feel like being in a crowded Metro. There is a canal outside Vitebsky Station and I walked alongside it, kicking at the slush. It was mottled; white, translucent and mud. I hummed a little Russglish ditty of Annya's, '*Sovietsky Sayous*, it gives me the blues.'

When would spring come? It was late March, it had to come soon. She'd been flirting with us for weeks. A temperature hike and the whole city would be dripping in anticipation. Snap and the temperature would drop to zero again, the pavements would freeze over and the snow would arrive, sailing in on heavy, low-slung skies. On off, on off, I craved sunshine, warmth, food and fruit. Pyotr had said he'd seen butter last week. Fruit was slowly trickling into the city from the south. It was on its way.

Nevsky had lost the impression that it was a film set waiting for its cast. It was crowded. People jostled each other past lines of street artists, stalls and money changers. Stray dogs jogged possessively down the pavements, sniffing up the girls' skirts, the hairs on their backs bristling.

A French perfume shop had opened up. It had been painted white and acid green, clean real colours. The faded ochre, russet and powder blue buildings neighbouring the shop had the unreality of an oil sheen on water. Pouf! If I blew hard enough they would disappear.

Babba Lenna was watching television when I slipped through the door. I could see it flickering from the hallway. President Bush was on the news. I could hear his faded voice beneath the Russian dubbing. I made myself an omelette and a pot of tea and listened to it through the walls.

I think it was Alexey who first suggested that I should visit Nikita. He had introduced me to a new student so I went around to his flat on the Fontanka and thanked him. We sat in the room facing the canal on one of Alexey's endless sinking leather sofas. Behind us a fax machine squeaked and whirred. He had heard from the gallery in Berlin that Nikita had arrived safely.

'I hope you won't take it personally if I remark that you are not looking very full of health,' Alexey said as, bending rather formally from the waist, he handed me a glass of tea. 'Tea with bergamot, I believe you call it Earl Grey. I don't think that you should be surprised, Natalie,' he said, reverting to the subject of my health. 'It has been, after all, an extremely hard winter and we are not yet over it. Natalie, if you ever require a holiday I am always in need of responsible couriers to deliver paintings to Berlin. After all, it is no problem for you to cross the borders.'

'When does spring come?'

'Here or in Berlin? In Berlin I think it must already have arrived. Here, well here it takes its time, it always does that, but when it finally arrives it will pounce on us.'

Maybe, I thought as I walked home, I should take him up on the offer. In Berlin I would be able to stroll around the corner and buy a banana, I could laze by the lakes and go for a walk.

I sat the next morning in the *molochnik*, having porridge and sweet fake coffee, and watching the feet of the pedestrians pass by the window. An old lady shuffled across the floor in a tremendously elegant coat with a fox collar. Two women stood by the stack of used trays with wrinkled dirty-white aprons. Behind them I could see a new cook at work, who was too slender to fit his regulation cooks' trousers. I returned my dreaming gaze to the windows. Would the feet in Berlin look different?

All that week the wind blew in from the sea, and most days it rained. I did very little, visited very few people. I spent days in the Hermitage getting lost in its palatial corridors. I went to the Hertzen Institute and drank coffee in their canteen, while eavesdropping on the Western students on language placements. Some of them came from the Oxford Poly where I had been. I went up to their rooms but it was no use; I didn't belong and I had forgotten how to make conversation. They were on their way back to England so I gave them some letters to post and they gave me their books and their ration tickets.

I patrolled the streets like someone revisiting old haunts, as if I had nostalgia. The haunts weren't mine, they were Pyotr's. The wind made me anxious and the rain washed most of the sludge away, leaving stubborn lenses of ice in the corners of the courtyards and in the dips in the mud. The river agitated at its granite embankments. I walked down to the Sphinx by the Academy of Arts and she looked tired and uncertain as well.

One day, walking in the streets near Pushkinskaya, I came across a drunk dead in an archway. He had leprous sores on his turgid swollen arms and his face was the colour of window putty. I didn't touch him. My breath gagged in my lungs and I only seemed to be able to breathe from my neck. I felt ashamed: before realising he was dead I had been indignant at his lying there. So many drunks in Peter's beautiful city. I had been revolted by his dirt-stiffened clothes and the reek of old urine.

What could I do? I just left him in the archway. I didn't go near that area again. I couldn't bear the thought of him still lying there. It was the first dead body that I had ever seen and that seemed shameful as well. If he had been alive I would have forgotten about him. He moved me far more because he was dead. I didn't think there would be dead drunks in Berlin.

As I walked the streets I fretted about Pyotr. The city was getting more dangerous. I wished Pyotr would take the money for the lawyer from me and not get involved with Oleg and his aquaintances. Pyotr's attitude was so cavalier, he seemed to think that he was on a winning streak, Sam Golod favoured him and everything was going to be OK. Sometime in the future his luck might turn but he would deal with that when it happened. He evaded all my questions and teased me when I got worried until I began to think that yes, I was being silly. After all, he had been living like this for years. He had managed to dodge the old Soviet system. He had spent all his life in squats and basements, declaring himself insane, getting out of the army, avoiding work. He was a master at it. He had laughed at the system, because he could see quite clearly what was wrong and joking helped keep it at a distance. But the Soviet Union was over, and a new system was crystallising in Russia that was far more subtle and insidious, and I wondered how long he would be able to avoid it.

There was also the other Pyotr, the one who was terrified of going back to prison, the one who refused to discuss it. The Pyotr who had made the welts, not long healed, across his wrists. It is not possible to laugh while you cut yourself with a slab of plaster. But with Alexey behind us I was confident he wouldn't ever have to return to prison.

The rain on the pavements made me think of London.

I tried to visualise Pyotr at home having Sunday lunch with Simon and Mum and Dad and I squirmed at the thought. I could imagine them looking at him like a curiosity in a museum, 'a real Russian', and Simon would tell him how he had been to Moscow on a package tour with his school, and everything had been incredibly cheap but the food in the hotels had been revolting. Pyotr would be so uncomfortable, it would depress him. I didn't want anyone to look at my home and think it quaint, point out the faults, see the smallness of Granny England. I knew its failings but I was of England. Even running to the other edge of Europe couldn't change where I was born. I didn't want anyone to show me how narrow it was, not even someone I loved, especially not someone I loved.

I went over to Annya's flat one evening after the clinic had released her. Leszek was dining with a business contact at Sadko's, the new rouble restaurant in the Hotel Europa. We cooked macaroni cheese and ate it off the crates that formed her kitchen table and washed it down with a couple of beers.

'Leszek wants to drag me off to Poland for a holiday. He just doesn't believe that anybody can take care of me apart from his mother, sister, aunt and his entire bloody female tribe.'

'You'll have a lovely time. They will fuss over you and cook proper meals and everything. You need pampering right now. There is no point in underestimating what has happened to you, Annya. You were stabbed, you've been very ill. Don't be tough about it, give yourself a break for a bit.'

'Yeah, you're right Natalie, it would be great. I just don't want Leszek to get the wrong idea.'

'Don't be stupid. Take advantage of him for the moment.

He wants to do this. He is not asking you to marry him, for Christ's sake.'

'How's Pyotr? Have you heard anything more about the lawyer?' she asked, changing the subject.

'I think the situation is pretty much the same. He hasn't said anything about it for a while.'

'What does Alexey say?'

'I don't know, I can't really ask him. It's a bit of a sensitive subject with Pyotr. As far as I can make out the lawyer is bent and he is demanding quite a lot of money, but Pyotr point-blank refuses to take it from me.'

Annya looked at me severely with one of her eyes, the other squinting over to the right of my shoulder. I never feel that Annya trusts me. She thinks I'm a little girl playing at Russia. I once heard her dismiss an American she'd met in Moscow on the grounds that he wasn't leading a 'Russian life'. 'Might as well be living in fucking New Jersey, except the winter's colder,' she'd said disparagingly.

I wasn't going to get any sympathy from Annya. Being frightened of the life that Pyotr and I were leading was weak. Stand by your man, stand by Russia and her bleeding heart. To be a dilettante, a middle-class dilettante was, to Annya, the worst crime you could commit. Annya, sitting there with a stitched-up stab wound in her belly, would fight for Russia. 'We have to be witnesses,' she said, handing me another beer. 'The world needs witnesses to what is happening here.'

She drew on a Belamor and opened her bottle by jabbing the edge of the top down onto the crate. I envied her conviction. Annya is so clear and certain about what is wrong and what should be done. The longer I live in St Petersburg the more the confusions and complexities multiply. I knew the city with much more certainty when I first arrived and ate my lonely cabbage suppers. Now I see the city like one of those dreams where the characters quietly transmute at whim. I know that whatever I understand now about St Petersburg will be overturned as I learn more, that nothing stays true for very long.

Two days later Pyotr was standing on my doorstep with a grapefruit in his hand, just off the morning train. 'You see I hurried back, I hurried back to you.'

I hadn't got up yet, I was in my pyjamas. I perched on the windowsill in the hall and watched him take off his boots; Babba Lenna looked out of her door to see what was going on and smiled indulgently at us.

'Did you survive without me then, little one?'

'Just about.'

'I brought you back some supplies.' He tossed the grapefruit in the air and caught it again with one hand. 'You wouldn't believe how much food there is in Lvov. I tell you I am getting positively fat.'

'Looks like it!'

'I've got some real coffee, and condensed milk. I'll bring you some in bed.' His gold tooth flashed in the corner of his mouth.

We sat in bed later and he smoothed the hair away from my face, slowly curling it around my ears, and kissed the crown of my head. 'I'm going to have to go back again soon Natalie, there are problems with the papers.'

'But you've only just got here,' I whined.

'I know, I know, but the Sovietsky swine in these offices, they take their time, they take all the time they want.'

'Pyotr, while you've been away I've been thinking.'

'You can do that, it's good to think, little one.'

'Don't call me that, I'm not little. Now listen, I've been thinking.'

'Mmmm, so you said.'

'I've been thinking, maybe I'll go on a holiday. I could go to Berlin and stay with Nikita. Alexey says that if I deliver some paintings for him he will pay for my train fare and I've got some dollars which I can use while I'm there. But first I need to know whether you'd be OK and whether you need that money for the lawyer.' It was a very stupid way to ask him, I should never have blurted it out like that. I could have found out whether he needed the money in a much more subtle way.

'We can manage without you Natalie, Russia won't fall apart.'

'Seriously Pyotr, don't joke, I mean it, I need to know.'

'Now you're being silly,' he said. 'It's a great idea. You need a holiday. It would do you good. You can tell us how Nikita is doing and while you're away I will go to Lvov and organise my papers. There is your answer, now Natalie please can I stop being serious?' He rolled me over and kissed me.

9

I was on my way from school to the studio. It was a baby-blue day but the trees down the Seventh Line were still bare and ice lingered in the crannies of their roots and the edges of the pavements. I jumped on a tram as it passed the Metro and got off at the next stop. There was a queue outside the *gastronomia* on the corner. They were selling milk. I hadn't seen milk since arriving in St Petersburg. Pyotr would be delighted.

A woman with a dirty white overall and a blue cap covering her hair was selling the milk off a metal rack outside the shop. It was in cartons decorated with a blue and white corn pattern.

I'd forgotten about milk, forgotten we didn't have it, forgotten that it was something I normally did have. The queue was moving fast. Men and women were fingering their string perhaps-bags. This was a find, this was treasure indeed. Half an hour later I was standing on the pavement with a carton in my hand. I'd only been allowed to buy one. I wanted to open it up, gulp at it straight away, right there on the pavement opposite the basement beer hall where men were queuing up with their jam jars. I stuffed the carton into my bag and scurried down the street to the studio, banging unnecessarily loudly on the window.

'OK, OK, OK, I'm coming as fast as I can,' responded Pyotr.

'Look what I've got,' I said as he opened the door. 'Wait until you see, look, look, milk!'

'Wow, go on in I'll get some glasses.' He'd been to see the lawyer that morning but I didn't want to ask him about it. We drank the milk slowly and reverently without saying anything. It was cool and fatty and it tasted very good. We had a glass each and saved some to give to Annya, and some so that I could have milk in my tea. English tea.

'I've got a surprise for you as well,' said Pyotr, putting his empty glass down with satisfaction.

'What's that then?'

He took me through to the next door room and there, leaning on a table covered in mediæval pottery, was a German pre-war bicycle. 'Look how well-made it is. Like a genuine English policeman's bicycle!' he boasted.

'Where did you get hold of it? Let's try it out now!'

We took it outside and he bicycled up and down the street in front of me, turning across the tram tracks. Then he did a turn with no hands. 'Now you too,' he said pointing to the back.

So I levered myself on and sat side-saddle. I felt unsafe and unbalanced and I had that screaming, unsure sensation of riding whirligigs at a fair. We waggled down the street and then turned into an untarmaced alleyway. I could feel us falling as we turned; I began to wobble, pulling us further off balance. I leapt off the back to stop the whole bike going with me and as I jumped I caught my foot painfully in the spokes of the back wheel.

Pyotr braked and the black metal bike rattled to a halt. 'I'm so sorry Natalie, are you OK?'

'I'm fine, honest. I've just torn my shoe, dammit.'

'No problem, I can sew that back together again,' he said, turning it over in his hands. 'Easy.'

I limped back to the studio. The spoke had bruised the inside of the arch of my foot. Pyotr bicycled very slowly beside me.

'Natalie, I hurt you.'

'No you didn't, not really. I'm fine. I'm pissed off about the shoe though, they were my London loafers.'

'I'll make them like new again, better than London. You won't even notice the difference.'

He sewed the shoe up with an ordinary needle and some button thread. He sat in the Captain's Chair with the light behind him seeping in through the dingy satin curtains. I watched him from the table and sipped tea with milk in it. I stalled time as I watched. That scene is one of the mental snapshots that I keep of him.

'How long do you think you will be in Berlin?' he asked without lifting his head from the shoe.

'I don't know, depends on how far my money stretches and what I feel like when I get there. Are you sure you don't mind me going?'

'No! Stop asking!' he growled and then more quietly, 'of course I don't mind you going. You don't come from here, it's hard for you.' That got to me, he wasn't being ironic, that's what he really thought. He might even have been right.

Every day of that week we slept at the studio. I wasn't very comfortable there; I never really got used to the dirt and the discomfort. The mattress lay beside a hot-water pipe which made me sweat in my sleep. Pyotr's studio suffered from mosquitoes even before spring broke, I suppose because it was a basement close to the river. They whined in an infuriatingly slow radio pitch that kept me awake and they bit ferociously, but they never touched Pyotr. He laughed and said that he liked sleeping next door to me, I was his decoy.

Twice that week he left at midnight for Moscovsky

Station to unload nickel for Oleg. I lay in bed listening to the mosquitoes and the scratching of the mice in the chest of drawers behind my head and waited for him. He would come back exhausted at six in the morning, but he still wouldn't come to bed. Instead he painted big brightly-coloured paintings of Sam Golod and little mechanical humans. I would wake up later to find him standing by the table or sitting in the Captain's Chair, watching me and smoking. He didn't sleep, wouldn't sleep, for several days at a time. 'It's not necessary for me, Natalie,' he said.

One morning while trying to wash myself in the dingy light of the kitchen, standing on the rotten floorboards in front of the sink, Pyotr clapped his hands on my wet shoulders. I jumped, I hadn't heard him come in. 'Natalie,' he said grinning with pleasure at the prank, 'I want to show you where my safe is, my personal Fort Knox.'

He knelt down beside the door at the back of the kitchen by the racks where he stored his old canvases, paint pots and general junk. He pointed down to the bottom rack. 'Down here in the wall you will find a hole about half an arm's length back. If you need to get something from it make sure that there is no one else in the studio. OK?' The top half of my body was naked and wet and I was shivering. Pyotr handed me my towel, which was hanging on the back of the door, and I nodded vigorously in assent.

I went with Annya to the Georgian market on Petrogradsky; she had decided to go to Poland after all. Leszek came from Krakow but they were going to visit friends of his in Warsaw first. She gave me his address in Krakow. She said she didn't know how long she'd be gone.

We wandered around the marble slabs of the market hall. There were piles of small yellow apples with little black spots on them and pyramids of pomegranates. We walked past *sala*, the slabs of white salted pork fat that Ukrainians are so fond of, and enormous cabbages, straw nests of eggs as well as vats of sour cream and honey. I bought five kilos of potatoes for Pyotr so that he wouldn't starve while I was away. Annya accompanied me back to the studio, and while Pyotr was still out we put the potatoes in the bottom of the chest of drawers.

Pyotr was in one of his strange moods, the laughter had suddenly stopped and he withdrew to some place where I couldn't reach him. He was more than usually secretive; he was cooking up some deal with Alexey but I wasn't allowed to know what it was. He went to the flat on the Fontanka whenever I had lessons. We used to walk together as far as the Metro, then he would catch the number 33 tram and I would walk down the Seventh Line to my school.

When I got back after lessons he would be sitting at the table in the studio, staring into space and smoking. He sat there for hours. It irritated me. I wanted to know what was going on, I felt that I had breathed the air of that studio too many times.

'Pyotr you have got to tell me!' I cried, striking my fists on the table with frustration. 'I can't just sit here and watch you rot away. What is it, what's getting to you? Please Pyotr, you've got to let me in.'

He hated me badgering him like that but I couldn't help myself. I could hear the hateful sound of my own voice nagging but I couldn't stop it. I was desperate to find out what he was brooding about, what was the matter. Why couldn't he trust me? The more I probed the further I drove him away into whatever black lands he'd gone to. He would sit, his face stiff, staring across the table, whilst in the background Radio Europa Plus played continuously.

'Pyotr, if you don't want me to go to Berlin I won't.'

'Of course go to Berlin. Natalie, I am OK. It's just the atmosphere, I can't always be happy.'

*   *   *

Five days before I was due to leave he said wearily, 'Natalie, go out on your own, leave me here. Please.' So I went out and wandered the streets like I had done when he'd been in Lvov. I walked for miles across the city, along the canals. I found a strange comfort in knowing that all the people I saw, all the people who passed me in the street and sat next to me on the tram, would forget me. I dreaded seeing someone that I knew. Once I spotted one of the other teachers from school with his wife and little girl and I slid off down a side street before they noticed me. I slipped like a cat around the corners of the city and it gave me a release, a freedom from Pyotr's black moods. When I returned he was still sitting there, gazing across the table at the rust spots on the wall.

I wish that I could say that those last days were happy, that we laughed a lot and the world spun, but they weren't. They were mute and damaged and Pyotr at his most bloody-minded held me hostage. Often when the silences became too strong the only release we could find was in bed. We made love under the hard abrasive blankets, our aching bodies knocking and sliding against each other.

I felt that I was losing him. I was afraid to talk to him, afraid that my words, or even just the sound of my voice, my bad Russian, would irritate him. I became hesitant, I would repeat my opening words to test their effect and I know that annoyed him. When I suggested cancelling my trip he snapped at me. 'Natalie, you can't drop out now, you've promised Alexey you will deliver his paintings and the gallery in Berlin is waiting for them.'

His mood turned the day before I left. He had been out with Alexey buying my ticket. He came dancing in waving it in the air. 'Go West Young Woman, Go West!' He grinned and I could see his gold tooth again. That night we went visiting friends in Pushkinskaya. On the way back we bought bread from the back of the bakery. After midnight the bread lorries unload ready for the next day. If you know where the unloading bay is and you arrive at the right time you can get them to sell it to you. It costs more but you don't have to queue for it. The bread was still warm and we ate it here at this table, spreading the slices with some cranberry jam a student had given me.

It was the first time that we had slept at my place for ages. Pyotr said he wanted to do some work. He got out some paper and sat at this table. He was still sitting there when I woke up the next morning. He saw me stir. 'We must have a party.'

'Pyotr you haven't been to bed yet, it's bad for you not to sleep.'

'We must have a party to see you off properly.'

'I'm not going away for ever, I don't need a party. I'll see you again in a couple of weeks' time.'

He wasn't going to budge about the party. He brought a glass of tea over to the bed; he must have made the pot just before I'd woken up. He put it on the floor beside my pillow and gave me a thorough kiss.

'Good morning Natalie.' He perched on the pillow. 'I'm going to go now. I was just waiting for you to wake up. I have got lots of things to organise. Do your packing now and then bring your bags to the studio. I will make some potatoes.'

I nodded in agreement and after he had drunk his glass of tea he went off to do his mysterious chores. I tried to puzzle out the change in his mood as I pushed my clothes into my rucksack. Whatever the blackness was, it had gone away and for the moment that was good enough.

So I had a farewell party. Everybody came, the artists, the dealers, the dancers, half of Pushkinskaya and even my private pupils. A lot of them gave me presents, which was embarrassing as there wasn't a proper excuse for presents. Alexey, with some ceremony, gave me an English book on

Russian art before the revolution. I don't know how he got hold of it but it was very generous of him. Yelena gave me some orange gladioli and a sketch of a haggard-faced woman with a hole in her belly like a Swiss cheese. A dealer, nicknamed Moriarty and rumoured to be the nephew of a general, gave me one of the cigarette cases awarded to the volunteers on the Baikal-Armenian railway.

I got drunk that night and sentimental. I fell in love with them all. With Americansky cigarettes and men drinking medical spirit, 'it's cleaner than vodka I promise you. Try some Natalie'. With soapy beer and potatoes eaten communally out of the frying pan with bendy nickel forks. Even with Annya ranting on about some plot that was pushing up inflation, an organised international effort to destabilise the rouble and ensure that a communist regime could never recover. Later she impersonated a drunken Brezhnev and everybody laughed. When I had had too much I lay down on the mattress and went to sleep while my farewell party whirled around me.

For breakfast Pyotr bought pastries filled with grapefruit jam from a new shop opposite the studio. I had a hangover from bad vodka, my bones ached, my eyes ached. It seemed too much effort to drag myself across the dusty floor to wash my face in the sink that wobbled precariously on its water pipe, or to face the revolting hole in the floor of the unlit room that was the toilet.

But after all that there was a beautiful breakfast and Pyotr fussing around and asking me what I wanted. We took a taxi to Alexey's place on the Fontanka to pick up the paintings. Under the modern chandelier in his kitchen he gave us coffee and Marlboro cigarettes. The paintings weren't too large and he had wrapped them up very neatly with masking tape and padding and cardboard, so that they wouldn't be bashed. He gave me the address of the gallery but he said that Nikita was working there now and so he could take me.

Alexey came with us to the station. Pyotr was strained in the taxi. I think it had occurred to him that I might not come back. That I could leave it all behind and, because I could cross borders when I wanted to and he couldn't, he would be helpless. He was sitting with me in the back and he leant forward to watch the road in the gap between the two front seats. He held his right arm across his chest with his hand inserted flat under his left upper arm, as if he were warming his fingers on a cold day. I looked at his face, gaunt and intent on the road.

When we arrived at the station Pyotr insisted on taking the paintings and my rucksack from the boot of the car and carrying them down the platform. Alexey and I followed his long, tall figure. We found my carriage and he checked out my compartment and pronounced it satisfactory. I followed him back down the corridor of the train and out onto the platform to have a last cigarette.

Annya arrived and gave me a packet of a Polish brand called Bond Street. 'Take them, cigarettes will cost a lot more in Germany and you are going to get bloody bored on that train. You'll want to smoke on the journey.'

'Come back won't you,' pleaded Pyotr, 'come back soon Natalie, don't desert me.'

'I'll come back,' and I knew that I would. Walking fancy-free into Europe and leaving Russia behind me wasn't really an option after all.

Then I was gone, out of the station and out of the city, rocking with the rhythm of the train through the dead forests to Berlin where there would be spring.

10

Nikita had been drawing cartoons while he waited for my train to arrive. He presented me with the results as he kissed me hello. I've got one of them here, drawing-pinned to the wall by the window. It's titled 'The Heroine of the Heroes' and it shows a large triangular figure with a puzzled expression on its face, floating above a crowd of smaller, bored-looking triangular figures.

The train came into a station in the east of Berlin. I struggled out with my rucksack and Alexey's paintings and breathed the warm air. We got lost trying to find Nikita's flat in the west of the city. I carried the paintings and Nikita carried my rucksack, and we found ourselves on a street lined with lime trees dropping sticky juice onto the Trabants close-parked beneath them like boiled sweets.

'I'm sure it's down this way,' Nikita said. 'I'll know where we are once we get to the canal.' And a little further down we found the canal. Not like a Petersburg canal at all. It meandered like a river and its banks were grassy and lined with ash trees.

Nikita had been lent a flat by one of the artists who exhibited at the gallery. It was in a good area close to the canal and in a block built around a courtyard like a Petersburg house. By the arch there were four different kinds of bins in different colours for different kinds of rubbish.

'I have a new Fräulein,' he informed me as he trotted up the stairs in front of me.

'Already!'

'You will like this one, Natalie. I think maybe I am in love. She plays the piano and she is very romantic. She is studying Russian, but we speak only English because it is easier.'

'How's your German?'

'Oh German's boring, I can't be bothered with it.'

'Nikita, you lazy slob!'

Her name was Sarah, she met us at the door. She was a redhead and so thin you could have pulled her through a wedding ring. She was dazed, bemused by this visitation with his flaying arms that had been placed at her feet like a baby in a basket.

Nikita jostled me into the kitchen in a hurry to show me all the Western treasures. I had never been to Germany before but it seemed very familiar. I knew the smell: Western cigarettes, plastic packaging and lemon-scented detergent. Nikita opened a bottle of beer and put it in front of me with a vanilla-flavoured yoghurt and a banana. The window looked out over a garden with daffodils in it.

'What else do you want, Natalie? We've got everything here.'

'It's so good to see you Nikita and you are looking so well. Honestly, you look miles better than when I last saw you.' He did, he looked more healthy generally, but it was hard to say exactly what the difference was. He was just as thin as ever, but his face wasn't so grey and his red nose had lost that purple tinge.

'I feel better. I eat better here, I breathe better and I even sleep better, but when I sleep I still dream of Petersburg.'

That night Sarah said she had to study so she stayed in the flat while Nikita took me out. We walked along the canal to an area called Kreusberg. There was a long street with bars and aluminium chairs and tables sat outside. The first one we went into was called the Bar Madonna; a large cage hung over the bar with a weird papier-maché animal inside it. As we leaned on the brass lintel of the bar I caught Nikita trying to look cool in the mirror behind the bottles of spirits. He giggled when he saw me. We were like children that night, both pleased with ourselves for being so clever, for being in Berlin.

'Now you've got to have Krystal, that's the beer they drink here and they put lemons in it. No, stop it Natalie, you're with me and I'm paying.'

'Don't be silly Nikita, you haven't got any money.'

'Yes I have, the gallery pays me. I really have got some money now.'

The woman behind the bar was tall and handsome and she smiled at us. We took our beers over to a tiny copper table on spindly legs by the window. Outside dusk was settling and the punters were parading the pavements. Over the road there was a more crowded bar with lights that spilled out onto the street. On the other side of the glass a blonde woman was earnestly picking her nose, frowning and pushing her fingertip right up into her nostril. I looked at Nikita and we got the giggles again.

A morose Frenchman called Bruno joined us. He was an architect. He said that because of the Wall coming down there were lots of architects in Berlin right now. They were thinking of making Berlin a capital city again, but they didn't know what kind of capital city they wanted to make and so architects were coming to Berlin from all over the world to draw plans and advise the authorities. He had curly brown hair and blue eyes that sagged like a bloodhound's. He sipped his beer carefully and said he had a family in Marseilles, but he thought they were better off without him.

'I was born in Algiers,' he said, lifting his eyes but not his

face from the rim of his beer glass. 'Before I was half a day
old a woman stole me from the hospital. My mother was
hysterical and the hospital authorities were embarrassed.
They searched Algiers and they found me after a month, in
the flat of an Algerian woman who had four other children.
I think of it sometimes and I think maybe they found the
wrong baby. I am not a good father myself and I don't like
France. So I have come to Berlin which is not a country
at all.' Then he resumed sipping his beer. He didn't say
anything for the rest of the evening.

Bruno came with us when we left the Bar Madonna and
in the bright street light we toured more bars. We went
down some stairs to a room that was painted black, and full
of tall Germans with dreadlocks dyed in fluorescent colours
dancing to thrash metal. Nikita and I joined in, while Bruno
hovered by the stairs looking uncomfortable.

At midnight we bought kebabs from a Turkish takeaway.
I got a vegetarian one because I thought the meat looked
like horse meat; the hot sauce dribbled out of the pitta bread
and down my arm. We toured a couple more bars, buying
one glass of beer in each just to see what they were like.
At half-past two in the morning we had coffee in a bar with
wooden sculptures and wooden chairs and a tree made of
wire with painted in birds in it. Bruno left us after that and
Nikita and I went back to the flat. Sarah was asleep when
we tiptoed in, fully dressed and lying limp diagonally across
the bed like a rag doll.

I had a hangover when I woke the next morning. Sarah
went to college and after she had left Nikita and I dragged
ourselves from our beds to the kitchen and eyed each other
balefully as we tentatively sipped at cups of tea.

'I must deliver those paintings for Alexey today. When
do you have to work?' I asked.

'I'm not sure. I only work occasionally. We will go in

today and they will let me know when they need me. Do you want to wash first?'

Nikita didn't have a shower in the flat so we went to a spotlessly clean communal baths a block away and I tried to scrub away the remains of my hangover.

I was very grateful for the shower. The gallery was a large expanse of elegant pale stone floors and white floating walls. The husband of the couple who owned it was in Naples on business and Nikita introduced me to his wife, Marie-Teresa. I was very conscious of how scruffy I looked and how worn my clothes were. To make up for it I was effusively friendly towards her. She treated me to a frozen smile and I immediately regretted being so gushing, feeling foolish and gauche. She was dark, chic and very polished; she could have been dipped in plastic. She wore stylish gold jewellery over a perfectly ironed silk shirt and a pair of slacks. I felt like a tatty teenager in comparison.

She thanked me for the paintings and then enquired about Alexey. 'We do a lot of business with Alexey. Such a cultured man, don't you think. He has a real "eye". And Nikita has been very useful. I think he finds it very strange here,' she said implying that Nikita was slightly simple. I didn't go back to the gallery again, the rarefied atmosphere made me feel too uncomfortable.

Nikita also helped out with some of the Russian traders whose little tables lined the streets in the Zoo district selling Red Army uniforms and lacquer boxes. He said that he had gone there when he had first arrived for companionship, so that he could talk to other Russians. There was a middle-aged lady called Veka. We minded her stall one afternoon while she went shopping. She told me that she used to live in a *communalki* on Nevsky. Her husband was an engineer but he hadn't found any work in Berlin yet and business was getting more difficult because the gangs were moving in. She said that she already had to pay protection money.

'There was a Belorussian who sold fur hats. He refused to pay the money. He said that this was Berlin and he was not going to take orders from Russians in Berlin. They set fire to him and all his hats. Oh it was awful, I shall never forget the sound, he screamed like a pig going to slaughter. The thug who came around collecting last week said it was a warning to us all.'

We left her selling Lenin badges to the tourists and took a bus to the lakes and walked along the shore. Sarah sometimes joined us on these trips and we would hire a boat and row it out into the middle of the lake, lie on our backs and smoke cigarettes.

One day Bruno turned up at the flat and we all had lunch together in an Italian restaurant, sitting at a table on the pavement. The weather was warm, the air limpid and the birds in Berlin sang.

Later we went and lay on the grass by the canal and then, because I hadn't done it and it seemed the right thing to do, we went and gazed at the Brandenburg Gate. In Berlin and St Petersburg people were only now emerging from the shadow of the war – a shadow that, until I had left England, had seemed to me to be well buried in history. Bruno remarked that it always seemed bigger than he remembered it and Sarah, the only German among us, said that even now, a year later, it was a shock to realise the Wall had been bulldozed away. Our chatter petered out and we stood in silence: Cold War children thinking their Western and Eastern thoughts.

On the Friday, a fortnight after I arrived, Nikita came back from working at the gallery at six-thirty. Sarah and I had spent the afternoon together, she'd been studying and I had been writing letters and prying gently into her life with Nikita. Then the man himself came dancing in with beers and Middle Eastern pastries.

'Sarah, you will wear you brain out with all this studying.

You must have a beer. Natalie, there was a message for you from Marie-Teresa at the gallery. She said you must ring Alexey at the Fontanka tonight.'

'How strange. Maybe he wants me to bring something back with me? Do you have his number?'

'Yeah sure, I'll do it, it can take hours getting a line into Russia. Once I tried for half a day but it's normally easier at night.'

We got a line after twenty minutes and Alexey answered straight away.

'Natalie?'

'Yes, hi, I got a message from Marie-Teresa to ring you.'

'Is someone there with you?'

'Yes, Nikita's here with his girlfriend. Do you want to speak to him?'

'Presently. Natalie, I am afraid I have some tragic news for you.'

'What is it, Alexey? Something to do with Pyotr?'

'Yes, yes it is. Natalie, Pyotr is dead, they found him in the Ukraine, near Lvov. Natalie, I can't tell you how . . . Natalie are you still there? Natalie?'

Nikita was looking at me, questioning, not understanding because he didn't know what had happened. It was obvious that there was no sense in me. I was dry. He uncurled my fingers from the receiver and took it gently from me.

'Alexey?'

I couldn't hear myself think. The roaring in my head was too loud. I could only hear the roaring. I couldn't hear anything else at all.

I was dimly aware of Sarah and Nikita moving me around like a doll. I let them undress me, put on my pyjamas and brush my hair. They lay me down on their bed and pulled the duvet over me. Nikita slept with me, I felt his body beside me and his voice in a repeating whisper, 'Natalie, Natalie, Natalie.' That's all I remember: the roaring in my head, the warmth of Nikita's body and his voice on a repeating tape. The rest is blank. White noise.

The next day we walked to a sand dune on some derelict land where the Wall had once been. We took a bottle of Johnny Walker Red; 'mother's milk' Pyotr called it. Sarah soon left us. We frightened her. Nikita and I sat silently looking at the East and passing the bottle between us.

The whisky tasted good; I was so numbed that the fact that I tasted it at all was good. It burnt on the back of my throat and that seemed real in a way that nothing else at the time particularly did. We broke down halfway through the bottle. Nikita triggered it off by talking about Sam Golod. It was late afternoon, there were a couple of clouds in the sky – not many but enough to cast a shadow – and there was a light breeze that didn't look like it was reaching the dark tenements in the East.

'Sam Golod gives and Sam Golod takes away,' said Nikita. It was a phrase that we had both heard Pyotr use so often. I stared blankly at the baubled spike that pokes through Berlin's eastern skyline, reflecting the sun in an ironic cross. As I stared, I felt the tickle of a tear as it slid around the base of my nostril. I turned to Nikita. He was crying as well. Realising this, I began to sob properly as if violent things were trying to make their way out from my chest.

We sat there, amongst the debris of the old Wall and we sobbed. We sobbed in great ugly burps. Nikita took my hand in his bony, feverish one and squeezed hard.

The tears were coming in crashing waves and my head was roaring but nevertheless I felt strangely disconnected and unreal. Even the sobs seemed to be happening to me rather than coming from me. I didn't believe that Pyotr was dead, sometimes I don't even believe it now, but then nothing at all seemed true or solid. Only the burning of Johnny Walker in the back of my throat was real, Pyotr's death was not and my tears felt autonomous.

On the third day after I had rung Alexey I decided to go back to St Petersburg. I remembered Pyotr's face in the taxi on the way to the station and I decided to go back. My reasons weren't any clearer than that, and I wasn't sure what I would do when I got there. Alexey had said they found his body near Lvov. I thought of going there or to Kiev or to Borshtshevice, the small town that he came from, but none of these places had any meaning for me, they were just names of places that Pyotr mentioned and that he didn't particularly like.

Nikita told me that Pyotr had parents and an older brother who was a doctor. That was so unexpected and so utterly normal: I couldn't imagine Pyotr as a child, washed, neatly brushed and in a uniform behind a school desk. The Pyotr that I knew must have arrived fully formed as he was.

Nikita thought I was making a big mistake. Because Pyotr was his closest friend, and I think not only because of that, he felt responsible for me. *'Hey Rabbit, will you take care of my* feministka, *my little English lady?'*

In the morning I went out with Sarah and bought the ticket. Nikita was in the flat when we returned. He begged me not to go. 'Fly to England from here, it doesn't matter, just leave your stuff in Petersburg, just leave it. Don't go back, Natalie. This is a hood killing. It's classic, just like an old KGB killing. Don't look for any sense in it. Listen to me, I know. It is dangerous and it will drive you crazy if you try and look for sense in it.'

He was very agitated. He walked around and around the studio in the flat, rebounding off the walls, kicking at an unframed canvas, twitching his thin body while his face went red. 'There is no reason in it, it's just history, politics, Sam Golod whatever you want to call it. But it's not Pyotr. If you want to come out of this with a mind, grieve for him but don't look for sense in his death. Go home Natalie, but don't go to Petersburg.'

On the train I closed my eyes and I could hear Nikita's voice in the beat of the wheels as they carried me back to St Petersburg, 'Natalie, Natalie, Natalie.'

Through Warsaw and Poland. We changed our wheels at Brest-Litovsk. The train stopped for a while two hours east of the Estonian border, by a village of worn wooden houses and a concrete factory that straggled into the forest. The iron train didn't move and the early summer heat stood heavy around it. Four small boys stared at us from the trackside.

I shared my cabin with two gangsters and a prostitute they were retrieving from Warsaw. She hadn't uttered a word since she joined the train; just lay on the top bunk and stared at the ceiling. One of her minders was small and wiry. He had black eyes that were constantly on the move and I didn't like it when he looked at me. The other one was more obviously a heavy. He was muscular and almost placid, and he had a habit of sniffing that I guessed came from a nose that had been broken too often.

They didn't talk much. At the border they had bought beers which the girl had refused. When they had drunk them they stripped to their underpants and lay down on the two bottom bunks. The smell of white hairless chests was threatening in the cramped cabin of the stationary train. So, angry and sulky, I moved out to the corridor and sat on the flip-up half seat observing the measly village.

I sat there and wondered whether it was thugs like them who had murdered Pyotr. I wondered in dull fury if it was because of people like them that Pyotr had been found lying in a ditch on the road to Borshtshevice. What a sordid way to die. Pyotr, of all people, needed to die with a grand gesture. Then I couldn't think of a grand way to die. Maybe there isn't one, maybe death is always sordid, maybe to be found shot and ant-ridden is as good a way as any.

11

I perched on the plastic seat and let the grief wash through me to the pulse of the train. Pyotr was dead. When it was long dark and all I could see through the window was my own reflection lit bright, I had a last cigarette in the gap between the carriages and went to bed. Like the prostitute beside me I lay on my back, the ceiling an arm's length away, and was coaxed to sleep by the beat of the wheels through the night.

The guard rattled our door at seven o'clock in the morning, a full hour and a half before we were due to arrive. I peered over the edge of my bunk to find that the girl and her escorts had gone. When? How did I sleep through it?

In their place were two badly shaved men. The one immediately below me had a shining bald crown to his head and the fat of his neck bulged slightly, threatening to topple over the collar of his greasy jacket.

They were playing cards at the table by the window, with between them two opened bottles of beer and half a *kalbasa* on some greaseproof paper. The garlic and pig fat smell of the sausage swung itself slowly upwards towards me. Beer smells sour in the morning.

I did up the belt on my jeans, swung myself down to the bottom bunk and was received by a curt good morning as

I fished around underneath the bottom seat to find my shoes. Taking my wallet from underneath my pillow and my sponge bag from the side pocket of my rucksack, I slid back the door into the corridor and joined the queue for the toilet.

We were still travelling through forest. Forest that had been monochrome, dead or dormant every time I had seen it before now fizzed acid green in the early morning mist. Through an open top window I could feel the cool dampness and the promise of the heat the sun would bring when it had risen. They had burnt the winter rubbish on the trackside. Out of the damp black-charred ground, green needled grass and luscious yellow king cups were growing.

The guard was hammering on the doors and shouting for the bed linen. I pulled mine onto the floor and then pushed my bunk up against the wall and fastened it. An object fell on to the bottom bunk; it had been jammed between my bunk and the wall. The man beside me picked it up and when I looked down I saw that he was slowly turning over a pistol in his hands.

The two of them looked slowly from the pistol to me, then to the pistol again. Foreigner, pistol, foreigner, pistol. I smelt foreigner fear; too long bred to be lost in one winter. I was a spy, a saboteur, no matter that there was nothing to spy on, no secrets worth knowing, nothing to sabotage. It was not important that I was only a young girl with a rucksack. They are cunning these foreigners, cunning as the devil. She is foreign, she speaks Russian and she has a gun.

'It's not mine,' I said and I enunciated it slowly as if the gun was pointing at me. 'It's nothing to do with me. There were mafyosi here last night. With a girl. They got on at Warsaw.' There was a pause and the two of them looked at the gun again. And then at me.

'Bed linen, come on, hurry up, bed linen now!' The guard appeared in the doorway. 'Come on, bed linen!'

'Guard,' called the man nearest to me. He placed the gun gingerly on the table next to the beer, on top of his hand of cards. 'Look what we found. Fell out of this foreign girl's bed.' I could see it more clearly now. It was gas-powered and it had a pale green cartridge, like a thin box, behind the trigger.

The guard took a step into the cabin and peered at it on the table. I was getting worried by this point. The guard had to believe me or I was going to be in a lot of trouble, trouble that I didn't feel strong enough to deal with. I remember thinking with relief, thank God it's Alexey who will be meeting me because if it comes to it, with his contacts, he would be able to get me out of any fix.

'It's nothing to do with me,' I pleaded. They had to believe me. It was ridiculous, why would I want a gun? 'It was here, it must have been pushed up from below.' I demonstrated how it must have come from the bottom bunk. 'It must have belonged to the people who were here last night,' I said looking directly at the guard, 'the ones that got on at Warsaw.' The ones, I thought to myself, who probably bribed you for the berth.

The guard picked the pistol off the table and shoved it into his jacket pocket. 'I shall confiscate it,' he proclaimed rather grandly. 'Now hurry up, girl, and get your bed linen ready.' He left self-importantly and quickly, as if we surely had to realise that he had more important things to do just before the train arrived in St Petersburg than dealing with guns in the bed linen. I sat down, feeling weak, on the bottom bunk. A pistol. I suppose I must have seen one before, on a French policeman's belt or something. The guard carried on down the corridor while the card players puffed righteously at me and I returned to folding up my sheets and blankets.

I sat on the corridor seat and watched the women up and down the carriage struggling with their luggage, red, white and blue Chinese bags woven out of plastic, shoddy suitcases, cardboard boxes tied up with string and great big bundles of cloth all being organised and piled.

We were passing by brightly painted wooden dachas with gardens of raspberry canes and potatoes. The forest around the dachas began to thin and the train emerged onto the sour mud of the blank marshes that surround the city. Soon we would meet the first grey concrete blocks of the Brezhnev suburbs.

The platforms of Varshavsky Station are in the open air. As the train came to a halt crowds mobbed the carriage doors. I pushed my way through them and, harnessing myself into my rucksack, walked with as much dignity as I could find towards the main body of the station. Pyotr should have been there, standing slightly away from the swarming relatives, smiling, sauntering and waiting for me.

Instead there was Alexey, his voice beside me before I saw him. 'Nikita rang and informed me of your arrival.' I jumped.

'Christ I'm sorry Alexey, you gave me a fright. I didn't see you. I was thinking of other things.'

He nodded knowingly, his face a picture of understanding. He tapped at my rucksack. Russian chivalry is very strange: Alexey is short, he is only just taller than me and the women here dig roads. Nevertheless I unclipped the belt and wriggled out of the shoulder straps. He picked up the rucksack using the arm straps like a handle and strode off to the street where he hailed a car.

He took control in the same firm, unobtrusive way he had that night at the Tam Tam Club and I, wandering in shock, was very happy to let him do so.

We didn't talk in the taxi and I stared glazed-eyed at the city as we drove through it. I was surprised how much had changed. I was expecting it to be exactly the same but the ice had all gone and, as in Berlin, there were leaves on the trees; they'd slipped in while I had been away.

The mask of Goethe hanging from the wall in Alexey's hallway stared at me in disgust as we came through the door. There was a new hall table and on it lay a pile of 'The Experimental Laboratory of Life' pamphlets.

'Natalie, sit down please and I will make you some coffee,' he said, courteous as ever. I drifted into the room overlooking the canal and went over to the window. Alexey returned with a bottle of vodka and two glasses. 'I think that perhaps we will find it necessary to have a drink as well.'

I joined him on the leather sofa and sank down into its scented depths. I felt tired and limp. 'Tell me how he died,' I asked.

'I am not in possession of all the facts but I will attempt to tell you everything I know.' He sat sideways and poured the vodka. He handed me a glass.

'Last Wednesday I received a telephone call from a man called Artiom Anatoliavich.' His face was shielded from me and his voice was exact and unemotional. It occurred to me that he had practised this speech and he probably hadn't looked forward to making it.

'I was aquainted with Artiom Anatoliavich when I lived in Kiev. Artiom informed me that Pyotr had been staying with him over the weekend and on the Monday Pyotr spent the day in the Lvov City Council Bureau, trying to sort out some problems he was having with official papers. Lvov is now part of the Ukraine and therefore there were many complications and the business was made considerably more difficult because Pyotr had a bad past record, you understand. Artiom says that when Pyotr came back to his flat in the late afternoon he looked tired and haggard. He says that they visited a friend's studio where they drank a lot of vodka, and then they bought another bottle and went back to Artiom's flat and talked. He says that they talked about you and Pyotr said you were in Berlin visiting Nikita.

'Artiom says that Pyotr seemed very depressed. They discussed his problems with the lawyer and with his papers. Pyotr apparently said that he didn't think that he would ever be allowed a foreign passport and he complained that even now when Communism was over he was imprisoned by papers and bureaucracy. He said that if he couldn't sort out his papers there was a chance that he would have to go to prison for two years and he didn't think that he could bear that. He said that you, Natalie, were so young and pretty and he didn't want to ask you to wait that long. He said that you weren't Russian and you shouldn't have to experience the Russian system. He said that even if he didn't go to prison the swines in the offices would still keep him here because he didn't have the right papers. He said that for people like him there could never be freedom, because for as long as they remembered the past it would always keep hold of them.

'Artiom has been aquainted with Pyotr for many years and he knows all the facets of his character very well but he told me on the telephone that he had never known Pyotr quite so depressed. Artiom says he possessed the air of a man who has been left behind. Artiom recalled a childhood holiday they had spent together in the Young Pioneer Camp where Pyotr had sabotaged an activity by faking an epileptic fit. The teacher, who suspected that Pyotr was play-acting but could not prove it, kept Pyotr behind for observation when the rest of the group went to play. Artiom told me that Pyotr wore a similar expression that Monday night as they drank vodka to the day they left him behind in the classroom.

'Artiom said Pyotr talked of his remorse for the terrible things he had done in the past to allow him to be free of the authorities. He talked about selling himself to the devil, so that he could become a member of the underground, of making friends with the worst kind of people so that he wouldn't have to be part of the system. He said that in the Soviet Union only the insane, the violent and the immoral were free, and he said that in the new world these three groups would be the system, they were the new rulers. He didn't want to be part of this new system but he felt he was already implicated, he was already of it. Artiom says that they both went to bed very drunk and very sad.

'In the morning Pyotr was up before Artiom. He told him that he was going to go and see his parents and his brother in Borshtshevice for a few days and maybe he would come and see Artiom on his way back to Petersburg. Artiom says that he was feeling the effects of the alcohol from the night before but that Pyotr did not seem to be suffering at all, in fact he was extremely organised.

'On the Wednesday evening there was a knock on the door of Artiom's flat. There were three militsia men outside. They requested that Artiom accompany them to the bureau, where they informed him that Pyotr's corpse had been discovered that morning in a ditch on the road from Lvov, about five miles outside Borshtshevice. The corpse was punctured by a bullet wound in the temple and the militsia surmised that this was the cause of death.'

I gagged on my vodka, splattering it all over the surface of the glass coffee table. This was not easy stuff to listen to. Alexey held up his neatly manicured hand like a policeman stopping traffic. 'I must apologise, Natalie. I assumed, maybe mistakenly, that you would like to know the facts, but of course it goes without saying that if you would prefer it I can stop here.'

I shook my head, 'No, go on, Alexey.' I did want to know but not quite so brusquely as this.

He rearranged himself, wet his lips with vodka and

continued. Artiom informed me on the telephone that the militsia had briefed him as follows: the bullet went straight through an artery and into the brain and therefore Pyotr would have died instantly. As far as it is possible to tell in these circumstances they were of the opinion that he would not have suffered any pain. The gun was located in the ditch beneath the corpse. It was a drainage ditch and the water had obliterated any fingerprints. In the vicinity of the corpse they located a small military-style rucksack containing a few clothes, and in the pocket of the jacket worn by the corpse they located Pyotr's internal passport, a small amount of money and Artiom's name and address.

'As Lvov is extremely close to the border the militsia were treating this as a mafya killing. They informed Artiom that the body had already been handed to Pyotr's parents for burial. The militsia then questioned Artiom. He did not mention their conversation on the Monday night, or the fact that Pyotr had been depressed and suffering from *tosca*.

'On the telephone to me, Artiom proffered the opinion that Pyotr had tragically decided to take his own life.' I closed my eyes to block him out but Alexey carried on relentlessly. 'Artiom, you understand, was of the opinion that it was unnecessary to burden the militsia or Pyotr's parents with this notion. Artiom told me that he thought it would be much easier for his parents if they assumed that Pyotr had been shot by an unknown and violent criminal element. The militsia would quickly forget about the case. It would be a waste of their time and resources to search for the killers of some scruffy artist who had a terrible KGB record, and in any case was normally resident, illegally, in St Petersburg.

'Moreover, Artiom told me that when he visited Pyotr's parents to pay his condolences they told him that they had almost expected it. For many years now they had worried about the life he led in St Petersburg and they had, on numerous occasions, pleaded with him to get a job and settle in Lvov, where he was legally entitled to live and where they felt the world was less capricious and violent.

'The following day I contacted Marie-Teresa in Berlin and asked her to get an urgent message through to you. It is a terrible tragedy, truly terrible. Pyotr was such a great artist and a noble man. Maybe this was a noble death, the only death fitting for such a man.' Alexey stared down at his vodka and shook his head lugubriously from side to side.

'Now Natalie, you must excuse me, this is a delicate subject but I feel I really have to ask you: what was Pyotr's mood before you left him to go to Berlin? His lawyer, his passport, did he discuss these things with you? It is really terribly important that I know.'

The sun was high enough now to leave a lazy patch of yellow on the wall of the far side of the room. My stomach was churning acid and I felt nauseous. Using the Zippo lighter that I had bought as a present for Pyotr I lit a Marlboro from a packet that I had brought back from Berlin. I didn't offer Alexey a cigarette. Why was he telling me like this? What was the point in asking me these questions? I looked at him but I could read nothing in his pale eyes. I exhaled, hissing the smoke through my teeth. After all, in the week before I had left for Berlin Pyotr had seen Alexey every day, Alexey must have known what his mood had been as well as I did. So why ask?

I sucked hard on the cigarette. I felt a sudden loathing for him. The strong tobacco was making me feel slightly dizzy. I rolled the brown-flecked paper around the filter between my thumb and forefinger. An undigested, uncomfortable lump of time had passed since Alexey had asked his question and he was becoming impatient.

'Natalie?' he enquired. Something stubborn inside me didn't want to answer him. I felt like he owned all the facts about Pyotr's death and I didn't want to give him my thoughts as well, so I still didn't answer.

'It is not necessary to say anything,' he allowed graciously and so to be contrary I did. I felt suddenly and irrationally angry. I talked fast, snipping off my sentences.

'Alexey, you know what his mood was that week as well as I do. I don't know why you are asking me this. I will go to my flat now. Thank you for the vodka. I will come and see you later on this week, but for the moment if you don't mind I would like to be alone.' I was aware that I was being rude, doubly so as Alexey was trying to be kind, but I hoped that he would realise that I was distraught and he would forgive me.

'But of course, forgive me Natalie, I have been thoughtless. You must rest. But I insist that you come visiting on Monday. I have organised an *actsia*, an art performance. It is entitled "Food, Art and Sex" and although I say it myself, I am certain that it will be most interesting. A famous Italian art critic from Milan will be present, who is a close associate of Marie-Teresa and Guiseppe from the gallery in Berlin. All the most notable figures of our own small art world will be present – the ideas will be most refreshing. I hope that you will be able to join us.'

I nodded and said that I would come. He had hung my jacket on a coat stand in the hall in view of the mask of Goethe. As I went to retrieve it I saw, sitting by the new fax machine, a pale green rectangle. It was the second time that I had seen one that day. The first had been behind the trigger of a pistol in my cabin on the Berlin train, and a passenger had accused me of owning it. It was the cartridge of a gas-powered pistol.

I continued my journey into the hallway walking lightly on the balls of my feet. Goethe regarded me suspiciously from above the coat stand. I said nothing to Alexey and gave him no indication that I had seen or recognised the cartridge.

Alexey insisted on carrying my rucksack down the staircase. The entrance to the street was freshly repainted with a thick brown paint that smothered the poor plaster cherubs that decorated the walls.

In silence he accompanied me along the canal and up into Sadovaya Street. He stopped a car and gave the driver my fifty roubles and my address.

'Thank you Alexey for everything,' I said as he kissed me on both cheeks with his tickly little beard. 'I'll see you at the *actsia*.'

Babba Lenna was in when I got back. She bustled out into the hallway on her old bowed legs. 'So here you are back again *dotchinka*. Did you have a good holiday? Look, the spring has come back with you.' I smiled and said that yes I had had a good holiday and I asked her how her leg was. Then I let myself into my room which was the same as I had left it. Nothing had changed at all, it was all there just waiting for me.

12

Suicide. *Sam Isdat*; self-publish; *Sam Golod*; self-hunger. *Sam Smiert*; self-death, suicide. Oh God Pyotr, how could you? And what am I meant to do now? Your mood, your *tosca*. How could I have gone to Berlin? How could I have gone on holiday and left you?

Then I heard a voice howling in my brain, protesting, pleading that it couldn't be true, that despite the moods Pyotr would not have done it. He had begged me to return, he had made me promise that I would come back, so why wasn't he here now I'd come? There was too much swagger, too much of the exhibitionist in Pyotr to shoot himself on a lonely road. I didn't want to believe it was true. I refused to believe it was possible. It made me incandescent with rage. I felt a bolt of anger searing through me. I wanted to be obscene, I wanted to make something tremble, be violent with my mind.

I was lying in my half-empty bed. Outside in the city the air was fat and humid and behind me I could hear Babba Lenna sweeping the corridor. She banged her old broom against the skirting boards. It had lost its bristles long ago and she had replaced them with a towel that she used like a snow plough through the dust.

I reviewed the previous day, rewound and replayed again. I am not angry in public, in front of other people, because it frightens me too much. Anger makes me brittle so I carry it away, afraid that I might shatter like a vase under its stresses. Here in the safety of this room I let myself go, I let myself go so far that all the guilt, rage, grief and confusion of the previous few days unhinged me slightly.

If Pyotr had killed himself then I had deserted him not understanding the full extent of the *tosca* that he had been suffering from. Alexey didn't seem to realise that when he suggested suicide he was accusing me of a kind of murder. How could I have gone to Berlin if I had even suspected that this was possible? I thought of his wounded wrists the day he got out of prison, but that hadn't been suicide, that hadn't even been an attempt, that had been a demonstration of frustration. I had seen scars on so many Russian wrists. I remember Nikita telling me that in the mental homes they think it shows that you have a soul.

Another wave of anger crashed over me. I bit into my pillow and thumped my fists pathetically on the mattress. Oh Pyotr you bastard, why didn't you ever say goodbye?

'I've never told Babba Lenna what happened to Pyotr. She was fond of him and I wanted to save her feelings. I also wanted to save mine. In this flat at least, Pyotr is still alive, and when I need the opiate of fantasy I can pretend that tomorrow or the next day he will arrive off the overnight train with a grapefruit in his hands.

I waited for my emotions to subside and when they had, leaving me feeling barren and flat, I pulled myself together and set off for the studio. It was a warm muggy day and the sky was cloaked with a white haze. The climate here is too extreme to allow much time for the intermediate seasons. Summer had already arrived. Spring, violent and quick, had happened in my absence.

The contrast in light as I stepped from the sunlight into the dark foul-smelling hallway of the studio's apartment block temporarily blinded me. When the blue shimmer from my unadjusted eyes had cleared I saw that there had been a break-in. One of the double doors hung tentatively from the lock and the bottom panel was broken to reveal jagged white wood edges. The padlock was untouched; the intruders had simply smashed the door by the hinges.

This was an unnecessary insult. Pyotr used to complain about the burglaries; he said it was because he was on the bottom floor. The last one had been at the same time as the *putsch*, while Pyotr was in Lvov holding his breath and waiting for the news from Moscow. How long ago had it happened? Was it just another random burglary, a simple coincidence?

I stepped gingerly through the gap by the broken hinges, the rest of the door swinging on what remained of the lock. I could hear the skewed beat of my blood in my ear drums. I found that I was holding my last breath in a lump in my mouth. I fumbled for the light switch by the door, which gave a blue spark as the light went on. Pyotr used to joke that the wiring would get him before the police did.

In front of me were the familiar alcoves full of rubble, the same nail-spotted plaster walls. There was no sign of anybody having been in the kitchen and the dust in the storeroom where the archæological pottery was stacked was undisturbed. Every sound that I made seemed to be magnified in the eerie quiet of the corridor.

I opened the door to the main room, turned on the light and, out of habit and because the silence was getting to me, I walked across the room and switched on the radio. I listened to the comfortable, familiar hum as it warmed up.

It took time for me to register the difference. It was nothing dramatic, nothing had been smashed up like the door, but something had happened. The drawers were open and all Pyotr's papers, even those from the top of the tin stove, lay in a pile on the table. The objects on his work table had been rearranged: nothing seemed to be missing but they weren't in their normal pattern. Pyotr's paintbrush jar was standing up the end where he didn't work, and his white spirit was too far from his paint. Somebody had been looking for something. They hadn't been rushed and they had known Pyotr well enough not to bother with the other rooms.

Radio Europa Plus was playing 'Money for nothing, kicks for free'. The Captain's Chair was empty, the whole room was so soaked with his personality that his absence was as palpable as if he was shouting to me, but I could only hear the echo. I returned to the kitchen. Down one side of the room were the racks which stored his empty paint tins, old newspapers, rolls of wallpaper and rubble. A naked lightbulb swung on a frayed wire, and because of the rotting floorboards around the sink and the adjoining toilet the air smelt manky. I used to be frightened that rats might nest in the racks so I had avoided them before.

On the bottom rack next to the wall was a pile of newspapers tied up with string. I crouched down, moved the newspapers and felt along the wall. An elbow's length back I found a square hole in the wall stuffed with scrunched up newspaper and an old tea towel that was stiff from being used as a paint rag. I pulled out the rag and then, one by one, the newspaper balls. In the back of the hole I found what I was looking for – a tin cash box and a plastic freezer bag, Pyotr's safe, his 'Fort Knox'.

I laid them out on the round table in the main room and perched on the edge of the Captain's Chair. There was grass in the plastic bag and in the cash box there were four Belamor cigarettes, some more grass stuffed into one of those plastic pockets that banks give you change in, $120 dollars in small denominations, aproximately one thousand roubles and an external passport.

I turned the passport over in my hands and then opened it. I don't read Russian very well and I find official Russian particularly difficult. The photograph was very recent, his face staring sternly back at me from the little lacquered square. He would, I know, have thought it demeaning to smile for any official photograph. I began slowly to decipher the entries, letter by letter. I feel like a child when I read Russian. I have to say each letter out loud and then hopefully I recognise the word. I checked the front again: it was embossed with the corn head crest of the Soviet Union and inside it stated that it was an external passport for a citizen of the USSR. Pyotr always carried his internal passport with him, so why wasn't he carrying this one as well? I figured out his name, Pyotr Sergeivich Morozof; St Petersburg was easy as I knew what the words looked like; and then the date of issue, 28 May 1992. The passport had only been issued ten days earlier.

I leant back on the old chair and tried to make sense of my find. A passport was such a momentous thing. How come he had one and one that was so recent? I rolled myself a joint because I knew that Pyotr would have approved. I would have remembered if he had mentioned an external passport to me, and according to Alexey he had thought that he would never be able to achieve one.

I looked around the room. A casual burglar would have wrecked the place, turned it upside down and shat on the mattress. Whoever had been here had known Pyotr and had come straight to the main room and ignored all the others. That suggested that they had been looking for something specific.

The paintings. The stack of his most recent paintings that normally leant against the wall by the easel was gone. I got up and checked the racks in the kitchen; they weren't there either. Had the intruders been after the paintings or had Pyotr taken them to Lvov? Pyotr's paintings had been big, double the size of the canvases that I had taken to Berlin. They would have been too heavy and awkward for him to have moved on his own. He was supposed to have gone to Lvov to sort out papers; there was no reason for him to take his paintings with him. All the same the paintings had been there and now they weren't. If thieves had taken them there must have been two of them. There had been about ten canvases if I remembered right, and most of them had been at least six foot across: you would have needed two people to handle canvases of that size.

Pyotr was a fine artist but he wasn't a great artist. He was well known in Petersburg, among the other artists anyway, and maybe he was well known in Lvov, I don't know, but no one had heard of him anywhere else. Pyotr wasn't Tornikov. Why steal the paintings of a small-time Russian artist?

I didn't understand. I wanted him there to tell me what had happened. I could feel his presence so strongly. I closed my eyes and clenched my fists and willed him to explain but he wasn't there, he wasn't there. I went through the pile of papers on the table. There were photocopies, articles that had amused Pyotr, sketches by himself and by friends, diagrams of English grammar, old documents, telephone numbers and cigarette packets. There was a postcard I had given him of the Tower of London, across the back of which he had written in English, 'a British prison!'. Pyotr was like a magpie, picking up anything that appealed to him. I hadn't known what was there when I had left for Berlin. I had no way of knowing what was missing now. If anything was. I looked at the passport, maybe that was what they had been looking for, but why?

I finished my joint and put the papers along with the passport, grass and the money into my bag and then, switching off the lights and the radio, I left. I tried to prop up the door behind me but the broken half swung loose again, dallying on its hinges. It wouldn't deter anyone now.

When I got back to my room I stuffed Pyotr's things inside

my winter boots and laid the papers out on this table. I would decide what to do with the money and the grass later. I didn't want to use them but it didn't seem right to throw them away either. The passport was different, it was a puzzle, it lay like a question mark in the toe of the boot. An external passport without an entry visa for the country you intended to visit was useless. There was no point in having one without the other. It didn't make sense.

I slept very badly that night. The White Nights around the summer solstice had already begun and there was no darkness, the dusk slipping straight into dawn. It was hot and muggy but I had to sleep under a sheet because the mosquitoes macerated every available window of skin. Their maddening, reproachful sonic whine kept me awake for hours. I wrapped my sheet around me like a cocoon and coiled a T-shirt about my head and shoulders, leaving a small breathing space for my nose.

When I finally fell asleep I dreamt of Pyotr wandering in circles around the streets of St Petersburg, his nose and his eyes streaming with ants. He was muttering, 'It's the wrong kind, they're the wrong sort, not the right kind at all.' Then he was standing by an embankment and a body came flying out of the window above him. It floated for ages like a dead leaf that refuses to land and I realised that it was the tramp that I had found near Pushkinskaya. Pyotr watched the body slowly drifting through the air and he shook his head from side to side, as if he had water in his ears, and I thought that maybe it was blood. Then suddenly the body speeded up and hit the ground with a heavy slap and I woke up.

I listened to a mosquito and waited for the dream to fade away. I released my arms from the sheet cocoon and pinched myself: I didn't want to go back to sleep and risk the dream returning. I found an old sheet sleeping-bag in my cupboard, which I tore up and pinned taunt around the window frame to keep out the mosquitoes. It had a strange blinding effect on the room, like living in a drum. I could hear the noises coming from the courtyard but I could no longer see what was causing them.

I spent an exhausting morning hunting down the mosquitoes left in the room, leaving little smears of blood (no doubt mine) where I splatted them against the walls. Then I sat down and started sifting through the papers I had brought back from Pyotr's studio. I found the bits and pieces comforting; solid evidence of his life that I could hold on to. There were notes that I had left him, misspelt and in my lousy Russian script, a photograph of Pyotr on a venerable motor-bike waving his helmet in triumph. His hair was longer and he looked much younger: it must have been taken about five years ago. It struck me how little I knew about his life – was this his bike, when did he cut his hair shorter, where was the photograph taken? – and how it hadn't seemed to matter very much while he was here, but that now it seemed very cruel. I picked up a postcard of a tank in Prague that had been sprayed light-pink, addressed to Pyotr care of the main post office on Nevsky Prospect and signed Ivan. Who was Ivan? There were three monthly transport passes and an article out of an art magazine about Dada and then I found a note from Oleg; 'Can you work next week?' and in the top right hand corner he had put the time: 6.30 pm, but frustratingly there was no date.

13

That night I went looking for Oleg and the nickel smugglers. Pyotr used to leave for the Moscovsky Station at about half-past eleven so I planned to arrive there at midnight. At ten o'clock I showered and made a meal which I ate by the diffuse light of my home-made mosquito screen. I dressed in clothes that I had bought in Russia; a pair of black fake Levi's, a dark-blue cotton army shirt and some black rubber-soled gymshoes. I tied my hair back in a ponytail. At eleven o'clock I put a roll of four fifty-rouble notes in my pocket and hid my key underneath the mat on our landing. The preparations seemed rather silly to me, like a childish ritual, but I found them comforting. I also had a sense of pilgrimage, to see where it was that he had gone during those dark nights while I waited for him on the mattress in the studio.

I walked. I had over an hour to spare and the rhythm of walking helps me to think, turning the blood in my brain like a water wheel turning the river. As I crossed the bridge the sun sat fat and orange on the rim of the Gulf of Finland. The light was iridescent and unearthly. The azure and gold of the Winter Palace floated above the river and its windows flamed in the reflection of the sinking sun. Young families were still strolling down Nevsky, no hurry to sleep, this was summer. I meandered along beside them, taking my time and pausing on the bridges to peer into the quicksilver water of the canals. I sat on the steps that spread out from the busty imperial statue of Catherine the Great and smoked a cigarette.

I crossed the street before I reached the turning off to Pushkinskaya, and found myself walking more and more slowly the closer I came to Moskovsky Station. Outside Ploschad Vostannya Metro I bought a beer from a kiosk. The stalls were all still open, selling beer, vodka, champagne, sticks of chewing gum, magazines and flowers. Old women were selling cigarettes in singles or by the packet, holding them up in their cupped palms as if they were receiving communion. I drank my beer on the steps and returned the bottle for the deposit.

It was a quarter to midnight. Moscovsky Station was on the other side of the square. The sun had gone and in the half light that remained the station resembled a grainy photograph which has been too enlarged for the details to be clear.

The main hall of the station was busy with passengers, ticket touts, beer sellers, bookstalls and, lurking in the corners, shifting with the dry wind in the litter, the shaven heads of the runaway children. There was no nickel here, it was too public. I walked back into the square and turned down Goncharnaya Street. The houses were close together and they sat in shadows dark enough to discourage the families strolling in the square. About two hundred yards down the street I passed a large pair of light-blue metal gates under a two-storey Stalinesque arch. On the other side I could hear the gruff throbbing of a Soviet-built lorry engine. Was this where Pyotr had come to earn his five dollars an hour?

A block further on I found an archway leading into a small courtyard and I knew that if it was anything like Vasilievsky Island there would be a back courtyard through one of the staircases. There were four doorways; I tried the one in the furthest right-hand corner to begin with. A naked bulb exposed a stone staircase and black wrought-iron railings. Next I tried the door in the furthest left-hand corner. This time there was no light inside and the stairwell was black, except for the pale wash of an open door behind the staircase. It led to a narrow alleyway in which stood four large, overflowing metal rubbish bins against a high brick wall, behind which I could hear the faint rumbling of the truck engine.

The smell of the rubbish had an acrid punch to it. I could hear the radio pitch of the mosquitoes and feel them biting my ankles. I pushed down on one of the lids and clambered up until I was crouching on top of its foul-smelling contents. I tried to stand up but it felt too unsteady, so I stretched upwards and grabbed onto the top of the wall, which from the summit of the bins was just below head height. Hauling myself up with my hands I swung one foot over the wall and hooked my heel on the edge of it. Then using my hands and my heel together, I heaved myself up on top of the wall.

In front of me was a yard, basically rectangular but tapering slightly towards my end. To the right of me the lorry that I had heard earlier was moving through the metal gates. Another truck was parked up by a platform at the top of the yard. A ramp led from the platform to the top of the truck, where a man was straining up with a hod on his back. He paused at the top, twisted the hod upside down over the hold of the truck and I watched, fascinated, as a stream of grey granules poured out glittering dully in the strange half light of the summer night. This was how Pyotr had worked, this was the nickel that I had rolled around the palm of my hand, that he had saved for me as a souvenir.

On the opposite side of the yard some passenger sleeper carriages stood in the sidings. Another man with a hod emerged from behind them and passed the man now

coming down the ramp with a small nod of acknowl-
edgement.

I heard a shout. Damn, I had been spotted, I had been
so entranced by the nickel I hadn't even thought about
hiding. There was a furious babble and I saw a squat,
slightly bow-legged figure striding from the gate towards
the wall that I was perched on. I looked behind me and
dithered hopelessly. The alleyway was very narrow and I
was frightened that if I tried to jump I would break my leg
on the rubbish bins. I turned back to the yard, where the
man was waving his hands around in the air. He was much
closer now and I could make out his features. He had dark
hair and a walnut-creased face. It was Oleg.

'Oleg! Help, it's me Natalie. I can't get down, I am
stuck.'

'Who is there? Give me your name?' He came a bit closer.
'Jesus Christ, it's little Natalie, Pyotr's girl isn't it? Do you
want to tell me what the fuck are you doing up there.'

'I'm stuck, I can't get down, there is no room to jump on
the other side.'

He walked to the base of the wall. 'Do as I tell you. Lower
yourself down and I'll catch you.' The yard was on a lower
level than the alleyway. I peered at Oleg nervously and
grimaced, it looked a very long way down. My muscles
were trembling from holding my position for so long. I
crouched down on my hands and knees and hesitated.

'Come on Natalie, I'm here to catch you, it's not that far,
you can do it. Are you sure it's not better on the other side?'
he said testily.

'No, no it's not. There are rubbish bins and there isn't
enough room to jump clear of them.' My voice came out
unnaturally squeaky.

I turned around so that my bottom was facing him,
shuffled my knees backwards and, gripping onto the top
of the wall tightly, I let my body fall. The edges of the

bricks were sharp and they cut into the veined undersides of my wrists. Oleg's voice came up from below me. 'You're still too high, let yourself fall, you can't go wrong, I'm right beneath you.'

I didn't have any choice; I had to trust him. My arms were straining and I wasn't strong enough to hold out much longer. I took a deep breath, let my fingers go and dropped. There was a jolt as Oleg caught me around the knees. Once he had broken my fall he lowered me to the ground. I stamped my feet to get rid of the worst of the rubbish and massaged my sore wrists. 'Thank you,' I gasped, leaning against the wall.

'It is the *Anglichanka*. What the bloody hell are you doing here? Are you crazy or something?' He started walking away. 'On second thoughts don't tell me,' he tossed over his shoulder. 'Don't move, not even a centimetre. Crazy woman. I don't know. Where did Pyotr find this one, I ask myself? I will be back in just a second. Now wait here and don't you dare move.'

I leant against the wall and my stomach sank. I had really dropped myself in it. Whatever Pyotr had said, there was no getting away from the fact that this man was a mafyosi.

Oleg reappeared behind the wheel of a luminescent white Volkswagen Golf GTI with no number plates. It was a brand new car, probably stolen from some rich Berliner and driven east.

'Jump in!' He leant across the gear stick and opened the passenger door from the inside, pushing it open with his stubby fingers. I hesitated, but I didn't really have an option. Oleg treated me to a non-stop sales hype on the car. He pointed out the leather seats, the compact disc hi-fi with its graphic equalisers, the electric windows, the sun roof. 'In my opinion German cars are the best. What do you think, hey? It is pretty good, isn't it? I only picked this one up two days ago, it is almost absolutely brand new.' He raised an eyebrow as he watched me do up my seat belt. 'If you ask me they are not worth it, I never bother myself,' implying that seat belts were a sign of weakness.

The gates were opened for us and we passed out the same way as the lorry had. Oleg turned the car up Ligovsky Prospect and proceeded to cruise through the city. He continued giving a running commentary on the virtues of German cars in general and Volkswagens in particular. I sat, tensely waiting for him to come to the point. Having important conversations in cars is a very Russian thing to do. Nobody can overhear you in a car.

We drove north down Liteyny Prospect towards the river then, bringing his muscular arm right across the steering wheel, Oleg turned the car down a side street running off to the left. A hundred yards down it he turned right and then left again almost immediately. At the end of this last street he pulled up by the pavement. In front of us on the other side of the Fontanka Canal were Peter the Great's Summer Gardens. Oleg had finally stopped talking: inside the car there was an exaggerated and ominous calm as the engine died.

'OK, Natalie, now do you want to tell me why you were spying on me?' His voice had dropped in tone.

'I wasn't. I promise you Oleg, it wasn't like that.'

'So, excuse me for being stupid, but just what the fuck were you doing?'

'I know it sounds silly but I just wanted to see what Pyotr got up to. He would never tell me, you see. All I knew was that he went to Moscovsky Station and I was curious.'

'Well why the hell didn't you ask Pyotr then?'

I looked at him sharply. Surely he knew? His face was like a carapace, it was impossible to read anything from it. In that weird ultraviolet light I could only see the creases that ran down from his nose and the chinks of his black eyes. I decided that the wisest action was to play dumb. 'You don't know then?'

'Tell me what it is I should know first and then I'll tell you.'

'Pyotr's dead.'

'What!' he exploded, slapping his hands on either side of the leather covered steering wheel. It was very hammy: he could have been acting.

'He's dead,' I repeated. 'I don't know what happened. I wasn't here, I was in Berlin staying with Nikita. I got a message to phone Alexey.'

Oleg snorted derisively 'Yes, you would do.'

I ignored him and continued, 'A mutual friend had rung Alexey to tell him Pyotr's body had been found on a country road near Lvov. There was a bullet wound in his temple. Alexey thinks it was suicide but I, well I don't think . . .'

'I tell you, that Alexey Andreev is an evil manipulating little toad,' spat Oleg. 'He has cut me out on two deals already this year and I swear to you, Natalie, that he has got Nikita tied up in little bloody knots. Oh those artists are so stupid sometimes I want to shake them. They just won't listen to me. Honestly, they don't live in the real bloody world, they just don't see what is going on around them. I don't believe a word that Alexey Andreev says; nobody fools me with smooth words and slick clothes. Suicide, to hell with suicide, it's only ten days since I paid off his bloody lawyer. Pyotr was not going to commit suicide. In my opinion Alexey's behind this. I tell you girl, don't trust that man, don't trust him at all.'

'So he couldn't have gone to prison after all?'

'No, he was cleared. He was free. I'll make sure fucking Alexey Andreev pays for this with his skin. Damn him, Pyotr was my client!'

And the man I loved, I thought with a sharp pain in my gut.

I wound down my window and let the silence come pouring in off the canal. I hadn't realised before how much rivalry there was between Oleg and Alexey. Pyotr obviously hadn't trusted either of them or he wouldn't have got Oleg to pay Alexey's lawyer.

I asked Oleg about Allia and he told me that she and the little girl Olga were now in a reception centre in eastern Germany. 'I wish she hadn't gone. But she would take it into her head that St Petersburg was bad for Olga and nothing I could say would change her mind. But I tell you I don't know if this place she has gone to is any better, any better at all. Allia's been ill and it breaks my heart to know that she is there and I'm here and there is nothing that I can do. She was telling me on the telephone that they took her to the hospital. It was pneumonia she had and she is all right now and she is back in the refugee centre, but I'm still not allowed to go and visit her.' Allia was so chic I found it hard to imagine her in an institution with crowds of frightened people. I remembered her talking about the little girl, *'It isn't a place for a child'*.

Abruptly, Oleg changed the subject back to Pyotr. 'OK, as far as I can see it you have satisfied your curiosity now and you know what Pyotr got up to. Now keep your mouth shut and don't go snooping around any more. This isn't the place for it and I'm telling you straight, Natalie, you will get yourself into trouble. Big trouble. Not everybody is as trusting as I am,' Oleg said sternly. He slid his hands around to the top of the steering wheel then took his left hand away and turned the key in the ignition. 'OK girl, I'll drive you back. You live on Vasilievsky Island as well, don't you?'

I nodded, 'Seventeenth Line, just off Sredny Prospect.' He slipped into gear and started down the canal embankment.

'Don't let Alexey know you've been talking to me, he wouldn't like it.' I looked at his face but there was still no change in his expression.

He handed me his telephone number on a scrap of paper. 'Why did you come back? You should have stayed away.

It's not too late to leave now, you can go across the border whenever you want to. Hey?'

I didn't reply. After a pause he asked me how he could get in contact with me. I wasn't sure that I wanted to tell him but I didn't know how to avoid it.

'I live with an old lady,' I told him. 'She doesn't like strangers coming around. It makes her nervous. You can leave a note on the door but she doesn't read, so write my name very clearly in capitals or she might think it's for her and get her grandson to read it.'

He drove with one hand lying casually on the steering wheel and one resting on the gear stick but he watched the road extremely carefully. His eyes flickered constantly between the mirrors and he didn't look at me once during our journey back here. This didn't stop him treating me to a constant stream of comment.

'OK, I'll tell you what, I've got contacts in Lvov. I will make some enquiries and I'll let you know what I find out. Hey, Pyotr was a grand man, one of the best. I'll look after you for his sake, you're going to need some friends. And I'll screw that little shit Alexey Andreev. This time he's gone too fucking far. He's not going to mess with me again. You did the sensible thing coming to see me. I'm the right person to help you. I have to give it to you, you're a brave girl but don't go fucking it up now by being stupid. OK?' I nodded obediently.

I watched the sun rising behind the thin gold splinter of the Peter and Paul Fortress as we crossed the river. He pulled up by the corner of the Seventeenth Line. I got out and heard the brakes screech as he forced the gleaming white hatchback in to a U-turn across the tram lines and drove away.

14

I sat on my bed and stroked my pillow in slow circles and let the tears smear my cheeks yet again. Who could I trust? Who should I believe? In my head I heard Pyotr's gravelly voice: 'Do you really think one kind of mafya is better than another? You don't understand, Natalie. You don't understand.' In the end I decided to see if I could glean anything more in Pushkinskaya, where rumours circulate through the dingy studios like vapours in the drains.

I took the tram: I like to go overground if I can. It was a hot day with a dusty sky and a low sun leaving long shadows. The tram went along the First Line and turned left down the embankment past the green cupola of the Kunstkamera where, according to Annya, they display Peter the Great's collection of pickled freaks, two-headed calves and babies with tails. We crossed the river which was sparkling sharply in the sunlight and I got off at the stop by the Winter Palace, then caught a trolley bus going down Nevsky.

The bus was crammed, people were treading on the edges of my feet and I struggled to keep my balance and my handbag. Nevsky was full too, with coagulations of stalls, sellers and Western tourists in brightly coloured gaggles. Nevsky's always crowded now; Pushkinskaya, in contrast, was empty and echoing. I stood for a moment under the arch that led into the dilapidated courtyard, trying to make up my mind which studio to visit first. I ran through the list of the artists I knew: they were all Pyotr's friends, not mine.

A tall man in a black silk shirt turned off the street. He walked past me and then paused and reversed. 'Do you know what room the exhibition is in?'

'Whose?' I replied.

'The photography one, Sergei Belinsky and the others.'

'No, sorry,' I said, 'I don't, I was looking for it myself.'

'I've got a feeling it's on staircase ten, but I'm not absolutely sure.'

'Well that's better than I can do, let's try staircase ten.' I attached myself to his tail and followed him over to a staircase in the second courtyard. He was right. It was on the top floor but you could hear the chatter at ground level, coming clinking down the staircase like bottles being emptied into a dustbin.

I recognised most of the faces. Boris, a film maker who also lived on staircase number ten, started talking to me in an affected, high-pitched voice. 'Natalie, I heard about Pyotr, what can we say? What can we do?' He shrugged his shoulders, frowned and shook his head dolefully. I winced. I wasn't feeling strong enough to cope with social sympathy. It seemed fraudulent but Pyotr had been a friend of his so presumably he was upset.

I braced myself. I was there to ask questions so I started with Boris. 'What do you think happened? What are they saying in Pushkinskaya?'

His face puckered like a baby's and he gestured vaguely towards the courtyard. 'Everybody is terribly shocked by this news, Natalie. We are all affected by it.' And I knew that I had made a mistake, I had transgressed a social rule: you should never ask anything specific, especially not if it matters.

Boris started talking about what was in the shops, which

is the Russian equivalent of talking about the weather. I felt sorry for him; he was looking very uncomfortable. The man I had come in with walked past and Boris stalled him by putting a foot in his pathway. 'Excuse me Natalie,' he squealed, 'I have to talk to Volodaya about something important.'

The red-haired girl, the one who had looked so young and had brought that tulip for Pyotr the day he got out of prison, was standing by the window. 'Pyotr,' she whispered when she saw me. There was no expression on her scandalously young face. Was this how you survived here?

I remembered the shocking red and black of the tulip. Pyotr had given her the key that night; had they been lovers? 'Do you know why?' I pleaded.

She didn't answer me either. 'There is such a feeling here in Pushkinskaya since we heard,' she said. 'Tornikov was different, that was a big man's death. Pyotr was *nash*, ours. His death has tipped the balance. Before it I believed that with the changes anything was possible, the best, the worst, who could tell what would happen here. Now the pattern has been settled, it will be all mafyosi and inflation and Pyotr is dead.'

'That doesn't help,' I said. 'That's all theory, it doesn't tell me anything.' I was on the route to the door and people kept on barging past me. I moved to one side.

'Are you going to Alexey's *actsia*?' she breathed. Her voice was so faint I thought it might evaporate before she formed a word.

'Yes, I promised him I would.'

'He has asked me to do an action in front of this foreign critic. I feel like we are performing dogs. I am glad you'll be there. To tell you the truth I am a little bit nervous.' She looked so young but I knew she had a job so she had to be at least sixteen. Her white nose was sprayed with pallid freckles. 'Have you seen

Sasha?' she added, pointing to a wheelchair behind the door.

I hardly recognised the creature slumped in the wheelchair as the man I had flirted with at Oleg's party. His skin was a dead pink-grey and it hung over the fleshless bones of his face like city washing. His big shoulders were wasted and buckled, his head had been shaved and his hair had grown back in an uneven bristle. Across the centre of his skull ran a glistening pink scar in a grotesque caricature of a parting. I heard the girl's hushed voice in my ear, 'He fell off the station platform, broke his neck on the rails.'

I left her and pushed through the crowd towards him. 'Hello Natalie,' he said in a tired voice.

'What happened?'

'I had an accident. Lucky to be alive really. Sorry to hear about Pyotr.'

I found myself staring at him like an idiot. I thought of the Tam Tam Club and Oleg and I wondered whose fault the 'accident' was. I could see the hurt and the defeat glittering blue around the pupils of his eyes. I felt the flutter of his hand pawing my forearm. I stopped myself flinching in disgust. 'Natalie,' he whispered, 'I want to warn you.'

I squatted down level with his chair. The bodies of the other guests were pushing around us.

'I've heard a rumour that he never went to Lvov.'

'How do you mean?'

'He died here.'

'But . . .'

'Shh, Natalie. Why don't you drop in at my place some time, I have a picture to give to you. Staircase three, flat 20. It's on the second floor.' I nodded and it struck me that nobody so far had mentioned suicide.

I stayed at Pushkinskaya until seven o'clock. No one was talking to me. I found myself constantly hovering on the edge of conversation clusters, standing behind somebody's shoulder blade. It made me sad. When Pyotr had been here we had been at the centre of all this; I had belonged to their group and been part of their discussions. Without Pyotr I was no longer interesting and I cringed as I sensed their pity. It is very humiliating to be pitied. I had the impression that I was a worry to people, because the way to treat me was no longer straightforward. I wasn't Russian and I wasn't somebody's girlfriend, I was a foreigner but I had been here too long to be treated as one.

I went straight from Pushkinskaya to Alexey's atelier for the *actsia*. I spotted the Italian critic the moment I walked in. He was easy to identify: he was dark and he wore a soft blue shirt and gold jewellery, his skin looked healthy and his clothes fresh. He sat on the sofa by the glass and aluminium coffee table and a crowd of people buzzed around him.

The large windows of the three main rooms had been opened. We were all gathered in one of the front rooms. I looked down through a window on to the canal, the rutted dust track of the embankment, the little iron footbridge and on the other side the deep, velvet-blue cupola of the church where Dostoevsky had been married.

Yelena was there; she raised her head on her long neck and smiled to me from the doorway. The room was beginning to go quiet. Alexey, his chest greasy in the heat under a black tail coat, cleared his throat, welcomed us and then welcomed the critic, 'who has travelled all the way from Milan to see our work. The themes of today's *actsia* are "Food, Art and Sex" because these are the essentials of human existence.' He then repeated the whole speech in stilted English for the benefit of the Italian.

A river taxi was motoring down the canal. In the front an old captain was laughing and I could see his big belly shaking, behind him four meek tourists sitting with their knees together and their cameras on their laps. The boat made a noise like a motorbike with the silencer taken off. The captain was entertaining his passengers by slaloming violently from one side of the canal to the other.

When the boat had passed I turned back to the room. The scene seemed very contrived. Art with Pyotr had been charged with hard, fresh ironies and everything had been invented for the moment, but this *actsia* was just a play directed by Alexey for the sake of the critic.

We stood in a semi-circle watching the first action. I wanted to sit down and looked around for a spare seat but I couldn't find one. There were two artists, a blow torch, sugar and a lot of white paint. I didn't understand what they were doing, it meant nothing to me. I leant my bottom on the windowsill. Alexey slithered around behind the audience. 'I'm so very glad that you came Natalie,' he hissed. 'How are you feeling? A little bit better maybe?' He looked at me questioningly and without waiting for an answer hurried back to attend to the critic.

There was some applause as the two artists finished their act and left the semi-circle. The redhead that I had been talking to earlier at Pushkinskaya walked over to the central window carrying a small sports bag. She didn't talk, didn't introduce herself and didn't tell us what she was doing. She took three glasses from her bag and lined them up on the newly painted windowsill. Next she took out a slightly rusty hacksaw and proceeded to saw across the underside of her left wrist. I gasped, I had been completely unprepared for this.

The saw was blunt. She rasped it to and fro across the thigh-soft skin of her inner wrist. The room focused down to the hacksaw and her slowly tearing skin. The audience was melded together with horror. Only one man walked away, unable to watch. It took a long time before she actually started bleeding. Her face was still, apart from her translucent eyelashes slowly blinking. She held her wrist above the first of the glasses that she had placed on the windowsill and two inches of scarlet blood poured out.

She padded her wrist with cotton wool and then tied a piece of white cloth around it which she pulled tight using her teeth. She broke an egg into the second glass and poured milk into the third. She whisked the egg with a fork, poured it into the glass of blood and using the same fork mixed the two substances together, then slowly added the milk and redivided the mixture into two glasses. She paused and if possible her face grew calmer, determinedly calm. She turned to us and thrust out one glass with her damaged hand.

There was no doubt in anybody's mind who she was aiming at. The Italian with his healthy skin and rich clothes looked terrified. He stared mesmerically at the glass. The rest of us watched and waited to see if he would accept the challenge. The girl drew back her hand, returned the glass to the windowsill and, picking up the other glass, drank half of the mixture inside it. Then offered the first glass to the critic again.

We waited with her through half an oppressive minute and the glass quivered as her arm tired. Eventually the Italian took it, he put his mouth down to the rim of the glass, funked it and drew back. He tried again and on the third go, with a slight intake of breath, he slammed the mixture down his throat. We cheered him like a war hero while she drank the other glass.

After that there was an outbreak of noise, everybody talking as a release from the tension. I saw the flick of Alexey's tail coat as he slipped out of the room. Outside the window on the canal another tourist boat was passing by.

Alexey glided back into the room clutching a couple of bottles of vodka and some glasses. He looked white but there was a pinched flush around his nostrils. I suddenly felt rather sorry for him: the Italian was his guest and by the looks of it the red-haired girl hadn't told Alexey what she was going to do. Alexey pompously toasted the critic and 'The Experimental Laboratory of Life' but he omitted to toast the girl.

I looked around the flat for Yelena and found her in the kitchen with Arkady. 'You'll come up onto the roof Natalie, won't you? We're shooting a film. Don't say anything to Alexey, this is Arkady's thing,' she said. She spoke in hurried little jerks and I guessed that she had asked me on impulse. She turned her enormous tawny eyes on Arkady, 'Shall we go then?'

We reached the attic via a flight of stairs in the next door flat. It was an empty communal flat similar to the ones in my courtyard. I could almost sense the presence of the families who had lived there. There would have been one family to each room and they would have shared the toilet and the kitchen. I imagined them gossiping, exchanging information on food supplies, pretending not to hear the farts and snores of their neighbours through thin internal walls.

'Why is this place empty?' I asked Arkady.

'Alexey,' he said sourly. Then he added, 'He wants to use it for a business.'

At the back of the kitchen a doorway opened onto a stairway to the attic. Discarded planks ran the length of the staircase. The stairs were covered with Belamor packets, bricks and plaster dust and, sitting on the bottom step for no reason I could think of, a chicken carcass.

The attic was very black but punctured by shots of sunlight that broke through the missing slates. The rubble was even thicker than on the stairs. Every now and then we came across a beam running the width of the attic at hip height. When we reached one of these Yelena would angle her torch at the ground to indicate to Arkady and me where it was. We followed a faint path through the rubble and by the corner of the building we climbed out on to the roof through a dormer window.

We clawed our way up the slippery slates and I perched myself by a red brick chimney. The night sun draped the city in an old transparent yellow, like last century's varnish. On the horizon red and cream striped factory chimneys trailed horizontal streamers of smoke. I looked down to the canal and the foot bridge a long way below, the light turning the water the colour of congealed blood.

I heard a flame catching and Yelena let out a triumphant yelp. I turned around. She was standing astride the peak of the roof thrusting an electric blue flare up to the sky. Arkady circled her with a camera. She laughed and changed position and began to spell her name in the sky like a child with a sparkler; when the flare started to fade she took aim and threw it down towards the canal.

Arkady had some vodka which we drank standing by the chimney. He held Yelena's hand and she smiled at him in a private thrill. It was obvious that they were having an affair. I thought it was very capricious of Yelena to let me know, but I was glad that she had, I was grateful to be included.

On the way down I carried the camera and Arkady took the torch. We'd just about reached the staircase when I heard him swear. He was standing ten paces in front of me, shining the torch against a stack of canvases leaning against the wall next to the staircase. The paintings were large, one of them at least six foot across.

I recognised them immediately. Brightly coloured acrylics of big machines covered with little lost humans. They were Pyotr's, they were the paintings that had been stolen from his studio.

Yelena came up behind me, picking her queenly way over the rubbish. She followed the beam of Arkady's torch and I heard her intake of breath. She looked at me, startled and I would have said frightened.

The painting closest to me was of a green triangle pointing up towards one corner, at the bottom in large stylised script Pyotr had written *sveeny idut*, the pigs are coming. I had lain on the mattress in the studio and watched him do it. I stepped forward and tipped the canvases towards me. I knew the paintings as well as friends, the grinning faces, geometrics and machinery of Pyotr's universe.

'What are they doing here?' I asked. My voice sounded too loud. I heard it jar and crash into the black shadows of the attic.

Arkady answered me. 'If anyone knows it will be Alexey. Who else would come up here?' He sounded jealous and bitter.

'I don't understand.'

'Well the Green Train comes in tomorrow . . .'

'Shut up Arkady,' interrupted Yelena softly. 'Natalie please, if you say anything to Alexey he will know who you have been up here with. Please don't betray us.'

I ran my finger along the top of the first painting. Yelena looked scared. I rubbed my eyes with my hand. Of course I couldn't let her down. 'No, I won't say anything, I promise.'

Back in Alexey's flat the *actsia* had turned into a party. I made my way to the kitchen and poured myself a glass of Soviet champagne. I picked it up, turned around and bumped straight into Alexey, who looked at me through his pale blue eyes and fingered his little beard. 'Natalie, there you are. I thought you had already disappeared. I have been searching for you everywhere. I would like you to meet my very good friend and aquaintance from Milan, Carlo.' I followed him down the corridor praying that I hadn't blushed.

The Italian critic was lecturing Yelena, 'Russia is so exciting. You see nobody knows what's here. It is as if it has been in an ice age and now the ice is melting we're just beginning to find out what has been going on for the last seventy years. I am sure that there are the equivalent of Picassos out there. The problem is how do we find them?'

Yelena's face didn't change when she saw me, as if she didn't trust herself with an expression. Alexey gave a small cough to interrupt the Italian and dismissed Yelena with a curt hand signal. 'Carlo, I would like to introduce you to my English friend Natalie who actually lives here.' I didn't like the Italian at all. I thought he was slimy.

'How fascinating,' he drawled. 'You must know Russia very well. I think there is a lot of money to be made here.'

15

Arkady had instantly made a connection between the Green Train and Pyotr's paintings in the attic and I wanted to know why. He had said that the Green Train was coming in the next day; my problem was to know when. Pyotr had met it at around midday, but it was a bought train and it would arrive when its buyers wanted it to.

At eleven o'clock I said a pretty goodbye to Alexey. 'If you need anything Natalie, anything at all, then please never forget that I am always here and I would be more than glad to be of service.' I thanked him and said that I would remember. I caught Yelena's eye as I left: she was still dutifully making conversation with the Italian.

I hurried to Ploschad Teatralnaya by the Kirov. The third telephone box I tried was working. I stacked five fifteen-kopeck pieces on the metal top of the telephone and rang Oleg. He answered just as a tram went by behind me, so I stuck my finger in my left ear and leaned into the box to try and cut out some of the noise. 'Oleg, it's me, Natalie, I need to ask you something.'

'I'll pick you up at your place.'

'Thank you. I will see you in a bit then.'

'In a bit.'

I put down the telephone and I wondered if I had done the right thing. I was wary of Oleg but I was certain he would know when the Green Train would be arriving. He was also Alexey's rival.

I took the 33 tram across the river and got off at the Tenth Line. Oleg was parked opposite the main arch of my building. He was looking out for me and opened the passenger door as I approached him.

'That was quick.'

'I do my best. Get in then.'

He told me we were going to a bar that a friend of his ran. We drove down Sredny Prospect, past the studio on the First Line and over Tuchkov Bridge. We parked up by the Arsenal, crossed the road and walked down to the Peter and Paul Fortress. In the little channel that separates the blank brick wall of the fort from Petrogradsky Island a small boat was moored. It was strung about with coloured lightbulbs and a hand-painted sign announced that it was doubling up as a café. Three couples were sitting at tables on the deck.

I followed Oleg's squat figure over the gangplank. He bent down and shouted into the kitchen, 'Aliosha, it's Oleg. How are you doing? Yeah, OK. I need a favour, undisturbed space for an hour, OK?' I couldn't hear the reply. Oleg turned back to me and smiled. 'Welcome to my office, it's good, isn't it? Now let us have a little refreshment. Would you like *champanskoy, kalbasa*?'

He escorted me out on to the deck and we sat at a table at the front. To the right of us the Winter Palace stretched and wavered across the wide river and directly in front of me, behind Oleg's back, stood the flaming gas beacons on the spit of Vasilievsky Island.

An adolescent waiter appeared, tall and awkward. He moved from table to table, bending over the couples, whispering apologetically. The couples behind us were grumbling. 'I don't believe it!' one man exploded. One by one they got up to leave. I watched them go and I swallowed nervously. I had put myself in such a vulnerable position. It would be so easy for me to have an 'accident' like Sasha, or to simply disappear into the Gulf of Finland. I shifted and sat on my hands to stop myself fidgeting too obviously.

Staring across the soft expanse of the river my craving for Pyotr swelled until it was so strong that I had to clench the edge of the table, digging my fingernails into the wood to prevent myself from crying. I had to find out what had happened to him. I couldn't just wallow uselessly in bereavement. Oleg and Alexey were the only people I knew who could help me, but which should I turn to? I realised that that had been Pyotr's dilemma as well.

The waiter was standing beside us now with an ice bucket of Soviet champagne and two glasses. He placed the two glasses in front of us and opened the bottle with a loud explosion which made me jump. I heard the gangplank being dismantled and the boat's engines starting up. Oleg had, for the last quarter of an hour, been treating me to a monologue on the iniquities of the vendors who sold lacquer boxes to the tourists outside the Peter and Paul Fortress. 'Can't you see what a scam it is. No way are these authentic Palik boxes, they're fakes,' he exclaimed in tones of genuine outrage.

By the time the waiter returned with a plate of *kalbasa* and bread we were in mid-stream. We left the spit of Vasilievsky Island to our left and headed towards the port with a regular hiss and bump as we hit the river waves. Once the waiter had gone Oleg asked me why I had called him.

'When is the Green Train coming in?'

'Why do you need to know?'

I hesitated for a moment. 'I want to find Yuri and Slava.'

'You don't want to talk to them. They are scum. You want to keep away from small-time street vendors like that.'

'Pyotr told me they were angry with him about something, I want to know what it was.'

Oleg grunted, 'Listen to me, I can tell you what that was.
I don't mean any disrespect but Pyotr was up to no good
when the police picked him up, I am sure of it. If you ask
me he told the *Mintey* where he had bought his grass. Don't
look so shocked girl, I tell you I bet any of us would have
done the same thing. Hey, we are none of us saints. How
else would he have got out of prison? That's what I say.'

My annoyance with this theory must have shown in my
face because Oleg leaned across the table and patted my
arm. 'Don't get on your high horse, dear. No one is really
a hero,' he said. 'Yuri and Slava had it coming to them, they
deserved it I promise you. If it hadn't been Pyotr it would
have been someone else. Might even have been me, you
never know. I wouldn't waste any sleep over them, they
aren't babies, they can look after themselves. So you think
Yuri and Slava killed Pyotr, do you? What are you going
to do about it? Tell them off? Go to the police?' He was
jeering at me.

We were right at the mouth of the river now, beyond the
port. The boat started on a slow arc to the left. The waves
were larger here and the spray came over the sides. As I
took a gulp of champagne I could taste the salt in the air.

'There is another reason why I want to see the Green
Train arrive,' I said. 'When I visited Pyotr's studio there
were some pictures missing. I was at an *actsia* at Alexey's
place today and I went up on to the roof with Yelena and
Arkady. On the way down I found Pyotr's pictures in the
attic. Arkady seemed to think it had something to do with
the Green Train but Yelena shut him up.'

'Remind me, Yelena is the blonde, good-looking one, isn't
she?' he asked.

'Yes, she's Alexey's girlfriend.'

'Hey you should listen to what I tell you. You don't want

to get mixed up with that lot. I've warned you before about Alexey.'

'I want to find out about these paintings.'

'God you are a liability, aren't you. Where did Pyotr find a girl like you?' He looked grumpy, the boat had turned around and was heading back to the gold spire of the fort. 'Well if you want it I'll give you a hand but don't let anyone see you. You'll have to promise me that. Whatever Alexey's cronies might tell you the Green Train is not a joy ride. But if you really want to know it's coming in tomorrow at eight o'clock in the morning. The bloody thing is coming into Platform 12, which is the closest platform to the sidings where we load up our metal. I've already got somebody watching it for me and if you get to the Goncharnaya Street Gate at five-thirty in the morning I will make sure he knows to let you in. You can hide in one of the carriages but you've got to promise me to stay there until at least midday. That way, if you are caught I won't get it in the neck and you won't be connected with the Green Train. The officials are jumpy enough about it as it is.'

He took a Marlboro lighter from his pocket and played with it, flicking it on and off. 'He frowned and looked abstracted. It was over a minute before he spoke again. 'I've heard all sorts of stuff lately. They say he's got a whole wagon coming up on the train.'

'What of?'

But Oleg didn't answer, he just grunted.

'Thank you Oleg, thank you very, very much. I am really grateful for this.'

'Yes, well I'm not sure that you should be.' From his other pocket he took out a half-empty packet of Bulgarski, offered me one, picked one for himself and lit it. He dropped the lighter inside the packet and put them both away.

He drove me back to the Seventeenth Line. His normal

stream of talk had dried up: he was quiet and sulky all the way.

I set my alarm for four o'clock in the morning but I was so scared of not hearing it that I only slept fitfully and eventually I got up ten minutes before it was meant to go off. Public transport doesn't start until five so I walked again, but I was much brisker this time. Only drunks stroll that early in the morning.

I was a quarter of an hour early when I rattled on the light-blue metal gates. *'Kto eto?'* barked a voice grated across a life-time of Belamor.

'Natalie.'

The gate was fastened by a heavy iron chain and padlock. The chain rattled as it was undone and then the gate opened just wide enough for me to move sideways through it. A short, hairy man nodded his head at me. He had been drinking fortified wine: I got a whiff of the sweet chemistry-grade alcohol on his breath. He laboriously threaded the enormous chain back through the two handles and relocked the padlock. He gave me another brief and rather disgusted look, and then stomped off across the sidings yard. He wasn't impressed.

I scuttled after him in the direction of the big green trains standing in patient lines at the far side of the yard. The man stopped in front of the train closest to the wire-mesh perimeter fence and, once I had caught up with him, set off down the sidings track. Five carriages down he stopped and swung himself up to the level of the door by gripping onto a thin hand rail. He wasn't much taller than the wheels so it was an impressive feat. He extracted a big jangle of keys from his pocket, selected one and opened the door. Still without looking at me he dropped his hand down and helped me up.

He opened the door to the main body of the carriage

and jerked his head in the direction of the corridor. *'Tam,'* he growled. Then he spat vociferously in the corner and grovelled around in his pocket before producing a manky Belamor. I got out my lighter and offered to light it for him. For the first time he looked straight at me, with a startled expression. Russian girls don't light men's cigarettes and I always forget about this because I am trying to be friendly. I turned the lighter over in my palm and handed it to him instead. He spent about half a minute sucking the end of his cigarette to try and persuade it to light. Once he had eventually got it going he grunted and handed the lighter back to me.

'The train arrives at eight-thirty,' he said and with the Belamor clamped between his teeth jumped down on to the track side and slammed the door. It was five-thirty, I had three hours to wait. The blind was down in the first cabin: I left it that way, lay down on the vinyl seat and thought about what Pyotr would have thought of what I was doing. He would have been worried, would have tried to discourage me. It occurred to me that Pyotr had tried to shield me from the business surrounding the Green Train and the rivalry between Oleg and Alexey.

I checked my watch about every ten minutes and watched the time pass slowly. At six-thirty I felt strong enough to deal with my first cigarette. On Russian trains you are only allowed to smoke between the carriages and I smoked it there out of habit. I had another at seven. At half-past seven the railway workers started arriving. They gathered on the other side of the wire fence, smoking and laughing and then moved off down the track in clusters. By quarter to eight the area on the other side of the wire was empty again.

The mafyosi dribbled on to Platform 12 from eight o'clock onwards. They were dressed up like members of a Brixton gang in bright shellsuits and box-fresh trainers. None of them looked at each other, and by twenty past eight there were thirty-four grown up men prowling the platform carefully ignoring each other. Yuri and Slava showed up at twenty-six minutes past. Business can't have been that bad: Yuri was dressed in an enormous aquamarine and purple sweat suit. Slava was dressed normally in jeans. Even they ignored each other. I watched them, to begin with thinking that they were just moseying with no particular aim. They looked very casual but in fact they were doing careful figure of eights the length of the platform and getting a good look at every other character who had turned up.

Then suddenly, quite close by, I heard Alexey's broken English. He was talking to someone, who I guessed had to be the Italian art critic. I couldn't decipher exactly what he was saying; I could only hear the angles of it. I reckoned they were standing in the small gap between my carriage and the next one. That way they would be shielded from the full view of those on the platform. They must have come across the sidings yard like I had and crawled under the standing sleepers. I wondered who had let them in. The old man?

I stayed where I was, peering out from beneath the blind. It was a dangerous situation to be in. How would I explain to Alexey why I was lurking in a standing sleeper waiting for the Green Train to arrive? I wanted to know what they were saying but if I had tried to edge closer they might have heard me moving about above them and I didn't want to take the risk.

We seemed to wait for hours. Occasionally I could make out a word from Carlo and Alexey's conversation but they were all trivial – yes, OK, maybe, it is not convenient. The train didn't arrive until twenty to nine. I knew it was coming by the way the men on the platform stopped milling, stiffened and oriented themselves to the east, down the tracks towards the low-slung sun that was warming the morning.

The train itself was an anticlimax. It looked like any other Russian train, rust-coloured goods wagons with Leningrad printed neatly on their destination boards. The only real difference was that you don't normally get passenger carriages on a mainly goods train. There they were with the blinds in the windows up and the curtains neatly tied back. A bleary, moustached face looked out of one. It was very close: fifty metres and a baggy wire fence was all that separated us. When the train eventually stopped I was looking out onto a goods wagon, which rather annoyed me because I remembered Pyotr's description of drunken, reeling mafyosi and wanted to see them for myself.

I thought again about tip-toeing closer to Alexey and the Italian and eavesdropping. They'd be less likely to hear me with the noise from the train engines. Then I heard Alexey's voice clear and right up close. For one insane moment I thought they were in the carriage with me.

'OK, OK, I understand,' the Italian was saying.

'This carriage is ours.'

'All of it?'

'All of it. And I can assure you that there is much more where this came from. You see, my supplies are plentiful but the market in Russia is immature. However that is not to say that the quality is not high.'

'I want to see it.'

'Naturally. I was assuming that you would. Please, follow me.'

There was a flap cut out of the bottom of the fence. Alexey bent it back and wriggled through the hole on his tummy. The Italian hesitated: he was taller than Alexey and his clothes looked too clean for this kind of operation, but he followed him all the same.

Alexey shouted and banged on the side of the wagon. He was so near to me that I could see the individual hairs at the edge of the bone smoothness of his bald patch. The side of the wagon screamed as it was pushed back on rollers: inside the walls were stacked with bales wrapped in hessian. There was a gap in the centre. Three dark-haired, bandy-legged men were sitting on the bales. Two of them had moustaches and between them were four opened bottles of beer, some cards and a neat pile of Belamor stubs.

They all leapt to their feet when they saw Alexey. He hauled himself up and pulled the Italian up after him. There was a lot of stiff laughter followed by a bout of back slapping. Alexey inspected the wagon, poked at the bales and showed them to the Italian. Since this was the Green Train I assumed they must be drugs of some kind. What impressed me was the quantity.

In front of me I had a smart Italian businessman inspecting a wagon-load of drugs from the Chu Valley. It didn't take a lot of intuition to guess that the Italian was buying drugs from Alexey. That in itself was enough to make me want to run. I had suspected that not all of Alexey's business deals were strictly legal but this was much deeper water than I had imagined. What still wasn't clear was the connection between this and Pyotr's paintings.

The two men were now standing in the doorway of the wagon. I found myself eyeballing their knees.

'I like your Green Train very much. Why can't we run something like this straight into Germany?'

'At present I don't think that it is feasible. From here to the Chu is a relatively simple operation and it does not entail crossing any international borders. To send a train into Germany would be considerably more complicated. It would be necessary for instance to alter the gauge, there are several borders to negotiate and many different criminal groups and these, especially in the Baltic states, are frequently hostile. They do not like anyone else coming through what they consider to be their territory. They are really quite insistent on this matter.

In my opinion the air option is preferable. Pulkova Airport is small and easy to manage, and should you decide that this is a profitable connection there are many airstrips in East Germany which we can use. They are very ripe, I would almost say that you can pick your barracks and then buy it.' He gave a dry little laugh and jumped down onto the tracks.

'Come Carlo, there is nothing more to see here, we will leave through the main station this time.' The Italian jumped too and I heard the scrunch as the leather bottoms of his classy shoes hit the gravel. Alexey banged on the side of the wagon with the flat of his hand. 'Close up! I will return later.'

It was quarter past nine. I still had to wait until midday. I lay down and indulged myself with memories. How much of this had he known?

At twenty past ten the Green Train pulled out of the station. The platform behind it was empty. At ten to eleven a slow train from Moscow pulled in, the windows framing luggage and passive faces. At midday I heard a bang on the door and my grudging gaoler appeared. He grunted at me and I followed him out into the open air. Open air was a relief. I felt I'd been locked up in the stale air of the empty carriage for centuries.

We crawled under the fence at the same spot that Alexey and the Italian had used. An empty train was standing at Platform 12, whose destination-board read 'Kirov'. We came around the back of it and then the man lost me in the crowds in the station. He melted away; I didn't even see him go. I didn't hang around either. I walked out and down Ligovsky Prospect.

16

I stood at an elbow-height table that ran along the window of the café with a cup of tea and a pastry. Hardly any of the cafés will let you sit down. I was the only customer. Two surly women in white sanatorium coats were posted behind the counter.

On that part of Ligovsky Prospect the trams running down the middle are separated off from the rest of the road by railings. From where I stood the tram passengers looked like busts on a production line. There was a man on the pavement outside the café wearing a light-blue Manchester United T-shirt. His hair had separated out into greasy clumps around an embryonic bald patch. He was selling magazines from a trestle table, some pornographic, some political or religious but mostly just fodder.

I felt tired and foreign, the same kind of mood I'd been in before going to Berlin, but this time it felt more permanent; I didn't think a holiday would cure it. I had become English. I am not English in England, I am Natalie. Here it was an excuse, when I made a mistake it was OK because I am English. The man whose cigarette I lit in the empty carriage would have thought I was a tart if I had been Russian. Russian girls don't light men's cigarettes and they don't swear, but I can do both of those things and get away with it because I have an excuse, I am English. Sometimes it's amusing and I can play on it. '*Oh that is so typically English, Natalie.*' By which they mean it is not a very Russian thing to do. There is a freedom in it, I can ask questions and people talk to me more than they would to another Russian. I don't think, for instance, that Yelena would let another Russian know she was having an affair with Arkady, but I am safe. I am an exception.

I am English here, but what will I be in England? So many things will have happened over there that I don't know about. My friends from Oxford will have moved around and got new boyfriends and new jobs and I won't be part of it any longer. I did the same as everybody else before I came to Russia; I went to school and then I went to college. I led a standard life. It had seemed too cloying and cramped and I had wanted to see something more but I was tied in tight by a loving cobweb of family, education and class. What will happen to me now after Pyotr, Nikita, the Green Train, Pushkinskaya, the Tam Tam Club? I feel that I am strange now, different, I've lost something since I have lived here. I will be like the *bezprizorni*, the runaway children in the stations. People will see through me, not because I have a shaven head like the *bezprizorni*, but because I've seen things, rotten things and I will stink of it.

I was tired and scared. Scared of what I was finding out and scared of what I had seen in the station. What should I do with what I had discovered? '*A terrible thing is knowledge that profits man not.*' Pyotr had gone and I was now sure that he hadn't killed himself; that he had been murdered. But he was still gone, he wasn't here and he never would be here with me again. Nothing could change that. Did I need to know any more? It was dangerous to try and find out any more, but the answers were coming in to roost on their own. There was nothing I could do to stop it now: I had asked too many questions, already set too much in motion, tilted too far.

When did it start, Natalie? Where did it all begin? When could I have stopped it? Before Berlin? I should have paid for the lawyer, I should have insisted. I wanted to go to someone. I wanted to hide behind my hands, watch between my fingers and let them tell me when it was safe to come out again.

A new girl has moved into one of the rooms on the second floor on the other side of the courtyard. She has got fanzine posters of rock singers up on her wall and a big shaggy dog. At the moment she and the dog are leaning their elbows on the windowsill and she is smoking a cigarette. She can see me looking at her, she has just waved. I'm glad I have taken the mosquito sheet away from the window. It was a silly idea. Stuff the mosquitoes; it is much better being able to look out.

Three days ago I arrived back here to find a note stuck into the plastic trellis work of my door. 'Annya returning from Poland. Berlin Train. Time of Arrival 8.50 am. Varshavsky Station. Yours Alexey.'

I didn't really want to see Alexey. I hadn't talked to him since the *actsia* and I was sure that he would guess I was up to something. The guilt would be written all over my face.

I was five minutes early for the train. Alexey was standing behind the ticket barrier. He must have stood the same way when he was waiting for me. I tried to discipline my expression but my face was difficult to stretch, like old chewing gum. I managed what I hoped was a chirpy smile and then I produced all the greeting phrases. Once I had got those out of the way it was much easier than I had thought it was going to be. There is a pattern to them and just saying them sets the pitter-patter of conversation into motion.

'Does she know about Pyotr?' I asked.

He pulled on his little beard, 'I have informed her, I thought it was wisest.'

'Oh.' I felt a little hollow. I had wanted to tell her myself but I had no rights on the information, or the grief. I was worried that she would be so sympathetic that I wouldn't be capable of handling it. She would gush it at me and I wouldn't be able to deflect it.

There was a disturbance down the long ribbon of track that grew first to a toy-sized train and then gradually larger as it drew closer. When it pulled into the track beside us it was twice as tall as me, a bulk of iron that smelt of hot metal, burnt air and brakes.

There was a crowd of meeters and greeters with us. The train disgorged its passengers and their lumps of baggage. A woman beside me gave a yelp of excitement as she spotted who she was looking for.

Annya appeared as a figurine towards the back of the train where the platform began to curve to the right. I set off from our staging post to meet her while Alexey tactfully stayed by the barrier. I couldn't see Leszek. She was struggling towards me with a barrel bag stretching off one arm, a large rucksack on her back, and an assortment of plastic bags dangling from her other arm. She looked like a human mule.

I met her halfway. She dropped the bags and squeezed me in a tight hug that was awkward to return because my arms didn't reach around the rucksack. 'Oh God Natalie, what can I say? We were fucking privileged to know him. Jesus, I can't believe he's not here.'

My cheeks felt pinched from the inside – like they do when you are about to be sick. I blinked and my eyelashes meshed damply together. I sniffed to hold it back. 'Give me some of those bags. Alexey is up by the barrier.'

'Is he? Fucking sweetheart.'

Annya has her own flat on Prospect Maklina, close to Canal Griboyedova. The instant she had unlocked the front door she stopped, blocking our way, and unearthed a bag of chocolates and bananas from halfway down her rucksack. The bananas were bruised and sweet and the chocolates had melted on the train and had wrinkles where they had set in their foil wrappings. We sat on wooden crates picking out the foil from the chocolates while Annya babbled enthusiastically about Poland.

'And Leszek?' enquired Alexey.

'He's on bloody business but I wasn't going to miss out on the White Nights for that.'

'Yelena sends you all her regards. She specifically asked me to say that you must visit her sometime. She would, I know, be delighted to see you both,' he said with a nod in my direction.

'And your injury?' he continued.

'As good as new. Leszek's female tribe were all fucking trainee Florence Nightingales. They had all these amazing folk remedies: herbs, teas and even leeches. Here have a Gauloise, yeah I know, aren't I fucking sophisticated or what? Leszek's sister is this superb woman who works in a joint enterprise in Krakow. And she was telling me all about these friends she's got in Warsaw who are something to do with a museum, so I thought why not take the exhibition there as well as London and Petersburg? She's going to look into it for me.' There was a lull in the conversation. I think Alexey, like me, was wondering which artist she was going to choose to replace Pyotr.

'Yeah, no we must go and see Yelena. That would be excellent. Hey Natalie, why don't we go this afternoon? Are you on for that?'

'OK, fine.'

'Alexey, what do you reckon? Do you know what she's up to?'

'Well, I am obviously not her keeper but I think it would be safe to say that she will be in my atelier on the Fontanka, although sadly I will not be present this afternoon. I have business commitments, you understand. Now you must excuse me, I will leave you two together. Annya, we are delighted to have you back and I will no doubt see you very soon. You must endeavour to raise Natalie's spirits, she has had a trying time.'

Annya and I stood side by side at the window and waved goodbye to him as he walked through the courtyard. 'What do you feel like doing?' I asked her. 'Well, I've been cooped up in a fucking train for the last two days. I'd like to get out for a start and I would also like to talk to you about Pyotr.'

I took her to the café on the boat that Oleg had taken me to. We ordered coffees and she updated me on her plans for the exhibition.

'I've managed to wangle some space for us at the St Petersburg Biennale and my old tutor from college, who is an excellent man, has got us exhibition space in the old market at Spitalfields in London. It's like hitting your head against a fucking brick wall trying to get anything fixed up in London from here but Chris has been a star. He is going to put stuff in the show, and he's a professor so we can use his name on the invitations for getting visas and stuff.'

The coffees arrived, brought by the same adolescent waiter. He also brought us a complimentary plate of *kalbasa* and bread, so he must have recognised me. I watched a speed boat come around the spit of Vasilievsky Island. I realised that if Pyotr had been part of the exhibition he would have got a visa to go to England. 'Who are you going to have instead of Pyotr?' I asked resentfully. The sun reflecting on the water made it brighter and sharper than the sky itself. I waited until the silence forced her to answer.

'Don't be like that, Natalie. You know he was my friend too,' she said reproachfully, which really rankled me. Pyotr hadn't been my friend, he had been my lover which just isn't the same thing.

'What did Alexey tell you?'

'He said that Pyotr shot himself on the road to his home town.' I winced as she said it.

'And so who are you having instead of him?' I demanded. I knew I was being unreasonable with her but, fuck it, I had a right to be. How the hell did she think she could understand what I was feeling?

'I couldn't think what to do when I first heard,' she said. 'Then I had this brainwave. I'm going to do the whole exhibition in his memory, name it after him and everything. What happened to Pyotr is like a symbol of what is happening here.'

It might be a symbol to you, I thought, but to me it is murder. 'Do you believe it?'

'What?'

'That Pyotr would kill himself.'

'It must be so hard for you.' She was being very sugary. It was quite obvious she was trying to calm me down. 'Believe me, I understand. What you've got to really make sure you don't do Natalie is blame yourself, because it is not your fucking fault. I mean Pyotr was an extraordinary man but he was pretty extreme. You know he lived on a fucking roller-coaster and that was way out of your control – there was nothing you could do to change that.

'Natalie, I've got a confession to make. That time when you came to see me just before you went to Berlin, I know I was a bit hard and I'm sorry. I just didn't realise how serious it was, how fucking tough it must have been for you.'

'Annya, Pyotr didn't kill himself. There is no way he would have done a thing like that, I'm sure of it. Somebody shot Pyotr like somebody shot Tornikov.'

'Like I say, Natalie, I know that this must be really tough for you but this isn't the way to get over it. You can blame anyone you like but you are going to have to accept it one day.'

She wasn't going to listen to me so I changed the subject. 'Do you want to go to the studio?' I asked her, remembering how that had been the first thing I had wanted to do when I had got back from Berlin. 'It's a bit of a mess because somebody broke down the door, but if you want to go I'll come with you.'

'No thanks, I think it would give me the creeps.' She had a brightly-coloured Afghani hat on and she shifted it slightly with the back of her hand and scratched the crown of her head. 'Come on Natalie, why don't we go and visit Yelena,' she said abruptly.

We took the Metro, got out at Ploschad Mira and walked. Antagonism crackled between us. I knew she was hurt by my attitude but I resented her taking over, assuming automatically that Pyotr had committed suicide and presuming she understood the confusion inside me. I felt angry and almost territorial about it.

Yelena asked who it was before she opened the door. 'How lovely to see you both, and Annya you're looking so well. Are you completely recovered now?' Annya said she was as good as new.

'I'm afraid I've got my little boy Kolya here and there is a friend of Alexey's in the kitchen,' she told us.

Kolya was five years old. He looked very like Yelena. He had tawny brown eyes and dark blond hair cut into a pudding bowl. He was sitting at the kitchen table with his tongue sticking out of the side of his mouth and he was drawing with some felt tip pens. He did not want to be introduced to a bunch of strangers, but he did break off long enough to tell me that his picture was of a secret forest.

On the table beside the little boy was a big five-litre jar of beer and a bowl of dill cucumbers. The beer was the kind you buy off stalls in the street and Russians often drink at breakfast as a hair of the dog. A fat man in a cheap, limp suit sat in the centre on the far side. 'Vassya,' said Yelena, 'these are two *Anglichanki*, Annya and Natalie. They are both friends of Alexey's.'

'They breed them better looking in England,' he leered. He had undone the first two buttons of his translucent white shirt and loosened his patterned tie. He slapped a meaty hand on the table. Kolya looked up and scowled at him and I watched the vinegar in the bowl of dill cucumbers shiver. The base of the hairs on the back of his hands stood out like blackheads.

'Beer?' he barked, but he didn't wait for anyone to answer and poured out two glasses, spilling it all over the table. Kolya gave the impression he was concentrating very hard on his drawing. Vassya pushed the glasses across the table and Annya sat down.

'Don't let's stay too long,' I said to her in English.

Yelena crossed her legs and disdainfully lit a cigarette. 'Vassya is setting up a bank in the next door flat.' She almost sounded as if she was taking the mickey out of him but, if she was, it was far too subtle for him.

I looked at him and he laughed a deep gut laugh with wet lips. 'Times they are a-changing,' he sang with a very thick accent. 'Bob Dylan.' He cut out more slabs of laughter from his chest. 'Five years in the gulag and now I am a businessman. The camps are the best business schools in the world, you have to be hard. You will see, soon nobody will be able to beat Russian businessmen.'

I asked him what kind of business he did and he treated me to a baby-eating grin. 'Banking, forestry, light metals, import and export, construction work. I will turn my hand to anything but you have to watch everyone. They are all crooks, everybody is a crook. They will steal your equipment, steal your grandmother. Everybody needs protection.' Was he threatening us? He fixed his eyes on me and slapped the table again.

'And what kind of bank will it be?' I asked in horror.

'International,' he said grandiosely. 'The International Bank of Friendship.' I thought of the decrepid flat next door, the worn wallpaper, dusty floorboards and naked wires. He watched my face with an expression of satisfaction.

'So, old-fashioned young English girl! Ha! What are you thinking of? Marble halls eh? This will be a private bank, just for friends. A fax, a telephone and a computer. We entertain our foreign friends in their hotels, not here. It is simple and it is more convenient for them. But sadly we need a lot of storage because the rouble is worth nothing now and so it takes up a lot of room.' He thought that was splendiferously funny and shook with laughter.

'It is a hazardous business so it is better to know the right people. Isn't that right, Yelena?' She nodded in reply but she didn't look very happy about it.

'You can't be too careful. Myself, I always carry a gun.' He got it out from a holster in his left armpit and pushed it across the table towards Kolya, who looked up from his drawing and stared at it as if it were a snake. There was something particularly unpleasant about shoving a gun in a kid's face. I looked at Yelena, whose arms were folded defensively across her chest. I saw her swallow nervously.

The gun was black metal with a blue menacing light. The handle part was squared and covered in a pattern of raised dots to stop a nervous palm from slipping. Behind the handle was a translucent green square; a gas-cartridge like Alexey's and like the one on the train.

Vassya enjoyed frightening us. He got a kick from it; I could read the pleasure in his fat grin. 'Maybe you've never seen a pistol before?' he said addressing us all. 'This one is different, it is fired by gas. You don't need to worry, it can still kill a man. Or so they tell me, eh!' He thought that was hilarious as well.

I was desperate to leave. I tried Annya again in English, 'I really don't like this. Can we go?'

'You were Pyotr's girl weren't you?' interrupted Vassya. 'He had a good eye, I'll say that for him.'

I stiffened but I carried on smiling. I prodded Annya between the shoulder blades. 'We are going now. I am not staying a moment longer.' Then reverting immediately to Russian I turned to Yelena and made nice to see you and see you soon noises. She looked embarrassed. I bent and said goodbye to the little boy.

'Why are you going?' protested Vassya. He was affronted, we weren't showing him sufficient appreciation. 'You must stay. Drink! We have plenty.'

Ignoring him I hustled Annya out of the door and into the lift, which had finally been mended. 'Who was that creep? How the fuck did he know about Pyotr?' The iron cage was rattling down towards the ground floor. The lift bumped as we stopped. 'What was that all about!' I shouted over the noise of the cables.

'That,' she said, snapping back the grilles and stamping down the steps out into the street, 'was nothing to do with me. So you can fuck right off. Christ, you have got a lot to learn, Natalie. I thought Yelena was your friend. Do you actually want to get her into trouble?' Annya's face was purple with rage. 'I don't particularly like Vassya myself. He is a fat slob and he's rough but there is no need to get your knickers in such a twist about it. This isn't fucking Clapham, Natalie.'

The insult hit home and I simmered as we stomped through Ploschad Teatralnaya and headed up towards Little Holland and the bridge over the Moika Canal where Rasputin was killed. I was riven with anger. I found my anger spilling over. It wasn't only Annya or even Vassya any longer. It was Pyotr's death. It was the questions that I wanted to ask but I knew that no one would answer. It was the changes, in me and in Russia. It all came spitting out of me. And on top of that I raged at my helplessness. As a

child I used to scream at my mother, 'It's not fair, 'snot fair!'
And I was screaming it again now as the sea wind knotted
at my hair.

'Why can't you believe in me for once, Annya. Why don't
you try and support me for a change, back me up. I had to
get out of there, I couldn't take that creep leering at me.
Wink, wink, nudge, nudge. Pyotr hey, nice bit of foreign
girl. No way was I going to stand for that. Can't you see
that? Annya, I loved Pyotr.'

She rounded on me. 'But you didn't, did you, Natalie?
You didn't really love him. It was a game, a traveller's tale
for dinner parties in Clapham. They will tell you about awful
loos in India and you'll be able to upstage them with stories
of romantic Russian artists. It was an experience, wasn't it?
You wanted to get out and see the world and now you are
a bit shocked, poor dear, because your holiday romance has
killed himself. He minded too much. That's not how it's
meant to happen, is it? That's not the fucking plan. When
you got tired you were just going to return to England and
never know whether he lived or died. Isn't that right?'

No, it wasn't right but there was enough truth in it to
make me smart. It was true that I had been seduced by the
scene as much as the man. If I hadn't loved him enough it
was because I wasn't big enough to take it all on, his moods,
the drugs and the constant circus that flowed in and out of
the studio. Maybe I didn't really try to understand his *tosca*,
to follow him into the blacklands he retreated to, because
to have done that I would have had to shoulder some of
the pain myself and I knew I wasn't capable of it. There
was too much history there and I think I shrank from it.
I wasn't Russian and it had seemed presumptuous to even
think that I could understand what it had all meant. I felt
a sense of awe when I thought of Pyotr's ability to endure
and survive. I, who have led such a soft life, could never
understand what it really felt like to declare yourself insane

and then continue to act insane, day and night in a filthy mental home watched by sadistic guards. To have grown up in a military zone where everybody had a relative in the gulags, and yet one in five was a paid informer for the KGB. To have lived all your life in the shadows, or to sit in a prison cell under a caged lightbulb and wonder whether it will be for two days or for years. I would have been a fraud if I had pretended that I could understand; it would have shown a lack of respect for what Pyotr had lived through.

My anger soaked away like blood in the soil and it left me with a flat, muddy resignation. I didn't say anything. We carried on walking, across the river and down to the Sphinx. I perched on the granite platform and Annya stood on the bottom step with her arms folded under her big breasts, the river lapping at the toes of her boots.

'Annya, he didn't kill himself. You have to believe that. He was murdered.' I was looking towards the Gulf, I couldn't see her face.

'Yeah, well, you can believe anything you like if it makes you feel better.'

'Annya listen to me, I'm sorry I screamed at you, Vassya freaked me out. Honestly, I did love him.'

'Maybe you did. I never understood what you guys had going. I think for Pyotr it was a kind of naïvety, a confidence that people like you have. Your sort have got the whole world to play in. Even Russia is a game. But I think in your own way you probably did love him.' Then as a footnote, almost a compliment, she added, 'Jesus Christ, Natalie, I never thought you could be so angry, never thought you had it in you.'

We went our separate ways after that. I watched her in her Afghan hat as she trotted over the bridge. I felt drained and I couldn't remember any longer what we had been angry with each other about.

17 ∫

Yesterday I went to Pushkinskaya. Sasha was in. I wondered how he made it up and down the stairs in a wheelchair, but he told me that his was the only staircase in Pushkinskaya with a lift that worked. 'Which is good luck for me.' He looked better than he had done at the photography exhibition, his hair had grown a bit and it now almost masked the ugly scar across his scalp. 'I thought you would come earlier,' he said.

His studio was white with painted daisies growing up the wall. His milk crate furniture was covered with Astroturf. The easel and the painting gear in the corner looked neglected. I wondered how he had got involved in the protection gang, when that had all begun. I strolled around the room rehearsing in my head what I wanted to say.

I gave him some ginger biscuits that I had bought as an offering from the bakery on Sredny Prospect. He thanked me and wheeled over to the kettle. It took me ages to get around to asking him any questions. We were at least halfway through our glasses of tea before I plucked up the nerve to begin.

'At the photography exhibition Sasha . . .' He wheeled forward and put his glass of tea on a milk crate.

'You said, you said . . .'

'That I had heard a rumour going round that your friend

Pyotr was killed around here and not in Lvov.'

'Where did you hear it?'

'It might be nothing. You know how rumours get around, but they've got to start somewhere haven't they? And this isn't even really a rumour, it's just something I heard someone say that made me think of him. He used to wear a red scarf, didn't he?' I nodded and folded my arms across my front. 'You know, don't you about my . . .' he stopped and shrugged his wasted shoulders, 'er, friends?' I realised that he was referring to the protection gang. I nodded again and bit my lower lip. I didn't remember him being this nervous that night at Oleg's but then that was before his accident.

'Erm, I don't know if you have heard of the Gagarin Party discos, but, erm, one of those friends does the lights for them. I heard it when I was with him, you see. He gets very good money for the discos, you have to pay for the tickets in dollars and they, erm, are not exactly what you would call cheap. My friend has a car. I've, er, known him for ages and ages, you see we did National Service together. Since the accident he, erm, has taken to, like, dropping around, you know, once or twice a week and, er, sometimes he drives me around in his car, it helps me to get out. Because I get kind of stuck in here, you see. He took me over to the Planetarium one day, when they were, erm, putting together a disco along with some other people who run one of those raves out of a squat on the Fontanka. I think it is quite close to, er, Alexey Andreev's atelier. You probably know the ones that I'm, er, talking about?' I had heard of them, Nikita used to go to them. He rubbed the wheel arch of his wheelchair with the sleeve of his jumper to polish it.

'The Planetarium is like an incredibly wild place to have a party. I mean there is this huge dome, all studded with lights and, erm, showing the stars and everything. When we turned up they were putting up even more lights, green laser beams with patterns on them and strobes. The whole thing just looked amazingly wild. My friend was really incredibly pleased with the effect and I was happy because I wasn't sitting here in this.' He tapped the metal arm of the wheelchair with the bottom of his glass of tea to show his disgust for it.

'One of the guys from the Fontanka had some, erm, tincture.' Sasha looked at me sharply but I didn't understand what he was talking about. 'Of opium,' he explained. I nodded and tried not to look judgemental.

'So we all took, erm, some of this stuff and there we were all sitting under the dome of the Planetarium with the lasers on and the stars lit up, feeling pretty good and everything. Someone went out and got some vodka and we drank that as well. We were talking and then things started to be not so good and one or two of them got a bit paranoid and stuff. One of the guys from the Fontanka started up talking about this, er, body. Up to that point I hadn't really been taking much notice of these blokes, but I kind of, er, perked up interest and asked him what he was going on about. His mate made noises like he didn't think that this was a very good thing to be talking about, but we were, er, all pretty far gone by that time and nobody took any notice of him.

'Anyhow apparently according to this guy they had all seen a, er, body in the Fontanka a couple of nights before. But the weird thing was that when they got up the next day the body had vanished and these guys were all being morbid and philosophical about it and, er, saying that it was a bit like capitalism. Somebody else's corpse.'

'What makes you think it was Pyotr? There must be hundreds of murders in this city that you and I never get to hear about. It was probably a drunk who fell into the canal and forgot to shut his mouth.'

'Yeah yeah, you are probably right. I was probably just being paranoid.'

'When did this happen?'

'Well I don't know, it, er, must have been about two or three weeks ago. I'm not really sure exactly, I mean I came out of the clinic and I remember hearing that you were going to see Nikita in Berlin and I suppose it must have been something like a week after that, ten days say.'

'I still don't understand what made you connect this with Pyotr.'

'It was the scarf, you see. They kept on talking about this scarf. What they said to me was that they had seen this dark, er, body bobbing around in the black canal and how it had had this bright red scarf around its neck. Bright red with yellow threads in it is, er, what they said. According to them it was the scarf that made it really eerie and horrible.'

I thought about the scarf. It had come from Guatemala. A friend of his, an artist who had been to Cuba, had given it to him. He was wearing it the day he got out of prison.

'A red scarf is not that unusual,' I said, flattening my voice to a deadpan. He apologised and slouched his big boxer's shoulders against the canvas of his wheelchair.

'Could he show it to me?' I asked.

'What?'

'Your friend from the Fontanka raves, could he show me where he saw the body?'

'I expect so, I suppose if I, er, asked him he wouldn't mind. I can't think why not. But, er, I mean the body's not there any more so I can't really see what good it would do.'

'Doesn't matter, I'd just like to see the place.'

Poor Sasha seemed to get tired very easily. His face was sagging like an old woman's neck and he looked washed out but he still agreed to go and find the man from the Fontanka raves.

Sasha was adept at propelling his wheelchair but it took time and even more energy. I walked beside him as he manoeuvred his wheels over the rough terrain of Pushkinskaya courtyard. I found that I had to pull back my stride to walk in time with him. I felt ridiculous taking my measured slow steps as he strained away beside me. I did offer to push him but he didn't like the idea.

The pavement was much easier and he wheeled down to Nevsky pretty fast. I stood facing the traffic and stuck my arm out. Three official taxis passed us but eventually a little red Neva stopped. The driver was in his mid-forties with a belly that his shirt didn't really meet over and skin the colour of uncooked dough.

He got out and volunteered to help get Sasha into the back. There wasn't any grace in his offer. He picked Sasha up, taking hold of him under his knees and his armpits, in the practical way a country man takes a dog by the scruff of his neck. It made me feel uncomfortable to watch, but I wondered if it wasn't easier to receive help that way than from my whimpering sensitivities.

I collapsed the wheelchair, got into the front seat and held it in front of me. It was heavy and awkward and the metal bars bruised my shins as we went over the bumps.

The guy from the Fontanka raves turned out to be Arkady, which short-circuited me. In my head he belonged to Yelena and it confused me to have him popping up where I wasn't expecting him. He lived in Krasny Armerskaya in a room in a third-floor flat. He picked Sasha up in a fireman's lift and I climbed up the steps after him with the wheelchair. He lived with his mother, an old lady the same vintage as Babba Lenna. She fussed around the stove and then left the kitchen to us.

'Did you hear about the shooting last night?' asked Arkady once she had left the room.

'Two Caucasians killed a policeman at half-past midnight. It was down by the Sovietskaya Hotel. I heard the shots from here. The corner where they were killed is like a shrine now. People have bought flowers, cards and banners.'

'Erm, no I didn't know about that but we have actually come about the same kind of thing,' said Sasha apologetically. 'I hope you don't mind, but I told Natalie about that body you saw in the canal a couple of weeks back and, erm, she wondered, you see, she wondered if you wouldn't mind showing her where it was.'

'The one with the red scarf?'

'Pyotr is meant to have committed suicide but I don't believe he would have done it. He had this bright red and yellow scarf that he wore a lot and I know it's tenuous but well . . .' The end of my sentence trailed away. The coincidence of the red scarf seemed rather foolish now but sweet, mild-mannered Arkady didn't seem to mind humouring me.

'Sure, Natalie, I don't mind showing you the spot. I warn you there is nothing to see though. Sasha are you happy sitting here, we will be back within the hour?'

It's not far from Krazny Armerskaya to the Fontanka Canal. We took the back routes and came out behind the blue Dostoevsky church, then walked through what must once have been an old market. High up on the stucco walls were classical plaster moulds of bulls, pails of milk and wreaths of corn. We passed through a sheet metal gate and came out onto the canal. We were almost opposite Alexey's atelier, just slightly to the left of it. Directly in front of us was a wrought-iron footbridge.

I was out of breath. Arkady walked faster than I did and I had to jog occasionally to catch up with him. Arkady stopped at the summit of the bridge as it curved elegantly over the canal and pointed to the side. 'The body was there,' he said. 'We were coming back from a party. I noticed it first. It was the scarf that caught my attention, it really stood out against the dark water. Whoever it was, they were face down in the water so we couldn't see their face. I think that would have really freaked me out.'

'And you think it was a man?'

'Oh yes it was definitely a man. It was very long.'

'Sasha says it wasn't there the next morning.'

'No. It wasn't even there later on that night. I went home at five in the morning and it wasn't there then. I know because I looked for it. So somebody fished it out of the canal in the three hours that I was visiting my friends.'

The spot he had pointed to was directly below the window I had stood at during Alexey's *actsia*. Arkady saw me look in the direction of Alexey's atelier. 'He's not in,' he said. 'He's taken the Italian to see the director of the Ethnographic Museum. Do you want to go on? While we're here I'll show you where the policemen got shot last night.' I glanced once more at the spot where the body had been and followed him off the bridge.

The embankment on the Hotel Sovietskaya side of the canal is in a bad condition. I scurried after Arkady, jumping over the potholes. 'How's Yelena?' I asked, in between leaps. 'Annya and I saw her the day before yesterday with Kolya and some creepy business aquaintance of Alexey's.'

'Yes I know, I heard about it. Alexey wasn't too pleased, he gave her a black eye for not being hospitable enough.' So it was Alexey who hit her. I knew it couldn't really have been anyone else but I'd always avoided admitting it to myself. This was the first time I had been forced to recognise it. I felt queasy. How could Alexey, who was so cultured and polished, hit anybody?

'Why doesn't she leave him if he hits her?' Even before the words left my mouth I clicked that this was not a tactful thing to be asking Arkady. I was hurrying to catch up with him and he didn't answer me so I thought that maybe he hadn't heard me.

In front of us was the concrete hull of the Sovietskaya

Hotel. Arkady slowed down as he got to the corner. Flowers and scraps of paper were strung in garlands around the lamp post. More flowers were piled up against the wall. The messages written under them were pathetic pleas from families with relatives caught up in the war in the Caucasus. There were dark stains on the pavement beneath my feet. I presumed they were blood.

'If she leaves him,' said Arkady staring at the dark marks on the concrete paving stones, 'he will kill her.'

'No, he wouldn't,' I protested. 'Alexey is not a killer. Maybe he is jealous, maybe he suspects that you and . . . Maybe he is trying to keep her through fear. I don't know, but I'm sure that if she told him that she was leaving he would respect that.'

He looked at me, his dark eyes unbelieving and bleak. 'I'm sorry Arkady, I shouldn't have said anything. I don't know what the situation is. I mean I feel as strongly about violence as the next woman. But there has got to be something behind it. I mean Alexey is not the violent type.'

He was still gulping me in with his eyes. He took a step towards me and seized me by the shoulders, and then he just let go and marched off down the street without saying anything.

'Arkady, I'm sorry!' I shouted after him. I'd realised how awful it sounded the moment I'd said it. 'Listen I've put my foot in it, forget that I said anything. I'm really sorry.' He slowed down a fraction and let me catch up with him.

'You fool, Natalie, he has done it before. Who do you think killed Tornikov?'

I came straight back here. This room felt like a box. I fluttered around it like a moth caught in a lamp shade. Arkady's accusation had rattled me badly. Could the same man that had helped me go to Berlin because he thought I needed a holiday have killed Tornikov? Alexey who was so generous, with his pretensions and his peculiar clothes. The man I had thought we took too much advantage of? I left this room again to walk and to think. I padded the streets, not going anywhere. This city is full of rumours, maybe this was just another one, Russia is a rumour machine.

Alexey got Pyotr out of jail. He was his friend. Did Pyotr know the rumour about Tornikov? There had been gossip that he was shot because of a habit but I couldn't remember ever talking to Pyotr about it. Did Alexey pull the trigger or was somebody paid? I remembered the slim green cartridge of a gas-powered pistol sitting by his fax machine. I thought of Yelena's face that night when Nikita and I had come in giggling with the vodka. Had she heard the rumour then? I felt sick when I thought about him beating her. He is so polite, so courteous, how could he hit somebody? But Yelena is proof that he does. Yelena like glass, fragile, elegant. Her pitiful, brittle mockery in front of Vassya. Holding her flare out to the sky when Arkady filmed her on the roof.

Lilacs, I could smell the heavy ether of lilacs. I found myself by the Academy of Sciences Library. There were students standing by the spitoons on the steps. Prim, resilient Russian girls. They would be searching for husbands already.

I think I went a bit off centre as I wandered around that night. Thoughts and images kept on racing through my head at jet plane speed, too fast for me to catch them or control them. Some of my thoughts were horrible. The sound of the dancer talking at the Tam Tam Club when everybody else had stopped, the oozing scar across Sasha's skull. I thought of trivial things too, a village I'd seen from the train, Babba Lenna asking me how my holiday had been. The images came in floods. I couldn't hang on to any of them, reject them, sort them. I needed someone to talk to, take me out of my head and away from my thoughts. I

missed Pyotr, I missed him badly. He could have laughed
at me and ridiculed my fears. He could have told me I was
becoming Russian and catching *tosca* as if it were flu.

I arrived at the embankment by the Academy of Arts. I
crossed the road and walked up the road to the Sphinx. I sat
on her paws, looked out to the Gulf of Finland and chewed
my knuckles. I sat there for ages and my head raced so fast
that I slipped into a kind of catatonic trance, so that although
I was aware that the wind off the river was growing cold and
the marble was uncomfortable I hardly felt it.

I stayed until the sun left the sky and the White Night
glowed blue, and then mechanically I came back here
and slept.

18

I ought to go and see Yelena and apologise for getting her into trouble with Alexey but I haven't been able to face seeing anyone today. I haven't been out at all, I've locked myself in here and lain on my bed thinking over what Arkady has told me. This afternoon I was a bit more active. I washed some clothes and Babba Lenna, who was delighted to have me in all day, helped me boil my underwear in a big metal bucket on the stove. She cackled at the smallness of my knickers and told me it was not surprising that I was always getting colds. If I wore knickers like hers, which come right up to her waist, then I would be much healthier. She then laughed uproariously at my attempts to squeeze the water out of my laundry. Useless. Just like a man. She took over the operation, and by the time her knobbly hands had finished with them they were virtually dry and the elastic was withered.

I don't think there is any point in me struggling on with this letter to my parents. I might as well stick it into an envelope right now. I can't see myself writing any more and I know it's short but at least it's something.

I take the letter out to the post office and on the way I buy some gladioli from the little market that has grown up around the Metro. After being inside all day, I find all these people quite disorientating. I am slower than most people, although definitely faster than the old ladies who inch with great determination between the shops and their rooms. The old women of St Petersburg are a powerful force. Old men are a rare sight thanks to the War and Stalin.

As I open the door Babba Lenna comes bustling down the corridor to inform me in a hushed and excited whisper that I have a visitor. Aware of the large, pink gladioli that I am holding in my fist I turn into the kitchen to find Yelena sitting by my cabinet. She's been severely beaten. Her right eye is the deep purple of a plum and so swollen that I doubt that she can see out of it. There is a graze across the bridge of her long nose, with a blue shadow behind it. Her top lip is split and one of her front teeth is missing. Basically her face is a mess.

I can sense Babba Lenna behind my shoulder. 'Horrible, horrible, this poor young lady has had a terrible accident.' Which is kind and tactful of her. Babba Lenna has seen a lot more of the world than I have and she must know that it is not an accident that has caused these injuries.

'Yelena you look terrible. When did he do this? You ought to see a doctor straight away.' I am not as tactful as Babba Lenna because I can't see the point in pretending any longer, and it sickens me that any friend of mine could do this.

'No, no doctors. Leave it be, Natalie. There is nothing that can be done.'

'At least let me clean it, I've got some proper antiseptic.' She aquiesces and I retrieve some Germoline and a First Aid Kit that I brought out from England. I want to do something because it is better than thinking about what these wounds actually mean. That I do not want to do.

Babba Lenna appropriates the First Aid Kit. I give her the aspirin and the gauze and explain what each of the tubes contains. '*Dotchinka*, a bowl of warm water and cotton wool.' I have to boil the kettle in order to get warm water because the hot water has been off in our building all week. She rejects the first bowl on the grounds that it is too hot. I squat beside her, feeling inept and superfluous, while she gently bathes Yelena's poor face and dabs Mercurichrome on to the cuts, which must sting like hell. Yelena is being stoical about the whole operation and the only time she does wince Babba Lenna ticks her off sharply.

When the old lady's finished I usher Yelena into my room and sit her down at the table.

'Just stay there for a second. Don't move, I'm going to dash out and get some *piroshki* from the Metro station. I won't be a moment.'

I snatch my handbag from the chair in the hall and sprint the two blocks down to the Metro station. It seems important to hurry although Yelena is hardly likely to run away. I get cabbage and meat *piroshki*, tomatoes, beers, yellow apples and then on impulse I join the queue in the *gastronomia* and get some cream cheese as well. The queue takes longer than I expect and I have to queue twice, once to pay and once to actually collect the cheese, but as soon as I have got it I hurry back, barging past the dawdlers on the pavement in front of me.

Yelena is, of course, still here and she doesn't seem to notice that I have been gone any longer than the moment that I promised. I give her a plate and some cutlery and open a beer bottle, then I put the food in the middle of the table and draw up a chair opposite her.

She picks delicately at the *piroshki* and then, seeing me watching her, puts it down.

'Alexey killed Pyotr,' she says. Boom, like that, out of nowhere. I ought to be shocked but I think I already knew, and have known at least since Arkady told me that Alexey killed Tornikov. I may even have known it for longer, but simply not wanted to recognise the fact.

'Why?' I ask. It's not the obvious question but it is the one that I haven't been able to answer.

'It started with Tornikov,' she says, and because her lips are swollen she mumbles as she talks. I abandon my meal and light us both cigarettes.

'Alexey smuggles opium. When he was younger he was sent to the camps for it. That is where he got his tattoo. A spider's web is the symbol of the drugs mafya. When he got out he came to St Petersburg. He must have made powerful friends in the camps because quite soon, after only one or two years, he was running the Leningrad Rock Club.

'Alexey began to supply the people who came to the club with grass. In the beginning he bought it all over the place: from the south, from Afghanistan and sometimes from the Kamchatka peninsula. He got to know growers throughout the Soviet Union but his best contacts were in the Caucasus. You see, Alexey has a strange background. He comes from the Ngorno-Karabach, which is difficult enough as it is, but to make things worse his mother is an Azerii and his father is an Armenian. Don't ask me how they met because I can't even begin to imagine it, but they did and the result was Alexey.

'In the mid-Eighties the Leningrad Rock Club became very popular and it developed into a sort of unofficial centre for the underground and the black marketeers. Soon Alexey was supplying a whole range of goods through it; alcohol, Western cigarettes, cassette tapes but mainly, as I said, marijuana.

'I used to work at the club as a waitress, that's how I originally met Alexey. He was well known even then and I had heard of him before I met him. But Alexey became too well known, and either the club became too noticeable or he bribed the wrong people. At any rate the authorities closed us down. Next Alexey set up the 'The Experimental Laboratory of Life' atelier, holding exhibitions of modern art. It was much lower key than the Rock Club so it didn't attract so much attention, but he still used it to deal in Western goods and Soviet grass.

'The area where most of the grass in the Soviet Union is grown and the place where Alexey developed the strongest connections is the Chu Valley in Kazachstan.'

'The Green Train.'

'Exactly, the Green Train. But marijuana is not the plant that grows best in the Chu Valley, opium is. In some areas of the valley the *kolhoses* grow nothing else but the opium poppy. Some of that is an official crop, which the state uses for medicines, but in that area and in some of the big cities people take it as a habit as well. They smoke it, they eat it and they make a tincture from it. In Petersburg they make mono-heroin out of it by using other chemicals and aluminium pots in the sun. In the summer you can see them on the roofs at Pushkinskaya. All the same it is rare. There aren't enough people using it even in this city to make selling it a profitable business. That was until recently.

'In 1989 everything began to change. You could feel the whole edifice begin to crumble. Natalie, you can't imagine how startling the first changes were. It felt like we were standing on the Neva after the winter, when the ice begins to crack and move down towards the Gulf. People started arriving from the West and here in Petersburg one of the first things they would all ask about was art. Art, art, modern art. Where is your modern art? Where are the dissident artists? What has been happening here for the last seventy years? So we showed them and the most famous artist at that time was Tornikov. But Tornikov had a secret, he was an opium addict.

'When Tornikov received his first invitation to go abroad, to Paris I think it was, I don't remember exactly, he panicked. He knew, of course, that heroin was easy to buy in the West. We were all brought up on stories of gangs of desperate junkies roaming the streets of decadent Western cities. But Tornikov didn't take heroin, he took opium. His addiction caused enough problems anyhow, and he didn't want to graduate to heroin, but he needed a regular supply of opium and he couldn't be sure that he would be able to find it or afford to buy it in the West. In the end he asked Alexey to supply him with a large amount to take with him and Alexey agreed.

'Tornikov got an amazing reception in the West; he was one of the first artists to arrive and they loved him. He got showered with invitations and he decided to extend his tour. He had by this time ascertained where to buy opium in Berlin, which is where he had moved to, but he found that it was extremely expensive. He was also worried that he might be found out and that would discredit his hosts and blow a lot of his chances amongst the respectable buyers in Berlin. He told his friends that he required more paintings to exhibit, and then he contacted Alexey who sent some paintings with blocks of opium hidden in their packaging. He sent it by train and fixed it all with the guard.

'Natalie, you have to understand about Alexey. He is a cold man and he is cruel. For Alexey, weaknesses, troubles, problems are like a currency which he will cash in when the investment is right.' Very gently she brushes the tips of her fingers around her swollen eye, as if she is checking once more the extent of the damage.

'Even now I can't make him out. He enjoys playing games with people, he likes to manipulate them and set little scenarios in operation. He is fascinated by how people react to problems. He likes to provide them with everything they want until they begin to rely on him. I don't know if you've ever noticed how, although he gives people things and helps them out, he always keeps his distance. Sometimes I think he is actually missing something, as if he is lacking a vital human element. Half the time it seems to me that he only acts through other people. Even when he hits me it's like he's worked it out. He's brutal but he's cold.' She pauses and gulps at her beer but I don't interject because I feel that she has been waiting to say this all for a long time and she needs to say it at her own speed.

We sit for a while in silence. There are footsteps in the courtyard, a television is playing in another room. Yelena, like me, seems to take comfort from these everyday sounds. Slowly she moves back into her story.

'Alexey sent more opium to Berlin than Tornikov needed and he told him to contact various people in the cities that he went to and to give them letters from Alexey and samples of opium. All the people he asked Tornikov to see were respectable gallery owners and they were also all Italian. Tornikov wasn't stupid. He realised what he was taking part in and what the proposition was.'

'What proposition?'

'That Alexey would supply raw opium to the Italian Mafia, which they would then convert into heroin in laboratories in Germany and Italy. According to Alexey at the moment they buy most of their opium from the Far East. That means that it has to travel a long way, and it has to cross a lot of borders – which makes transportation risky and expensive. Alexey was offering them opium in large quantities from next door. His opium would only have to cross one very easy border so, not only was it going to be cheaper to buy, it was also going to be cheaper to transport.

'Tornikov saw what a good plan this was and he was greedy, so when he returned to St Petersburg he started trying to develop contacts for himself in the Chu Valley. But Tornikov was an oaf. He wanted it too badly and it wasn't long before Alexey got to hear what he was up to.

'I tell you Alexey is cruel. He knew what Tornikov was doing, but all the same he organised an exhibition for him at the Ethnographic Museum. It was a big honour for Tornikov and Alexey had to pull a lot of strings to achieve it. That week he refused to give Tornikov any opium and by the night of the exhibition Tornikov was gagging for it. They had a stand up row in the middle of the reception, and afterwards Alexey shot him on the steps of the museum. He fixed it with the police. He wanted to make it public. He wanted to make sure that the whole underground knew who the new power was.

'Not long after that Vassya turned up in Petersburg. Alexey and Vassya are old friends from the camps. Vassya has a lot of criminal friends in the West who were finding it difficult to launder the massive amount of money they were making from selling drugs. Before they could use it, they had to make sure that no connection could be made between the money and the drugs, because otherwise Western governments confiscate the money from bank accounts etc.

'Vassya and Alexey contacted the people that Alexey had been planning to supply to and offered to launder their money at the same time. What they are going to do is buy huge amounts of roubles off Vassya and Alexey for dollars. Honestly it's crazy, they are going to buy hundreds of millions of dollars' worth of useless roubles. It sounds stupid, doesn't it? I mean the whole of Russia is desperately trying to buy foreign currency and these unimaginably rich Italian Mafiosi turn up trying to buy roubles which are worth less than loo paper.

'Now this is the clever bit. People like Alexey and Vassya have always bribed the authorities, but now they are bribing them in huge amounts, so that their Western friends can buy in roubles and export the only things that Russia is rich in – raw materials. Forestry, nickel, iron ore, gold, oil and diamonds; they are all going to flood out of the country, but they will have been bought legally in roubles using export licences that Alexey and Vassya have squeezed out of corrupt government officials.

'And of course they will also be buying opium and that too in huge quantities.'

'Did Pyotr know this?'

'Sorry Natalie, you have let me run away with my tongue. No is the answer. To begin with Pyotr did not know about this. Sure, he knew that Alexey sold Marlboro and cognac and he also knew that Alexey sold grass. Pyotr didn't buy his grass from Alexey. He got it from somewhere else and he even used to get some for his friends, so in effect he was in competition with Alexey, but he was so small and unbusinesslike that Alexey didn't see him as any kind of threat.

'Alexey already exhibited Nikita's paintings and he knew and admired Pyotr's work. He told me several times that he was going to get Pyotr to exhibit with him. Then he heard, I don't know exactly how, that Pyotr was in prison and in trouble. Alexey bribed somebody and got him out and fixed him up with a lawyer. The lawyer charged Pyotr an enormous fee which was Alexey's way of keeping Pyotr obliged to him, and keeping him in trouble. Annya and you were on the scene and Annya was talking about exhibitions in London. Alexey reckoned there was a strong possibility that he could replay the Tornikov scenario and get Pyotr to deliver opium to the contacts that he and Vassya were developing in the West. The lawyer's fee was Alexey's lever on Pyotr.

'Vassya's Italian friends have a network of art galleries in all the major European cities. They use them as depots for heroin. Galleries are a perfect cover. They often receive bulky shipments, they must have storage space and the value of the objects they are selling and buying is mutually agreed upon, it is subjective. The galleries are all perfectly genuine. They all deal in modern art but that is not the only thing they deal in.

The opium arrangement is set up and ready to go. They are going to fly the first shipment into Eastern Germany tomorrow. They have packed it up in crates of paintings which they are going to deliver to a gallery in Berlin. Up until now Alexey has only sent small amounts as samples, but the first real shipment arrived on the Green Train last week and it is waiting in Pulkova to fly out. That's why the Italian is here.

'Alexey wanted someone to go with the opium. He wanted an artist because that would fit in with the cover of the operation. He asked Pyotr. Pyotr didn't want to do it and so Alexey leaned on him. Pyotr managed to get someone to pay off the lawyer. When Alexey discovered that it wasn't you, which was what he suspected at first, but some Baltic mafyosi, he was furious. He went and fixed the lawyer again and told Pyotr that if he didn't go with the opium he would go to prison. Just before you went to Berlin Pyotr agreed.'

'Yelena, the paintings I took to Berlin they weren't . . . were they?'

'Oh yes, they were stuffed full of opium. I watched Alexey pack them up. I remember thinking if they search the train, even a little bit, at the border that poor girl is going to be in a lot of trouble.

'Once you had left it was all sunshine and smiles between Pyotr and Alexey. Alexey got Pyotr an external passport and then he got him a German visa; but he obviously didn't trust Pyotr completely because he kept hold of the visa himself.

'Pyotr came around late one night, way after midnight and Alexey told Pyotr he had the visa but he refused to give it to him. They were in the atelier at the time, I was in the kitchen and they were in the next-door room, the one that faces the canal. Pyotr was livid, I could hear him screaming and shouting at Alexey. I thought that there was going to be a fight but Alexey said nothing, or what he did say was so quiet that I didn't hear it. Pyotr carried on bellowing with rage and then I heard a shot.

'I ran next door. Pyotr was slumped across the windowsill. Alexey was sitting completely composed on the sofa by the coffee table, cleaning his gun with a handkerchief. The inhuman bastard didn't even look up when I came in. I don't think he had moved since he had shot him. I am pretty certain he actually fired the gun from the sofa, between taking a sip of tea and toying with one of those revolting pink iced cakes he is so fond of.

'I remember standing inside the doorway paralysed with fear. That's the awful thing about Alexey. You know, I mean I know what he's capable of. He just got up from the sofa and walked over to Pyotr's body, and told me to take it by the feet. He sounded disgusted, not with himself but with Pyotr's body for being a body. I gagged, I could feel hysteria bubbling up inside me. I just couldn't touch him. Alexey took the gun out of his jacket pocket. I was terrified, I thought he was going to shoot me as well, instead he wacked me across the face with it, very hard, which made me stumble backwards. He ordered me again to pick up the feet, so I did and together we pushed Pyotr's body out of the window. The most awful thing was the sound of it as it hit the pavement. It was a thwack, like when you do a belly flop into water. The sound echoed out across the canal and it came back and back and back. I went to the toilet and retched into the bowl.

'Alexey telephoned Vassya. He came around a quarter of an hour later. He has a white Mercedes. I watched him park from the window. He looked at the body on the pavement and then, as if it was animal fodder, he picked it up and chucked it into the canal. Then he drove his car around the block and walked back.

'He made some phone calls and an hour or so later a truck pulled up outside, they fished the body out of the river and took it away, I don't know where.'

19

Yelena slumps slightly in her chair and lets go of her breath. 'I wanted you to know,' she says.

But I don't say anything. What is there to say? What was it Annya used to insist on so zealously? *'We have to be witnesses to what is happening here.'* I have been an unknowing witness. Conversations have flowed through me, events have unfolded around me and Pyotr was taken away from me because I didn't know what I was witnessing. Murder is a foreigner in my world, I don't know it, I have no dialogue with it. A man has died and all I could be was a witness.

In front of me Yelena bends her revolting battered face down towards her lap. She tells me she felt guilty because she had a hand in Pyotr's murder, and she says that I have burnt on her conscience since I came back from Berlin. So that is why she invited me up to the roof on the day of the *actsia*. I am shocked but I am still not sure whether I believe her: after all she has very good motives for hating Alexey.

She is looking at the hands on her lap and fastidiously pushing back the cuticle on her left forefinger. 'I thought I should tell you,' she repeats. She puts down her hand to find her handbag and half rises to go.

'You can't go now. Where are you going?'

'I am going to my studio in Pushkinskaya, Arkady is waiting for me.'

'You will keep away from Alexey, won't you?'

'Yes, I think this time I really will. Every time he does this he promises me that it's the last time, that it'll never happen again. And he seems so genuinely sorry that I feel I've got to give him the chance. Of course I do, because half of me wants to believe him and the other half is terrified of what he'll do if he thinks I don't believe him. You know I think he actually enjoys other people seeing what he has done to me. I mean he always makes me go out when my face is all cut up. He's got a taste for it, I don't think he's ever going to stop. For God's sake of course, he won't, I mean he's killed a man. He's killed Pyotr. He's a murderer for Crissakes. I can't stay with him. I don't care what he does to me any longer. I've reached my limit. I can't live like this. When my face's better, I'm going to join Kolya at my mother's and we're going to start again.' She makes it sound so simple but I can't understand why she didn't leave Alexey the first time it happened: that too seems madness.

We walk together to the door and I ask her again when they are flying out the opium.

'Tomorrow from Pulkova. Be careful, Natalie, he doesn't trust you.' I offer her my First Aid Kit, but she refuses and says she must hurry because Arkady will worry about her if she is late. I tell her that I will come and visit her tomorrow in Pushkinskaya, and I hug her rather carefully and let her go.

Then because I can't think straight and I need somebody else, I ring Oleg. After all he has helped me before. I ring him from a phone box on Maly Prospect, which is the closest phone box to me that hasn't been taken to bits.

Oleg is in, and tells me to meet him at the boat café at eleven o'clock. He is there when I arrive, sitting at a table on the deck looking out across the water at the swollen fireball of the sun, his face creased into predictable patterns like the bark on a tree.

The other passengers are being cleared off the deck and so I stand by the gangplank to let them off. 'I hope,' I say to Oleg, 'that your friend doesn't mind us using his boat again.' Oleg looks amused. 'My friend doesn't mind. You must be crazy, believe me he does well enough out of me, I wouldn't worry your pretty little head about him. Sit down. I have already ordered us some drinks. What have you to report to me today?'

I slide myself sideways into the seat opposite him and draw a deep breath. 'Yelena came to see me today.'

'And what did she have to say?'

'She . . . , she said that she was there when Pyotr was killed. She said that she helped dispose of his body. She said that Alexey shot him.'

The boat moves off from the mooring and comes around the corner of the Peter and Paul Fortress, travelling upstream towards the cruiser *Aurora*. While the adolescent waiter serves us champagne and *kalbasa* I tell Oleg Yelena's story. For once he listens to me without saying anything. There is a light wind. The boat jars as each wave passes underneath it. When I finish Oleg orders another bottle of champagne and we sit for a moment in silence.

'So tell me, do you believe her? Do you believe this crazy story?' he asks.

'I think so, yes. But on the other hand if someone beat me like that I would blame anything I could on them.'

Oleg tells the waiter that we want to return to the mooring and waving him impatiently away he opens the bottle of champagne himself. He pours my glass and then his own. 'In my opinion we only have one way to make sure she is telling the truth. I think we should go to Pulkova Airport tomorrow. I want to know where that opium's going to and if it's there I bet they'll fly it out in the early morning. It's the safest time of day.'

The boat has turned around and we are now level with

the small beach that cowers at the base of the fort walls. 'I'll drive you home,' he says. 'I think we must be at the airport early. If we are going to go I do not want to miss them. OK, this is the plan. I will drop you off now. I would stay with you but unfortunately I have other business to attend to tonight. Tomorrow morning I want you to be waiting outside the main arch of your building at four o'clock.'

I feel that there is something rather old-fashioned in his insistence that he drives me home. I am comforted by it and by his planning. I wonder if in some indirect way he feels he is doing this for Allia's sake? We leave half a bottle of champagne on the deck. 'Why bother with it?' he says, 'we don't want it.'

I don't sleep. I don't think either, or at least not consciously. I sit at my table dry-eyed in the light of the night. Sit there dumb and stupid until the sun rises at three o'clock. Then I have a shower, which is cold as our building still doesn't have any hot water. At three-thirty I make a cup of tea, and at ten minutes to four I walk downstairs and stand in the archway that leads onto the street.

The route from the Winter Palace to Pulkova Airport is a mathematical radius of the city. It is like driving through the rings of a tree trunk. Since St Petersburg's foundation, each successive Russian autocrat has left his character on an area, from Peter the Great's centre through Catherine, Alexander, Nicholas, Stalin to the dreary grey monoliths of Brezhnev's suburbs.

Just outside Electrosila market Oleg stops the car. 'Can you see anybody?' he asks.

'No.'

'No, me neither, but then I'm always crap at spotting them.'

We wait for a minute and then Oleg draws back out into the road. No one pulls out behind us. He stops again outside the Pribaltiskaya Hotel, on the outer edge of the city. 'I have a friend here,' he tells me. 'We may be able to get some information.' The Pribaltiskaya is a towerblock built of brown marble and brown tinted glass. Clocks above the reception desk show you the time in Paris, New York and Vladivostock. In St Petersburg it is four-thirty. I loiter between a hip-high chrome ashtray and a plastic rubber plant while Oleg talks to the Night Manager. When Oleg turns back towards me he is smiling. He opens out his arms expansively and ushers me past a sullen porter and out through the automatic doors.

'This is crazy, I can't believe our luck. Come on get in the car, Natalie.'

'What's up? What did he say?'

He doesn't tell me until we are back on the avenue that leads to the airport. He is elated, as he drives one hand leaves the steering wheel and makes little curlicues above the gear stick. 'Your friend Vassya is well known around the hotels because he hosts a lot of foreign businessmen. The Night Manager, who is an old aquaintance of mine, tells me that Vassya came in yesterday and booked a room for an Italian transferring from the Europa. But this is where it gets crazy: the room was prepaid for one night only, and breakfast was ordered for four-thirty in the morning so we are only just ahead of him. Like I said before, they must be flying the opium out this morning and my guess is that the Italian is going to fly with it.'

Oleg turns the car off the avenue onto the narrow road that runs between billboards and pine trees to the airport. I sit heavy and filled with dread beside him. It is not at all obvious why we are doing this and I suspect, not for the first time, that Oleg has other reasons for knowing Alexey's business.

Pulkova Airport has two terminals situated half a mile away from each other. Pulkova One is for internal flights and Pulkova Two is for international flights. 'How do we know which terminal they are going to use?' I ask.

'I don't really but I reckon that they will probably use Pulkova Two. The runway is much less busy at the best of times, and I would be really surprised if there were any international flights at this time of the morning. I hope they do because this car won't stand out in the car park there, but it sure as hell will amongst all the crap parked around Pulkova One.'

The airport is a two-storey building the size of a small town railway station. A round flowerbed stands outside planted with stiff, red, official tulips. A black BMW and a Mercedes are parked beside two brown Moskvich. Oleg pulls up beside the foreign cars.

'It is crazy how much money they make in this airport,' he comments slightly jealously. 'OK, Natalie, listen to me. This is your story. The airport shop is an Irish joint venture, so if anyone stops you say that you are Irish and you are inspecting a delivery for the shop. OK?' And I nod obediently.

I leave the car reluctantly and follow Oleg, who seems to know his way around through a wooden door in the wall to the right of the building with a sign on it saying, 'Entry Is Forbidden. Staff Only.' In front of us are three runways. Two biggish aeroplanes stand side by side with their noses facing the main airport building. One of them belongs to Air France and the closest one to us is Aeroflot. There is no sign of any activity.

'Are you sure they are going to load here?' I ask, hoping that we might miss them.

'No, I'm not sure but if we hide ourselves here we will soon know.'

We find some luggage trolleys and, making a terrible noise, line them up together to form a small barricade. We crouch between the trolleys and the wall. Oleg's jacket flaps open and I can see a gun in his belt but I am not surprised. I am quite blasé about guns nowadays. Five minutes pass and I am convinced that we are missing everything. If they are loading at all it will be in the chaos and mess of Pulkova One, where families camp for days waiting for the chance of a seat on a plane.

My knees ache and I am cold. I begin to shiver. I ask Oleg what we are hoping to achieve by this and he replies that we need to know where they are flying the opium. This knowledge is useless to me but it is obviously important to Oleg. I wonder how he will use it. I am not used to squatting and my knees are hurting. I hear the sound of lorry engines and Oleg nudges me, unnecessarily because I have already noticed it. He is tense with anticipation beside me.

The sound of the lorries fades away again. 'Quick!' hisses Oleg. 'Get into the building. The lorry will come up this way to load. Move.' The building is divided into two parts. The first for administration and the second for the departure lounge, luggage retrieval and customs. There are four doors on the administrative side and each one is locked. The automatic doors leading into the departure lounge are switched off.

I can hear the throb of the lorry engines again, approaching from the far end of the first runway. I suggest to Oleg that we use the door we came through. We edge along the front of the building, past our barricade of trolleys and out through the wall. As I close the door behind me Oleg's hand pushes down hard on my shoulder, shoving me to the ground. A white Mercedes is approaching the bed of tulips. Following Oleg I inch crabwise into the small gap between the two Moskvich.

The white Mercedes pulls up beside the car on our left. I hear the doors opening and Alexey's sinewy voice. 'Have the lorries arrived?'

'They should be loading right now.' Vassya's voice is

heavier and it comes from further back in his mouth. He carries on speaking. 'Let's see if that swine of a pilot is sober enough to fly the damn thing.'

'No,' interrupts Alexey. 'First I want to inspect the loading.' They walk over towards the door in the wall which we have just come through. There are three pairs of feet and one of them is wearing Gucci shoes, which means the Italian is with them.

Oleg gets up almost before they have closed the door behind them. He pushes his car keys into my hands. 'Lie on the ground in the back seat. Don't let anyone see you. I'm going to find that pilot,' he orders.

I do as he says, fumbling with the keys. Once I am inside the car I lie down with my back bridging uncomfortably the ridge that runs underneath the gear stick and the hand brake. The carpet underneath my head smells new and synthetic.

I wait and I wait. Oleg seems to be taking forever. It is quarter past five by my watch. I will give him until half past. Then what? Do I drive away? Do I go in and find him? What if Alexey or Vassya have already found him. At twenty-five past five I hear the Italian speaking quite close by, but from my position I can't tell who he is speaking to or where he is going. It is half past five, there is still no sign of Oleg and I am now seriously uncomfortable. Then I hear Vassya and another man's voice that I don't recognise.

At twenty to six I hear footsteps running towards the car, followed by a rapid volley of knocks on the car window. 'Quick Natalie, let me in!' It is Oleg. I fishtail out of my awkward position as fast as I can, open the door from over the front seat and hand him the keys. He starts up the car as he sits down and thrusts the gear stick straight into reverse.

Once we are out of sight of the building I clamber over the seat and into the front. 'Jesus Christ, that was crazy!'

exclaims Oleg, letting go of the steering wheel and running both his hands through his hair. He is still buzzing on adrenalin. 'That, Natalie, was so close. Honestly I'm not joking, you're lucky to have me here. Phew!'

'Watch the bus Oleg!' He swerves and misses it.

'Well tell me then,' I ask.

'I found the pilot. He was upstairs in the canteen and he was pissed out of his mind. He'd been drinking with one of the controllers. I pretended to be an associate of Alexey's. He was so pissed he would have believed me if I'd told him I was his grandmother. I shouted at him for being drunk. I told him he was a pisshead and useless and I was firing him and I wanted another pilot. Then he got hysterical and started pleading with me that he wasn't that drunk, and begging me to remember his family etc. etc. I almost felt sorry for the bastard, I promise you I did, but I said to him, I said, 'You're so fucking pissed you wouldn't even remember where you were going.' And I tell you he was fucking pissed. I certainly wouldn't have let him near any bloody aeroplane of mine. 'No,' he goes, 'I might be drunk but I know exactly where I'm going. I'm going to the military airport in East Berlin.' Natalie this is absolutely crazy, they are flying the stuff straight into Berlin. They're flying it into the fucking Red Army airstrip.

'Wait, wait it gets worse. As he was telling me this I heard the door opening downstairs. So I left him gabbling into mid-air and ran down a corridor that led off the canteen on the opposite side from the staircase. I opened the second door I came to and hid in there. It was a secretary's office or something like that. I could hear Alexey, Vassya and the Italian in the canteen. It was crazy. They were getting at the poor bloody pilot for being drunk and he kept on bleating. 'You've told me all this before, I've explained, I've explained.' And I was sitting there thinking, Jesus fucking Christ, any minute they are going to guess that someone has been asking him questions but they didn't, they just thought he was being drunk and stupid. Then Vassya says that they are signalling from the aeroplane that they are ready to go, and there is a lot of shuffling and the pilot protesting that he is fine, and then I heard them go downstairs.

'Alexey and the Italian are still in the canteen and I heard Alexey ask the Italian whether he wants to telephone his contacts. They walked down the corridor and I thought they were going to come into the office I was in. I thought that was it, how the hell am I going to explain this? For Christ's sake Alexey knows me and he hates – you know there is a lot of history between us. I stood there and I sweated. It was a tiny office with a desk, a chair, a typewriter and a telephone. There was absolutely nowhere to hide. But then the footsteps went past me. I heard them fiddling with keys and opening another door further down the corridor. I waited until they closed the door and then I bolted out of the office I was in and down the stairs.'

20

Oleg drives me back to Vasilievsky Island. It is only eight o'clock in the morning and I have already been up for four hours. I lie on my bed, fully clothed, for the rest of the morning but I find that I cannot sleep and in the afternoon I keep my promise to Yelena and go in search of her.

There is some kind of festival going on in the courtyard at Pushkinskaya when I arrive around two o'clock. A stage has been set up at the end opposite the archway and on it stands a red and yellow, two-storey-high dragon made out of scrap metal. A thrash metal band are playing on the stage. They have spectacularly dodgy speakers that make the sound even rougher than they intend. Three symbolist canvases are strung from the roof and there is a crowd of sorts: thirty or forty Pushkinskaya types loitering around the rubble landscape in the kind of drooping-plant way that they have.

Sasha is there with quite a court surrounding him. 'Natalie, er, Yelena says she wants to see you. She's up in her studio. Tell her I, er, might get someone to give me a lift up later.'

I thank him and make my way across the yard. I have to go around the back of the stage to get to the staircase. The guitarist is off on a long ego-rip. The sound judders out through the static on the speakers. He is still going when I reach the top floor. Some people have climbed out of the landing window and are sitting on the roof listening to him. I rap on the door. There is no answer so I try again and after a couple of minutes Arkady opens it. He is wearing a frayed pair of jeans and his shirt is undone, looking thoroughly relaxed.

'Hi, come in. Yelena said you were coming. We're sunbathing on the roof out the back, come and join us.' I follow him down the dingey corridor to the small back room. It looks exactly the same as when I first came here with Nikita after Tornikov's opening. So much has happened to me since then but nothing has changed in the room.

Yelena's face is peering sideways through the window. It is against the light so I can't see how it is healing. 'Natalie, it is good to see you. Come out here, it's wonderful, I have the most incredible view.'

I stand on a chair and squeeze myself through the window. I don't really like heights but once I have sat down I am fine and Yelena is right, it does have the most incredible view. Slightly to the right of us is the thin gold splinter of the Admiralty spire and behind it, as if you are seeing double, is the second gold spire of the St Peter and St Paul's Cathedral. Straight in front of us is the hulking mass of St Isaac's and beyond the factory chimneys in the distance the port and the Gulf.

I light up a cigarette in the bowl of my hand. 'It's lovely.'

Yelena answers me, 'I can't imagine what it must have been like when it was Finnish marshes. What it must have looked like to Peter the Great when he arrived here. Nothing but swamp for as far as he could see. What made him want to build his new model capital on a swamp?'

Arkady breaks in. 'There is an idea,' he says. 'A theory that it's because St Petersburg is Peter the Great's creation.

I mean it wouldn't be here if it hadn't been for him, and if he hadn't been the kind of man he was. He was vile, he was a really brutal dictator – this city is like a concentration camp, it is built on bones – but he was also a complete visionary, you know. I mean he shipped in the best architects, gardeners, sculptors and engineers from all over Europe to build this. You know in a very real way this is Peter's dream and we are all of us living in his dream. We are all part of it. Often I think the city controls us, creates its own dramas. Do you ever wonder why you are here, Natalie? You see you too are part of Peter's dream, and maybe the city has caused you to act in a different way to how London would cause you to act. Every city has got its own character but with this one you can actually name him. You know he was six foot six and he foisted this city on the land, it's his. What's that quote from the Bronze Horseman; *"Or is all this a dream? Is all our life Nothing but an empty dream, heaven's jest?"*'

'Not new, Arkady,' says Yelena gently.

'No, it's not new,' I add. 'But I know what you mean, especially for me, maybe it's being a foreigner as much as anything else. I often don't feel in control here. Events seem to happen to me without me having anything to do with them.'

'One moment,' says Arkady. 'Is that the door?'

We all listen together. Somebody is knocking. 'It might be Sasha, I saw him in the courtyard, he said he wanted to come and see you later, Yelena'

'Your guest Yelena,' says Arkady. 'I got it last time, it is definitely your turn.'

'Oh please Arkady, I really don't want to open the door looking like this.'

'They are going to see your face anyhow. It might impress upon you how important it is not to go back to that murdering fucker!' says Arkady with some feeling.

'OK, I'll go, just don't lecture me, Arkady. All right?' snaps Yelena.

'Well go on then.'

The knocking comes again and she squeezes herself back through the window. 'I'm coming. I'm coming,' I hear her shout down the corridor.

'She's not really going to go back to him is she?' I ask Arkady.

'I don't think so, but I didn't think so last . . .' The noise that has interrupted him is a gunshot. Two shots, almost overlapping like a heartbeat. There is the same terrifying quality of a loud noise in a small box that I remember from the Tam Tam.

Arkady is already scrambling through the window. His bum is sticking ridiculously out into the air as he shoves his way through head-first. He is too tall to do it quickly and his frustration fans our panic. I follow, but turn around and go through legs-first to the chair standing below the windowsill. I am standing on the chair when I hear him scream. Not a scream but a maceration of her name that then chokes away, 'Yelena, Yelena.'

She has been shot in the head and the chest. The force of the shots has propelled her back along the corridor. There is a tang of gunsmell and blood. Human blood smells, in that quantity the smell pushes against the back of my throat like fingers.

I put my hand against the wall. I have to check first that there is no blood because there is blood and other stuff splashed across the wall in a lot of places. I don't trust my vision. It is refracting into spots of jiggering light in a similar way to when you stare directly at new snow. And her face, there is not much left of her face, only a crater for a forehead. I am on my feet. I have the acid from my stomach in my mouth, then I retch and can't be sick any more.

Arkady is kneeling but even he can't go near her. She is

repulsive. I suppose the only way to look at it is that she is not Yelena any longer.

'The bastard, the bastard. How could he? When she stayed for so long. I will kill him, I will, I promise, I'll kill him.' He is fuelling himself up on anger.

'Do you have a sheet?' I ask him. We can't just leave her splattered across the hallway. I realise that there are no friendly emergency services. We will have to deal with her. 'Come on Arkady, let's give her some dignity for the moment at least.' But it is not for her dignity that I want the sheet, it is for ours. The sight of her paralyses me; I know that until she is hidden I can do nothing. Arkady holds out his hand to me and I squeeze it. I am not sure where we will find the toughness to handle what we have to, but there is nobody else.

Arkady takes the sheet from her bed and we lay it over her. I think of Pyotr being turfed into the canal. This is better. Arkady has a tin bucket which he fills with water. With this, paint rags and a large block of brown, all-purpose household soap we scrub the walls and the floor. It takes us hours and it is horrific work. We don't talk except to organise the emptying and filling of the bucket and to allocate areas and tasks. When it gets too much we touch each other. Arkady's hands are long and loose with hardened palms. He chews the skin around his fingertips and it is ragged and sore in the places where he has torn the skin away. He wears three dirty bone rings and he has a mauve and blue friendship bracelet around his left wrist. I have not known him very well until now. For these hours we are together in what we are doing.

The best way is not to recognise what I am scrubbing, what lump is under my paint rag. To exclude my brain, not to think at all, this is just housework. Of course I don't believe this but the effort of pretending is helpful. I remember when I was nine, being sick and my mother making me clear up the vomit. I was very squeamish about it. I hated it and I remember thinking that it was unfair and cruel of my mother to make me do it. Clearing up the hallway is a bit like that, but it is worse.

By the time we have finished I am soaked, my clothes are dripping and stained reddish-brown all over. A crescent of blood is lodged under each fingernail. I stand in front of the sink in the kitchen and scrub my hands until there is virtually no skin left on them. It is as if Yelena's blood is poisonous in itself. Arkady hands me a pair of Yelena's trousers and a shirt. I strip in front of him – after the last few hours modesty would be insulting – and douse my body and dress in her clothes. They are too big and I have to roll up the sleeves of the shirt and the trouser legs. Arkady washes as well and then we climb back out on to the roof and we sit and smoke cigarettes.

'I have to tell her mother,' he says. It isn't particularly directed at me; he could be telling the view.

'And Kolya,' I add. 'Is he with his grandmother now?'

'Yes, she takes care of him most of the time. I don't know how I am going to do it.'

'Do you want me to come with you?' I offer.

He thinks about it and then declines. 'No Natalie, thank you but I don't think it would be a good idea. It is going to be hard enough for her as it is. It will be worse if she thinks there is a foreigner mixed up in it as well.'

The city lies spread out before us, as oblivious and calm as it was when I arrived, soaked in the oil of the low sun's light. I think about contacting Annya but I know that somehow she'll make me feel this is my fault; that Yelena wouldn't be dead of I'd understood what I'd been meddling in.

There is a rouble restaurant called Sadko's in the Hotel Europa. It is a mafya hangout. The decor is Scandinavian, you can buy German beer in tall glasses and it feels more

Western than anywhere else in the city. I go there even though I know I can't afford it. I haven't taught since I went to Berlin. I'm eating deep into my emergency money, the money I tried to give Pyotr. It won't be long before there's nothing left. A bouncer stops me at the door but he lets me through when I speak to him in English. It is seven o'clock in the evening and the room is relatively crowded. I order a beer and sit down at a small table. Next door to me is a group of visiting English businessmen. They are middle-aged, they wear light-grey suits, they have taken off their ties to relax and they are resting their pillow-plump bellies on their laps. They have Midland accents and they are complaining about the telephone system and discussing football.

I want to talk to them very badly. I want to say, '*Hello, can I join you? I couldn't help overhearing. I'm English too.*' But how can I? They will think that I am a weirdo, that I am trying to pick them up. I would be intruding and it would make them uncomfortable. Here for three days, dressed in their suits, assessing the business potential of St Petersburg and I, who have been here too long, dressed in a murdered woman's trousers that are rolled up above my ankles. They would be bound to ask me about Russia. '*What is it like living here?*' How would I answer that?

There are two heavies leaning on the bar. One of them has a bulge under his armpit. Three beautiful women are sitting at a table in the corner, scanning the room and paying no attention to each other. They are prostitutes. The Russians call them '*international girls*'.

I pay for my beer and walk down the white marble steps to the cloakrooms. The telephone here is never vandalised. I wait until the room is empty and then I ring Oleg but there is no answer.

I find that I can breathe more easily on the street. I wonder if the people crowding towards me down Nevsky can tell. I feel there must be something strange in my face.

I am sure that violence must mark you, brand you. Can they see it?

I try to ring Oleg again from the phone booths on Canal Griboyedova but there is still no answer so I walk on. I dawdle. I detour through the great expanse of Palace Square. There is a demonstration going on. When I get up close I find that it is the fascist group, Pamyat. They are not very impressive; ten or fifteen of them, about my age, dressed in black and the men with straggly beards. They have banners against communists, Jews, atheists. One of them is holding a large picture of Boris Yeltsin onto which is drawn a tail and two horns. Yeltsin looks rather nice that way. I walk on. When I look back a large group of tourists has blocked the demonstration from my view.

I try Oleg for the third time from the telephone booths on the corner of Sredny Prospect and the First Line. This time he is in. The booth is right by a tram line so I have to stick my finger in my ear to hear what he is saying.

'Oleg it's me, Natalie.'

'Good, I'm glad you've rung, we need to talk to each other.'

'Not tonight Oleg, there has been a terrible accident. Our friend's girlfriend has been extremely badly hurt.'

'How badly?'

'She's dead.'

'When?'

'This afternoon, in her studio. I was there.'

'Did you see anybody?'

'No, we were sunbathing on the roof. She went to open the door. By the time we got to her it was too late and the visitors had gone.'

'It sounds like an employee of our friend. Are you sure they didn't see you?'

'I don't think so.'

'Where have you been since? Has anybody come with you?'

'I haven't seen anyone but I haven't been looking. I went to Sadko's for a beer. I'm on my way home.'

'Natalie, I think it is very important that you go away as soon as possible. There is a train tomorrow at twenty past twelve. I think you should take it. Are you listening to me?'

'Yes, I'm still here.'

'Believe me, it is vital that you go. Ring me when you get there OK?'

'I'll definitely think about it.'

'Don't be crazy, Natalie. You have to go.'

'All right, I'll ring you. Bye for now.'

'Be careful, Natalie, good luck.'

Over the last week they have moved the market that has grown up around the Metro station across the road. It is now big enough for a street of its own. Stalls line the road on either side. It reminds me a little of the North End Road. There are stalls for clothes, jam, beer, fruit and veg. There are old ladies at the corners selling Bulgarsky and Belamor. There are booths selling Marlboro, probably fake, for roubles, as well as sticks of Hollywood chewing gum, squares of Polish bubblegum, newspapers, magazines, translations of Agatha Christie, James Bond and Hemingway, plastic-covered Bibles, English dictionaries, beans, eggs, sacks of rose hips. 'For your flu, for your flu,' calls the woman at the stall.

'I don't have flu,' I tell her.

'You will do,' she says confidently. 'Better to buy it now.' A little girl of about eight is selling bright green bottles of 'Bio-Activ Spirit' which is supposed to be for cleaning engines, but I know that some poor bastard will drink it instead.

On the corner there are three men standing behind flaming barbecues of shashlik kebabs. I ask for one, hand over my roubles and wait while it is cooked. The fat drips down onto the charcoal and orange flames dance up in the soft evening light. I am so tired that I sway slightly on my feet and I am afraid that the shashliki men will think I am drunk. I have not slept now for two days; I think that I am only walking and standing because it has become a habit.

One of the men turns the shashlik over the embers and periodically tests them with a two-pronged fork. If blood oozes from the wound caused by the fork he leaves them, but now clear fat is oozing and he takes the shashlik from the fire and, using the same fork, eases the lumps of meat off into a white napkin. As he hands this to me I notice his eyes widen over my shoulder and I sense a tensing awareness in him. I take the napkin of hot meat from him and turn around. My path is blocked by four men dressed in brightly coloured tracksuits. I start to move forward but the men do not move out of my way. I sense the danger, I have seen it in the shashliki man's eyes and now I can smell it.

I draw my head up and my shoulders back and I push out my chin. I know that it is very important that they do not sense my weakness. Weakness can smell like blood. Maybe it is just paranoia seeping from my over-tired brain. They will go away. I move forward. The two men in front of me move to the side. They are not particularly tall but they hold their arms away from their sides in a way that I find very threatening. Now I am surrounded and I realise that to pretend that I am not afraid is silly because these men do not care. The kebab in my hands is too hot to hold comfortably. The blond man at the back leisurely lifts his arm and slams his fist into my jaw. It comes at me small – fists aren't very large – but I stumble back under the force of it. I feel pain and I hear the crunch of my tooth and these two sensations are quite separate. There is blood in my mouth and it tastes like liquid aluminium foil.

As I stumble, the man to the right of me, who looks remarkably like Oleg, punches my eye and I go down onto the rotting vegetables on the tarmac of the market street. A sharp pain shoots through my ribs and I hear a crack. As I scream the hard rubber of a heel hits my mouth and a kick lands in my stomach. I jerk my body into a hairpin to try to protect myself. Then the men are gone.

There is a space around me on the road of the market. I am winded. I scrabble out my hand and painfully push myself up onto my knees and then upright. A flame shoots through the air from the shashliki fires. The two men standing behind the spitting meat gaze at me balefully. The street is looking at me and there is a certain unnatural silence but no movement. I am a spectacle to be avoided. I am blooded and dirty and I am trouble. Nobody wants to be involved.

I buy cigarettes from a woman who glares resentfully at me for having chosen her and spits lightly in the gutter. It is very painful to walk, the side of my body feels like it is burning. The men and women at the stalls stop and stare as I make my slow progress past them. I recognise the expression on their faces. They look at me with the same blank disapproval as if I were a drunk.

I make my way slowly up Sredny Prospect. When I reach the next junction I stop on the kerb and wait for the lights to turn in my favour. I hear a shrill woman's voice calling from behind me.

'*Dievushka, dievushka* – girl, girl!' I ignore it. I must concentrate on crossing the road before the lights change again. She catches up with me by the time I have reached the other side. '*Dievushka*, we must walk together, it is not safe any longer at night.'

She is in her forties and she is wearing a dress and

matter-of-fact shoes. She takes my arm away from the side that it has been clutching and tucks it firmly under hers. 'Where are you going?' she asks. 'The Seventeenth Line,' I tell her.

'What a coincidence, that is the way I am going too.' I lean on her and together we walk up the street. At the entrance to my building she says, 'You will be safe from here. You must be more careful *dievushka*.' And she marches off into the dusk before I can thank her.

21

Once we've got clear of the city, once we've reached the forest, then I'll be able to breathe more easily. It's two days' train journey to Berlin, it's too long, I should have flown. But if I had gone by plane I would have had to buy an advance ticket with my name on it. Anyone who was looking could have found that. Anyhow, Pulkova bloody Airport is one big mafya convention as far as I can make out. I'm less obvious this way, and if I think of it in steps I won't get so scared. It is one step out of the city, one step over the Latvian border and a big step at Brest-Litovsk when they change the wheels before we cross into Poland. For two hours we will be swinging around in a train hanger, and any bully in a uniform, any bully with dollars or a gun, will be able to get on. If I survive that I've got the long run into Berlin. But will I be safer in Berlin? With Nikita?

I'm sitting on the bottom bunk with my legs curled underneath me, pushed back against the wall by the window. I can see out, but someone looking in could only see me if they stood at a specific angle, and they would have to know which window to look for (the guard knows). We haven't picked up speed yet but we are moving and for the moment I think I'm OK.

I'm sharing the cabin with two women; one young and one old. There is a top bunk free and I could claim it. If I did it would be harder for anyone to see me but it would also be harder for me to see out. I would only be able to hear voices from up there and I know that I would feel trapped.

The older woman is sitting opposite me. We are ten minutes out of the station and already she has got her slippers on. She is leaning her elbows on the small Formica table, looking out of the window, challenging the view.

The young one is a country girl so I don't need to worry about her. She's not, as far as I know, their kind at all: hennaed hair, tight snow-washed jeans, white stilettos and a lot of eye make-up. Strange that she is going to the West on her own. Maybe she's got family in another cabin (no sign of them yet) or maybe she is getting off at Vilnius.

The guard and Babba Lenna are my weak links. I told Babba Lenna I was leaving and asked her not to tell anyone for at least three days. Then she could do whatever she wanted with my stuff. She was angry with me for leaving it all behind but her grandson will be delighted. He's a small-time black marketeer and there is all sorts of Western gear in there that he will be able to flog for lots of money. I hope he spends some of it on his grandmother.

She was frightened too – she thinks I'm in trouble with the authorities. I suppose I am, but not the authorities that she is thinking about. She didn't want to have anything to do with me. She wanted me gone, out. What will they say on the staircase? In the courtyard? She is frightened that she will be implicated: I lived in her room and that is enough. I don't think that she will be. Alexey just wanted to shut me up and Babba Lenna doesn't know anything anyway; besides, she has had a lifetime's training in how to be quiet.

What else could I do? Tell her that I was going out shopping and then never come back? Surely that would have been more distressing for her?

There is also the guard, but apart from my face he has

no reason to suspect anything. I bribed him for the berth as Oleg suggested. It was vacant anyway and the train was about to go; he will see it as a perk. He's got Pyotr's dollars safely in his pocket and he won't say anything unless someone pays him more or pushes him hard. On the other hand, if he has worked on this route for a while, he is bound to be an informer. But he won't inform if he doesn't think it's important, and he has got my bribe, for what it's worth.

I've made it this far, at least that's something. I'm one step ahead and I'm still alive; my lip's split, my jaw hurts like fuck and I think they've broken one of my ribs, but I'm here and I don't think they know it.

I have never been as scared as I was last night. People staring, the glow from the coals of the kebab fires and the shadows behind that were so thick that they seemed almost solid. I was so totally fucking helpless. What really scares me is how much more they could have done. They weren't drunk, they weren't angry, there was no emotion. They were just beating me up and that was their job.

I have no emotion either right now; I'm blank, rational, I'm on hold until I get to Berlin. It's not that I haven't been affected. I am still together but I know I am brittle. I can't even hold a glass because my hands are shaking so much and I need my whole fist to deal with a cigarette. My jaw thumps and I am slightly feverish from the pain. I keep worrying at my lip with my tongue, and when I breathe it feels like I've got a knife in my ribs. I think the only reason that I am not collapsing is because I have got to get out. It's a survival thing. I swear that this is the last time I take this train.

I must have looked awful when I got in. I'm glad Babba Lenna didn't see me, although I know she has seen worse. I took a shower; there was still no hot water so it was cold. My skin felt so sensitive and the water was hard. Afterwards I dried myself with a sheet because it was softer than a towel. I found the First Aid Kit that I had tried to give to Yelena, and I gently dabbed some Germoline on the bridge of my nose, on my lips and around my eyebrow and cheekbone. It stung but I found the smell comforting. It felt incongruous to put something as homely as Germoline on to the violence of my face. I was too vain to use the Mercurichrome, I really didn't want to look any worse.

I didn't have any problem sleeping, which surprises me. My brain blacked out. But my body hurt more this morning than it had last night and my eyelids were swollen and heavy to open. I moved carefully in case a bit of me fell off and, like I say, breathing wasn't easy.

Using the last of the coffee, I made enough for one very strong cup. I managed to avoid Babba Lenna while the coffee came to the boil. Normally when she hears me moving around she comes into the kitchen and we have a good-morning chat, but this morning I didn't want to see her and I didn't want her to see my poor face until I had decided what to do.

My bread was hard and cracking. I cut a centimetre off the end and it was still just about edible inside, but to get it past my lip I had to soften it by dunking it in my coffee. It was a bit like eating baby food. As I worked my way through it I thought of Oleg and how insistent he had been that I should leave. Oleg, I decided, knew Petersburg better than I did. Oleg, I also decided, was a dangerous friend to have. I made up my mind to get out and get out fast. I'd had enough.

Was it a softening up or just a warning?

I don't have enough money for them to bother about. I don't have enough proof about what Alexey and Vassya have been doing, and who could I tell anyhow? I am hardly going to go to the police, or even that nice lady from the British Consulate. You can just imagine the scene. 'I'm sorry to disturb you, I don't know if you remember me but I'm the one whose friend got stabbed. I wonder if you could help me. I've discovered an organisation that smuggles opium into the West, where it's made into heroin for Germany and France. The same people murdered my boyfriend, Pyotr Sergeivich Morozof, an illegal underground artist from the Western Ukraine, social undesirable and occasional grass dealer, who had a KGB record thicker than your address book and a stamp in his passport certifying him insane for missing his national service. Who told me this? Well I am afraid she is dead as well.' Somehow I don't think she would be very keen to help.

I came back from Berlin to say goodbye and I have done so. I have made my peace with Pyotr now and there is no point in me being here any longer. I have never loved Russia; I loved a man and I loved a city. The man is dead and the city is changing; the hope is running out of it. I don't want to hang around and see what happens. I want to get out now, with my life and my memories intact.

The last half inch of the coffee was sludge. I drank it anyway, sucking the grounds through my top teeth, carefully negotiating my bashed up bottom lip. I delicately checked my teeth with my tongue. A premolar on my lower right-hand jaw was loose.

I didn't have any time to waste. I didn't know if I had any time at all. For all I knew they could be waiting for me as I walked out of the door, or they could even come straight to the flat, but then again they might not come at all.

I went next door to tell Babba Lenna. She didn't ask about my face. She stared at my lip and listened. 'Babba Lenna, I have to go home to my family, I have to go home immediately. Give my stuff to your grandson, I can't take it all with me and he can sell it. There is an envelope on the table with the rest of my rent in it. Make sure he buys you some cheese with it. I know you like it. Take care Babba Lenna, you've been very kind to me. I will miss you.'

She had a strip of white muslin tied around her hair and she was wearing a housecoat. Her eyes did not leave my lip. 'It's better that you go to your homeland,' she said. 'Your mother must need you. Is it a long way that you have to go?'

'Yes, it's a long way. I've got to go to England.'

'England, is that east or west in the Union?'

'It's a long way.' I paused. It was true, I will miss Babba Lenna.

She was sitting at her table and I was standing in the doorway. I wanted to sit down and join her. I wanted to melt down and cry, tell her everything, tell her Pyotr was dead, tell her about the attack and let her dismiss it with one of her stoic phrases. But I knew that I couldn't.

'If anyone comes looking for me, don't tell them that I have left, at least not for three or four days.'

'Who will come looking for you?' Damn it, I had frightened her.

'No one, I'm just saying if . . .'

'Are you in trouble? There has been talk in the courtyard that there is a foreigner living in this flat. What does she do? Are the police coming here? I've worked all my life. I am a *blokadnik*. This is Leningrad, the hero city. I've done nothing wrong. I don't want the police here.'

'Babba Lenna, don't worry, don't worry. The police aren't going to come around here. I'm not in trouble with the police, it's not like that.'

It was no good, I'd rattled her. Her voice was getting higher and faster. Her grandson told me once that she had high blood pressure. I stepped back out of the doorway and went to my room but she was still going on. Her shrill old voice was a shriek now. I felt terrible, but what else could I have done? I had to let her know that I was going, didn't I?

I packed clean knickers, a book, toothbrush, money and my passport into my little rucksack. In the side pocket I put Pyotr's money and grass that I'd hidden in my winter boots, along with the drawing that Pyotr had given me the day he got out of prison. On the back he had written *Svaboda* (Freedom) and the date. Then, ostentatiously carrying a red string perhaps-bag, so that it looked like I was going shopping, I said goodbye to Babba Lenna, who was still angry with me, and walked out of the door leaving my keys behind.

My broken rib rasped as I walked down the steps but at least there was no one waiting for me. I took the back route through the courtyards. I tried hard to walk naturally; to remember how I naturally walked. I couldn't see if anyone was watching: too many people around the Metro station to be sure. I had to force myself to walk past the place where, last night, the kebab sellers had stood, their faces illuminated by burning charcoal, but I was intent enough on getting away from the city not to dwell on it too much.

If anyone was watching they would expect me to be shaky, to fall back on a routine, so I joined a queue. They were selling cheese in the *gastronomia* opposite the station. The shop is set below the pavement and you can't see into it from the street. From the queue I scrutinised the bodies of the customers entering the shop before I could see their faces or they could see mine. I bought a wax paper parcel of cheese and placed it in my perhaps-bag as a signal that I was shopping, scavenging, taking part in the daily search for food.

It was torture to move so slowly. The eyes of the crowds were on my black eye. My body was so sore and it took great self-restraint to stop myself sticking out an arm for a taxi to take me away from the unseen eyes that may or may not have existed. But I didn't because I knew that a taxi would be too obvious.

I took the Metro, standing on the escalators that go on for as long as a storey. The station at Vasileostrovskaya has doors that open from the concourse to the train tracks that line up with the doors on the incoming trains. It struck me as a sinister system. I was noticing the details that had become ordinary.

I changed at Gostinny Dvor, moving through the tunnels between the platforms. There are beggars now, grovelling for money on their knees, heads bowed, hands together in sham prayer to please the passers by. Only the drunks lie down, relaxed and oblivious. On the platform a clock counts the seconds since the last train left. They come every three minutes. I got out at Teknologichesky Institute and queued for bread in a nearby bakery, where I also bought some iced ginger biscuits. They joined the cheese in my perhaps-bag. I went back to the station and bought a cone of fresh raspberries from an old woman. It seemed that unconsciously I was buying myself treats, being kind to myself. It was four minutes past twelve, twenty-two minutes until the train left for Berlin.

A man jostled me as I queued at the ticket barrier, and a pulse of pain rose up from the dull ache in my side. One stop to Fruzenskaya. From there I moved fast. If anyone had followed me this far, they would guess where I was going. I checked the board and walked straight onto the platform. Halfway down the train I tried my first guard. Failure; two carriages down I tried again.

'Excuse me, do you have a spare berth for Berlin?' She pointed me next door.

'Excuse me, do you have a spare berth for Berlin?'

'Dollars?'

'Yes, dollars.' I got into the carriage. The guard showed me to his two-berth cabin by the samovar. 'Wait,' he said and closed the door behind me. Five minutes to go.

When the train lurched forward I hissed relief with the

steam on the brakes. The door pushed back. 'Fifty dollars to Berlin.'

'Fifty dollars is fine.' I pulled out Pyotr's coil of foreign currency. The money was in ones and fives. The guard counted it, licking his forefinger between each bill. He nodded and counted again, then he led me down the passage to the cabin with the two women.